THE UNRAVISHED BRIDE

The Unravished Bride

Terry Tucker

NEW ENGLISH LIBRARY
TIMES MIRROR

© Terry Tucker 1970
First published in Great Britain 1970 by Robert Hale & Co.
63 Old Brompton Road, London, S.W.7.

*

FIRST NEL PAPERBACK EDITION APRIL 1973

*

NEL Books are published by
New English Library Limited from Barnard's Inn, Holborn, London, E.C.1.
Made and printed in Great Britain by Hunt Barnard Printing Ltd., Aylesbury, Bucks.

45001437 1

CHAPTER ONE

'AND NOW *this*,' commented King Edward III testily, pulling at his forked beard, 'we've had enough trouble and scandal with her in the past. *Why* she has to be widowed just at this juncture, I can't imagine.' Sitting comfortably in Westminster Palace within sight of the fast flowing Thames, they were speaking of Joan of Kent.

'Beauty such as hers is a fatal gift,' acquiesced Queen Philippa, placidly continuing her work on an altar-cloth. She shot a glance at the King and wondered fleetingly if he was remembering how as a boy he'd been forced into signing his Uncle Kent's death-warrant, leaving this, Kent's child, at the mercy of the world. She, Philippa, had tried her best to bring the child up rationally with her own. But twelve offspring – seven sons and five daughters – and this adored yet difficult-tempered mate, had kept her hands fully occupied over the years. She recollected, a trifle guiltily now, that they'd made use of the child Joan to be company for Edward's mother, Queen Isabella, in the terrible years of her mental frenzy and decay. It was this thought that made Philippa add: 'Perhaps she feels the world owes her some recompense.'

I gave her love, thought Philippa defensively, but as she grew up into a ravishing beauty she always seemed to be on her guard against me – realising, no doubt, that my lord the King and I considered her no fit mate for our eldest son, Edward, the Prince of Wales, the very mirror of all chivalry, the idol of the people. For one thing she's his great-uncle's daughter, is older than he is, far more experienced – and of a flighty disposition. In fact, in hearing this unexpected news of Thomas Holland's death, Philippa had fervently hoped that stories of his wife's flirtations at Court had not embittered his death at Rouen.

'The world owes her?' the King retorted questioningly. 'Actually we've tried to give in to her on all her entanglements. You'll remember, my love, that the Earl of Salisbury and Sir Thomas Holland both wished to marry her and that she had a pre-contract affair with Thomas whom she certainly wanted. Then, when he was off to the wars, the Earl of Salisbury declared she'd been contracted to him – and *they* were married. And to cap it all, when

Holland returned she wanted him back – and Pope Clement VI gave judgement for *him*! Recompense? Ha! I'd say she'd always had everything her own way. And those aren't the only scandals she's been mixed up in by any means.' His voice had risen.

'Yes. Well – she's had four children, is Countess of Kent in her own right and is thirty-three years old. Let's hope she'll settle down to widowhood.' Philippa dropped a stitch and tut-tutted at her own carelessness. Like all married couples who have lived harmoniously together for many years, she and the King were in reality carrying on a deeper conversation far below this surface talk. He betrayed it now involuntarily.

'Our son is godfather to Joan's eldest, Thomas Holland – stood with him in his arms at the baptismal font. That is a spiritual relationship that the Church would rightly rule as even more disbarring than their being second cousins . . . No – no– never!'

'Of course not – it's entirely out of the question – always has been,' said Philippa serenely but her colour had risen. 'I don't know why you mention the possibility.'

'Nevertheless, it's high time he settled down and produced an heir. You and I had four sons by the time we'd reached his age,' said Edward complacently. 'I've been considering the Lady Margaret of Flanders, Duchess of Burgundy. What think you, my Philippa?'

'Shush! that is his footstep,' exclaimed his mother, 'I'd no idea he was in London.' To her, his footfall was totally different from any other.

The silken tapestry wall-hangings were pushed aside as the Prince of Wales stood framed a moment before he made his entrance. The hero of Crécy and Poitiers was at the zenith of his powers. At Poitiers, five years ago, he had indeed behaved with such nobility and generosity to a conquered foe that all had greeted him with adulation. His clean-cut features, wide-set frank eyes, high cheek-bones above a generous mouth, were all set off by his brilliantly fair Plantagenet colouring which he stressed by his penchant for wearing contrasting black. To ride white horses was usually a badge of royalty – yet even to this extreme Prince Edward carried his dramatic singularity: the horse that oftenest carried him was sable. In future ages, this exponent of the art of chivalry – that ideal which was already becoming debased and tarnished from its original objectives – would be universally referred to as the Black Prince. Learned, elegant and brilliant, he also had great strength and commanding height like all the children of Edward III and Queen Philippa – yet none of them

6

were to attain their sixties, all fell into premature old age. Even now at thirty, the Prince of Wales was showing a little of the excesses of the tilt-yard, the frequently-borne intolerable weight of plate-armour, almost incessant warfare, and even something of the cares of State, all entered into from early boyhood. It was a tread-mill display of gallantry and courage for which he was universally idolised; few yet realised that the chivalric ideals that had helped to lift Europe from its thousand-year eclipse, were themselves becoming stereotyped and superficial and only the prerogative of the wealthy.

King Edward shot an appraising glance towards his son who hastily crossed the rush-strewn floor and placed his sinewy hand on Philippa's shoulder, stooping to put his cheek against her lips. She dropped her needlework to lay her hand on his, her face glowing with pride.

'When did you come up to London?' asked the King with assumed gruffness.

'I was in Essex at Waltham Holy Cross till yesterday – January 16th – but I knew you'd be convening Parliament at the beginning of next month and that I should be here for the first session of 1361. Besides, I was anxious to see my Manor of the Rose.'

'You're overheated, my son,' said Philippa, caressing the hand on her shoulder, 'did you row up here?' Westminster, though the centre of royal administration, was but a village clustered around its abbey, west of London.

'Sculled here – in half an hour or less. Even the poor swans looked clemmed in this cold wind.' He sank on the bench beside the Queen, stretching his long legs across the rushes, and spoke directly to the King. 'Too bad that Sir Thomas Holland's health failed at the last. He'd done a wonderful job with the troops in Normandy, Maine and Anjou. We shall miss him. . . . He died at the Tour de Rouen at the end of December – I'd just arrived back from France myself and was at Waltham.' By the Treaty of Bretigny of the previous year, King Edward had agreed to renounce his claim to the French crown in exchange for that part of France that lies between the mouth of the Loire and the Pyrenees. As events were to turn out, this Treaty only provided a short breathing space, of which, at the moment, the Black Prince was taking full advantage.

Smoothly he now slid into a detailed account of the recent great storm in Essex. Trees had been pulled up by the roots, bridges swept away, houses blown down. An appalling gale!

7

Weather was always a safe topic.

Was Joan of Kent there? The Queen longed to ask, but wisely suppressed the urge. Long experience with seven Plantagenet sons – not to speak of an equally temperamental spouse – had taught her wisdom. Sensing the question in her expressive eyes, the Prince launched into a detailed account of recent forays in France and of the condition of his London house on his return. Two or three hundred yards west of London Bridge, his great Manor of the Rose had a superb frontage on the Thames and, with its attendant swans, was a show place. Below its slit windows, the panorama of London life and the artery of the river unfolded themselves.

'We shall have to settle something proper for Cousin Joan,' remarked the King heavily, following his own train of thought, 'not that it should be difficult. One hears rumours of Sir Bernard Brocas.' Looking across at the mature Prince of Wales sitting affectionately next to his mother, the recollection crossed the King's mind that thirty years ago the two of them had been favourite models for paintings of the Virgin and Holy Babe.

'Most suitable – after a decent interval,' assented the Prince. The devil, he was thinking, were those ribald stories of her and her admirers that had been the bane of Sir Thomas's last days, circulated so freely? He must warn her to be circumspect. Sir Bernard was a gallant knight; later on, when times of condolence were over, he, as Joan's favoured cousin, would speak up for Brocas. B'our Lady, he himself had once had an eye to Cousin Joan – but it never would have done.

Presently the Prince rose and pulled his cotehardie about him in a negligent gesture. 'I must take my sculler back before dusk,' he said, vaulted over the bench and was heard clattering down the steps to the river. . . . Well, with all that chatter of Joan, at least he'd escaped the usual hintings at his own marriage; he'd been afraid on arrival that he'd overheard mention of Margaret of Flanders. Ah no! not for him. There were plenty of wenches willing to obey his beck and call – no need for him to tie himself down yet to dull domesticity. With so many delightful creatures to choose, he'd never understood this overwhelming urge for one in particular that the poets prated. . . . He chuckled as he fitted the sculls in the rowlocks, glancing at the thinning traffic on the river. He'd make good time and exercise his muscles now that everyone was off home for the five o'clock evening meal. Yes, this was better than bringing the Royal Barge up the waterway – or even using the plying boatmen who awaited his pleasure by the steps, shivering in their cloaks muffled against the wind. God! he was hungry;

he'd do full justice to his supper at five o'clock – he'd naturally not had a bite since dinner at ten-thirty this morning, though he'd sat over that a full two hours enjoying the viands, the company, and the antics of his jester. He'd sleep tonight like the dead, unless indeed he fancied some wench to keep him company, but the household would be early astir and breakfast, at latest, at 6 a.m.

His last thought again, as his skiff's bow grated against the frontage steps of his own Manor, was that he must return to Waltham to condole properly with Joan and, later, gradually lead up to the suitability of her re-marriage. After all, Sir Bernard was a worthy knight and gossip had evidently already coupled their names.

CHAPTER TWO

THE LADY JOAN of Kent – she to whom future ages would always refer as The Fair Maid of that county – was bored to extinction. She supposed it was inevitable she should retire from Court circles for a short period of mourning, but, b'our Lady, she could not stand it for long. She was used to accompanying her lord on horseback, riding proudly astride with her skirts tucked into bags on each flank, when he went hunting or hawking, or even on whatever campaigns in France were in hand, and there awaiting his return from the battlefield. Or, as an alternative, when the latter waiting palled, she was accustomed to returning to the English Court as the cynosure of all eyes, the idealised Knights' Lady of the troubadour songs. Could she help it if gossip was often rife about her? She tossed her head now and gloomily inspected herself in a mirror. She would become dull, and old, old *old*, if she remained here with her women and stayed away from Court.

Suddenly two strong hands were clasped across her eyes. Someone was standing immediately behind her.

'Who is it?' she breathed. Was this danger? At least something was happening.

'Ah! little Joan,' said a deep voice. 'Tho' not little any more.'

'I shall call for my women,' she protested breathlessly – and mendaciously.

'Yes, do that, Lady Joan – I had not expected to find you alone.'

9

He was laughing as she whirled to face him.

'Edward!'

Ridiculous how disconcerted he felt at the impact of her beauty. Long ago, he'd thought himself inured to it. That she was still lissom, high-bosomed, of a wild-rose complexion and dramatically lovely, seemed absurd when one remembered she'd borne four children – or even recalled the chubby awkward child that his mother had brought up, and whom he'd seen occasionally at every stage of her development. Man-like, he'd always realised her adoration of himself, the beau ideal of English chivalry. And if, within recent years, that ideal had slightly hardened till, dazzled by his own career, he scarcely recognised his own latent cruelty and ferocity in battle – that too was accepted as part of the public image of his popularity.

He teased her now in self-protection of his own vulnerability. He had removed his hat on entering, and next pushed off the coif that enclosed his hair and ears. He noticed that Joan's surcoat was undone, showing the sleeved kirtle underneath, and that her hair was loose around her shoulders in unconventional disarray. 'Ah!' he said, fondly mocking, 'no wonder it's said that you're *la plus belle de tout la roiaulme d'Engleterre – et la plus amoreuse.*'

'*Who* dares say that?' she retorted angrily.

'On dit – on dit – on dit.'

'Bah! the coward's evasive reply. Tell me.'

Stung, he said: 'Well, I think it was young Froissart, if you must know. Doubtless he meant it as a compliment.'

'I can't imagine why your mother makes such a fuss of that young upstart – calls him her Chronicler – doubtless he's useful as a secretary. Personally, I mislike the idea that a mere Hainaulter seems to be taking notes on all of us.' Her tone softened: 'I don't care what he thinks of me as long as – as – I'm still "belle" to you, Edward.'

She had turned her back on him and leaning against one of the cusped lancet windows. After a moment's silence she added huskily: 'Why have you come?'

'I thought – well, I know this is premature but – but, in private, plans have to be made – at least thought of – well in advance.' He paused.

'Yes,' she assented softly: 'Oh, yes.'

'Sir Bernard Brocas is a chivalrous knight, we were comrades in arms at Poitiers – he was in fact my body squire.' As she remained in a frozen stillness, he blundered on: 'And you, Cousin Joan – like the rest of us – are not growing any younger – how old

10

are you now? – I always fail to remember these prosaic facts.'

Men! she thought furiously. Pah! they like to enjoy the mystery of sex and to be violently attracted to us who are the custodians of the power of love. And yet, when it suits them, they instinctively try to reject paying homage due to beauty, try to render us prosaic enough to forego the basic female rights of make-believe and magic. Demand the truth of us, forsooth!

She whirled round to him again. 'I've had enough of forced marriages,' she said coldly, 'or of arranged ones, for that matter. I shall not re-marry except for love and liking. And since that seems impossible – I shall never marry again.'

'Cousin Joan! I cannot imagine *you* retiring to a cloister,' he said brutally, goaded by her ridiculous assertion on 'forced' marriages. Who had ever managed to control this gay and flirtatious female? 'Your beauty has spoiled you – it imprisons you from all reality. . . . Well, I'm doing no good here – I must go.'

'My famous "beauty",' she cried desperately, 'I'd sacrifice it willingly for some appreciation of my real *self – me* – not my looks.' Her voice strangled: 'Yes – go then.'

And suddenly, to his astonishment, he was aware that she was weeping. Her face crumpled as she turned away with slow great tears rolling down her cheeks. Joanna – she who never wept, who had put a bright face on everything however desperate. His heart lurched in his breast.

'Jeanette!' he said then, brokenly – the baby name he'd used so often in their childhoods. 'Jeanette?'

If that last word were a question, the answer was here and now. She was in his arms, hers encircling his neck, pressing the back of his head, his lips down on her own. A liaison with this fantastically fair cousin was the last thing he'd counted on – but suitability, reason, circumspection were swept aside in the tempest of mutual passion and desire. 'Ah! don't you remember? It was always you,' she murmured in an ecstasy, and neither knew nor cared whether he had heard, so often had she reiterated these words to him in fruitless day-dreams.

It was hours later that again she leaned in the narrow window-slit, listening to the receding clip-clop of his mount, Morel, on the hard frost-bound earth. What was that he was singing so exultantly? She smiled when she recognised one of Laurence Minot's songs of triumph that celebrated the great military victories of the reign. How like him to think even of love in terms of war! But war would be her only rival; she was sure now that he would often return and that this spring would be a climax in their lives. As soon as a decent interval had elapsed, he would have to break it to his parents. After all, she was of royal blood too, and could not be treated as one of his serving-wenches – or even as he behaved with some of the ladies of the Court. Besides, she had fired his blood and he would not be able to keep away.

And suddenly she felt faint with joy. So – her private fantasy, that she would one day be a Queen, incredibly would come true when Edward III died. Edward IV and Queen Joan – how marvellous that sounded! And in addition, in fact the aspect that mattered most, mattered far more than that distant vision of absolute royalty, was the fact that theirs would be a love match – the greatest love match in all the world. One side of her mind was even saying – let him lose all, that I can prove how gladly I would share nothingness with him. . . . She knew that Edward III – her cousin Edward – would never be reconciled to the marriage, and that even Philippa, who'd been her foster-mother and had loved her, would find it hard to accept. But Queen Philippa, like most women, was a realist – she'd had to be in that great family of Plantagenets – and eventually she would welcome her with a good grace for her son's sake, and would in the end reconcile the King to accepting the marriage as well, once he'd got over his first rage. After all, the beloved Philippa always eventually won her kind and generous way.

When the Lady Joan rejoined her ladies in the Great Hall, her hair was bound back and confined in its wonted crestine ornamented with spangles, her surcoat fitted decorously over her kirtle, and her slim waist was emphasised by a low-fitting girdle complete with pouch. No one could have guessed the crisis she had passed through. Nevertheless she was very gay with them that evening and allowed them to take turns working at the great tapestry on its frame, while all joined in lighthearted songs and roundelays.

The Black Prince himself never forgot that spring. Since early boyhood he had been trained by jousts, tournays, singlestick, wrestling, archery, for the main and only purpose of masculine life; warfare. At sixteen years of age he had become the hero of Crecy; the chief honour of that day rested with him, and it was there he had adopted, as the badge of the Prince of Wales, the three feathers worn by the blind King of Bohemia who was killed fighting on the French side. A love of flashing colour, of movement, noise, excitement and glory combined to give men a fierce enthusiasm for war. The sheer joy of living expressed itself in violent action and in tests of personal courage that overflowed in patriotic song. Not yet was Edward's penchant for warfare to degenerate into an appetite for cruel slaughter. And this spring of 1361 saw an entire break in the continuity of his interests.

For the first time since his small boyhood, he looked at the green peaceful English countryside and learned to love it. It was as if his senses were opened to beauty, to the songs of birds he'd long forgotten, to scents that reminded him nostalgically of childhood, to sounds of waters murmuring by the rutted lanes, to scenes that touched his heart with pride and love. As he traversed the green uncrowded land, where game stirred in the thick forests and wild-fowl cluttered the wide marshes, he passed again and again through the repetitive pattern of the countryside: stretches of unbroken verdure, then the open strips of cultivated arable land around a few cottages and hovels clustered about a church, a castle or manor-house, and a monastery, then once again the unbroken verdure stretching as far as eye could see. On these continual journeys from London north into Essex, he marvelled at his own sharpened emotions. Can it possibly be, he wondered, that, at my age, I'm really loving for the first time, rather than merely desiring? Is this what is meant by being in love?

He noted that the landscape itself was slowly changing. The villages and hamlets had shrunk most pitifully with the terrible loss of lives due to bubonic plague and later recurrent epidemics. In a few places, the long open strips of arable land were beginning to be exchanged for separate holdings strangely enclosed by hedges. Then, too, some of the held-in-common folk-land was being converted to Royal hunting grounds, where game preservation was enforced by pitiless game laws; this was not only to reserve a selfish royal sport but to make it possible to obtain fresh meat for the huge Courts. What else could they do, Prince Edward wondered – and yet was newly aware of how hardly the poaching laws weighed on the common people who naturally liked hawking, or running after hare-hounds, and certainly enjoyed a chance at a haunch of venison. And when land was seized and enclosed that had really been common land, no wonder the peasantry was outraged. Ah! but however clumsy and unfair some of the laws appeared to be, at least they were a groping towards making order out of the chaos of those bygone terrible ages when there was practically no law at all.

But mostly, on his forays through the countryside in that

strange spring, the Prince of Wales was joyous in an entirely new manner to such as he. Next time he rode those twenty-five miles or so northward of London, he noted a few wan snow-drops already peeping out to meet the cold occasional sunbeam. Edward pulled his cloak around him as the bleak east wind whistled through the withered sedges and the dull leaden sky seemed to weigh on the north-western hilltops. His horse's hoofs rang on the frost-bound rutted roadway, and bare trees made a tangled tracery against the heavy clouds.

In February, heavy rains succeeded the snow, and wet slushy ground made heavy going. In places, miles of marshes lay under-water, broken here and there by the tops of trees. Soon, the fragrant primroses startled the infrequent passer-by with their flash of pale gold, making the traveller aware that spring was indeed on the way. By March the daisies were in bloom – the day's eye, as the country people always called them – and the birds began to return in this month of rapidly changing shower and sun. Some-times the woodlark startled Edward with his song so that he reined up his horse to listen. But the most heartening bird-sound came in April when the messenger of spring flew from tree to tree singing 'cuckoo! cuckoo!' Irrepressibly, he drew up his horse by the scalloped reins and burst into song:

> 'Summer is a-coming in, a-coming in, a-coming in
> Loud sings cuckoo!
> Grows the seed and blooms the mead,
> And sprouts the wood now.
> Sing, sing, sing cuckoo!
> The ewe bleats after the lamb,
> The cows lows after the calf,
> The bullock leaps, the buck goes to doe –
> Merrily sing cuckoo –
> Cuckoo, cuckoo, *cuckoo* –
> Cease thou never to sing CUCKOO!'

Laughing at his own exuberance – why! he hadn't felt like this since he was a boy – he wondered fleetingly what other youth, bemused and intoxicated with the spring and with the surge of his own blood, had shouted that most popular of spring songs during the last hundred years. He even found himself approaching Waltham with sprigs of May blossoms entangled in the reins. By now, sunrise was before 4 a.m. and the early breakfast hour was a blessing before the long stretch of daylight.

Soon the rough highways would be shadowed by heavy foliage,

the scent of the flowers all-pervading, the clamour of birds almost deafening in its intensity, while the continuous humming of bees was a reminder that England's early nickname had been Island of Honey. Beauty was everywhere, tugging at the heart-strings. High summer in the English countryside would be foretaste of Paradise.

Not that it was unnecessary to keep a sharp look-out against lawless marauders on these same rutty roads. Murderers, thieves and outlaws skulked in the underbrush where it was impossible for the King's officers to provide protection. The Prince of Wales passed the isolated manor houses, the infrequent noblemen's castles, and the log shanties of the poor with their bare earth floors and thatched roofs, or saw the peasants with their oxen cultivating the strips of land, with a feeling of safety. But once on the lonelier roads, a scuttling in the brush, the sound of approaching steeds, even the flicker of sun shade on the road ahead, made him instinctively touch the handle of his dagger. Sometimes his horse was startled by innumerable coneys dashing across the road, or a single deer or fox.

Groups travelled together for safe convoy, but when the approaching figure was alone, it usually turned out to be a travelling Friar, or a Pardoner, or one of Wycliffe's poor priests, intent on carrying the Holy Word to remote hamlets. The Black Prince saluted them with good cheer and reflected how strange it was that so great a spiritual leader as John Wycliffe appeared to be, should be so intent on reforming the Church. His idea of turning the Bible into the Common Tongue, when, of course, each book had to be reproduced with endless and incessant individual copying with pen and ink and brush, had become an obsession – an obsession that, though no one yet realised it, was to alter the whole religious life of an England that was rapidly being fused into a nation.

But sometimes the distant sounds materialised into a group of minstrels, jugglers, beggars, pilgrims – wayfarers of every kind and every degree of plausibility bringing the strangest breath of outside air to the untravelled villager; a villager who still knelt on the stone floor of his church on Sundays to hear his parish priest mumble the service in incomprehensible Latin.

When, after two or three hours hard riding, the Black Prince reached Waltham, the architectural beauty of the monumental cross struck him anew. What an ideal marriage his great-grandfather, the powerful Edward I, must have had to mourn his dead wife so passionately. This was but one of thirteen crosses – now used for outdoor preaching – that the great King had had erected in every spot where the royal bier rested with the body of his beloved Eleanor on its last sad journey from Lincolnshire to Westminster in that dark November of 1290, seventy years ago. The last cross of all in the funeral route was named the *Chère Reine's* cross, in the endearing words the royal widower had always used to describe his Queen; soon the phrase was Anglicised to 'Charing Cross' . . . But now the Black Prince spurred on his horse, reminding himself that his business was not with the past, however intriguing. For him, the present and the future, and perhaps, God willing, a marriage as fortunate as his ancestor's. He'd have to eat his words that women were all alike, that sex was a fleeting whim easily indulged with any pleasant woman. Perhaps, subconsciously, he realised that his heightened awareness, his prolonged trance-like state of ecstasy, had been induced by his belated falling in love.

But Joan was beginning to grow restive. Yes, she too felt a mad happiness watching the whole unfolding pageant of this particular year. But, woman-like she was more practical: *when* was their marriage to be arranged? Ah, yes, Edward swore, no man should ever again possess her but himself.

Women are greater realists than men. Inevitably, Queen Philippa realised what was engrossing her eldest son. At first her mind refused to accept the long-dreaded possibility. Then, her heart committed her to making the best of whatever Prince Edward claimed as essential to his happiness. 'Yes, yes,' she reiterated, her candid face lighted with affection, 'I promise you, Edward, it will be all right. Leave it to me.' She would not spoil his relief by betraying her own doubts and indecisions, or by showing what the struggle would cost her. Man-like, he then took it for granted it would be easy for her; yet, she thought, a trifle sardonically, as Queen-consort I am in reality the King's subject, not his equal – and then chided herself for such a thought: her husband had seen to it that she received homage and devoir as became one of almost similar importance to himself.

Philippa laid her plans carefully. She waited till they were at Windsor Castle, twenty miles west of London, that principal seat of English kings since the time of William the Conqueror. Edward III loved both its propinquity to the river and to Windsor Forest with its teeming wild life, so he had continued with its building. He boasted that it was becoming a worthy residence even for the Kings of England – and not only a State Residence, but a fortress

16

and a castle. Beneath the summit of the knoll on which the Round Tower stood, a riverside plain ran down to the limpid water. This was the ideal setting for tournaments and jousts when gorgeously-gowned ladies sat in tiers around the lists, and the eye was caught by the brilliant colours of pavilions, and of heralds in their gaudy tabards.

Now it was supper time in the Great Hall of Windsor – a scene of happiness and confusion. Servants scuttled back and forth with dishes and with lighted torches which they stuck in sconces round the walls, though it was not yet dark. Not only were knights and squires at many of the tables, but extra places were laid for any who cared to sup. Minstrels were making merry music, and every now and then burst into song. The King's jester passed between the tables, his cock's head cowl throwing fantastic shadows on the walls from the flickering torches, as he familiarly tapped some shoulders with his bauble.

Philippa looked lovingly across at her lord. He was fond of the fanciful dishes served up to him, and tonight was obviously enjoying the poultry, the good cheer, the songs and roundelays. Impossible to realise he is nearly fifty, she thought fondly, and was glad that of all their big family of children, the seventh and youngest son, Thomas Woodstock, was here with them tonight. It kept one young to have a child still barely seven years old. Difficult not to succumb to the temptation of spoiling the last one of the litter! Perhaps she did indulge Thomas too much – allowing him to be imperious in his childish rages, and even acquiescing in leaving him as Regent for his father two years ago when she and Edward III had been campaigning in France! Never mind, he'll have to learn moderation as he grows up, thought Philippa indulgently. Life itself schools us all in time. (Perhaps it was as well she could not foresee the dire consequences of giving free rein to Thomas's headstrong, predatory temperament.)

Two hours later, the King, repletely yawning, was ready to retire. Now, thought Philippa nervously, is the moment. She stepped up to the tapestry frame in a chamber off the hall and occupied herself threading a needle.

'Do not go yet, my lord,' she said faintly and was annoyed to see her hand was trembling.

'What is it, my Philippa?'

'It is high time our eldest son married.'

'Why, of course. I was speaking only recently of the Lady Margaret of Flanders as a suitable *parti*. Surely you remember? You and I will doubtless live many years yet, but I should like to see the grandson who will succeed our Edward – Edward IV as he will be – on this great throne of England.'

'In this modern age,' said Philippa softly, 'princes sometimes like to choose for themselves – no – no – let me finish.' It came out as a jerking spasm: 'Our son is desperately enamoured of the Lady Joan of Kent.'

The King had risen, was looking positively apoplectic, and almost fell over a faldstool – which he promptly kicked out of his path. 'Never – never,' he shouted, 'you yourself know the innumerable obstacles.'

'Indeed I know them all,' she admitted sadly, 'I also know we loved her as a child – and Edward loves her now.'

'Why, Salisbury, to whom she was originally contracted – to all intents and purposes married – is still alive. And that is not all, as you admitted.'

'Yes. But Edward will never marry anyone else. Now he will never be contracted to anyone except for love.'

'Love? *love!*' stuttered the King furiously, 'what the devil is the world coming to? Is there nothing to be said for the old virtues of duty, diplomacy and policy? . . . All this modern parade of love as the mainspring and incentive of courage and chivalry – bah! 'tis but a fashion imported from France that we bow to as an amusement . . . an idle fashion *pour passer le temps*. Dynasties are not founded on such decorative whims of an idle hour. Your Jean Froissart is one of those who believes in parading love as the *raison d'être* for every happening. He's young yet and will grow beyond that frivolous French phase. But as to Edward – no – never, never, never.'

She turned and looked at him – at his face blotched and darkened with rage, at his hands clasping and unclasping, at his foot pounding the rush-strewn floor. Holding her head calmly high she came and stood directly in front of him. Her compassion lent her courage.

'Ah! gentle sir,' she cried, in almost the same words she'd used fifteen years earlier when she begged for the lives of the burghers at the siege of Calais, 'I would kneel to you now as I did once before – but today I'm not so young and supple. You gave me then the lives of six good citizens. Now I ask for the happiness of our eldest son – as before, in proof of your love for me.'

He groaned and turned his head away.

'Alas! again. I cannot refuse you. Lady, you drive a hard

bargain. But – I cannot refuse you. God send we do not live to rue it.'

'No – it will be all right. You will see,' she comforted, stroking his hands with hers. Suddenly she laughed, the clear sweet laugh of her girlhood. 'Edward, you speak as if all love matches were weaknesses. Yet – what was ours but that, all those long years ago?'

'That was entirely different,' he insisted, smiling now. 'How would it be, my Philippa, if when those two are married, we bestowed Aquitaine on them to rule? Edward could hold Court there. But of course,' he added hastily, 'the wedding must wait at least till her year of widowhood is over.'

'Not even that,' she said gravely, still clasping his hand. 'We shall have to get a Papal Dispensation. And,' she added, her heart heavy at the prospect of the inevitable definite parting, 'I think your plan for Aquitaine most excellent. . . . Come now, my lord, I've kept you up far too late if you intend to go hawking in the morning. It must be all of nine o'clock.'

CHAPTER THREE

UNDER ALL these circumstances, the wedding was a fairly subdued affair for a Prince of Wales who was the hero of his day. Nevertheless it inevitably held some grandeur. The solemn handbinding or betrothal at Lambeth Palace before the Archbishop of Canterbury and the Bishop of Winchester was entirely private except for a few members of the bridegroom's household; it was followed four days later on Monday, 10th October, 1361 by the actual wedding in the Garter Chapter at Windsor. (To which previous similar occasions did the bride's mind revert – or was she able to forget the past in this consummation of her dreams?) Even this was attended mainly by some of the Royal Family since the King was still extremely upset about the whole business.

Young Jean Froissart saw little of these events, a fact which was frustrating to him in the extreme. A native of Valenciennes, he was only twenty-four years old, but had been writing the stories of the wars of his times and the history that had led up to them, since his nineteenth year. Twelve months ago, he had come to

England in search of further material and of adventure. France, England, Scotland, Flanders, Germany, Italy, Spain, were all to be the subjects of his pen. Though he travelled modestly on horseback with his portmanteau slung up behind him, and followed by his faithful greyhound, he was welcomed at Courts by lords and knights, heralds and squires who eagerly contributed their quota of fact and gossip to his rapidly accumulating mass of materials with which he would eventually affect the whole standard of history. That he loved hunting and music, dancing and all the amusements of the age rendered him acceptable in any company. Queen Philippa had made him very welcome at the English Court when he arrived in 1360 and he became her secretary. Sometimes he lightly amused her by composing amorous ditties and virelays; but in reality both of them realised the importance of his chronicles and for this he always held her in the highest respect and veneration. It was while he was attached to the service of the English Court that she urged him to continue travelling in order to gather contemporary historical material. He never forgot his great benefactress.

Another protégé of Queen Philippa's, one who was to shed lustre on the entire age, was the young Londoner, Geoffrey Chaucer. A few years junior to Froissart, Geoffrey had been page and then squire at the English court, and now had only just returned from France where he'd been taken prisoner of war at Réthel. The King, who liked to tease Queen Philippa about the retinue she gathered round the brilliant Court, made a point of reminding her he had contributed £16 towards the ransom demanded for this sparkling youngster. 'Ah! just you wait – you'll never regret it,' she'd retorted placidly.

Already this youth was crazed with cadences of poetry. Sometimes when he was sought for to read aloud in his melodious voice to the assembled company at Court, he would be found poring over some manuscript on which, to him, the written words were the symbolic gateways to a magic world. Bemused, he would lift his head from the tumbled pages of the hundred-year-old French poem, 'Roman de la Rose', with its enthralling presentment of the love philosophy of the troubadours – and the squire who'd run to fetch him would realise that Geoffrey Chaucer was deep in his dreams of the past. This bulky manuscript strongly influenced the young man, who soon, however, developed his own keen observation, sense of ironical humour and psychological insight, and, even more significantly, started to abandon the use of French and to write with such technical excellence in his own

20

clearly-formulated style that henceforth English was the only possible language for England's writers.

But though these young men were not at the royal wedding, Jean Froissart was staying at the Castle of Berkhamsted in the Queen's entourage just before the Black Prince and his bride departed at last in June of 1363 to rule over the English lands in France. Actually it was here they had spent their honeymoon in that October of two years previously, for this manor in Hertfordshire, once the seat of the old Kings of Mercia, belonged by right to the eldest son of the Kings of England and thus had been part of Edward's mighty inheritance at the age of seven as Prince of Wales. Here he had entertained, jousted, hunted, in the carefree days of his bachelorhood between the battles and campaigns on the Continent which, since Crecy, had left France bare and pillaged. To these familiar surroundings he was proud to take Joan as his bride in that mellow October of 1361.

They were very much in love. Compared with war-devastated France, the English countryside looked serene, peaceful, prosperous – fit background for their wild, ecstatic happiness. No longer could anyone consider the match unsuitable. Even the King was reconciled.

It was now a yellow autumn, with the first light frosts mornings and evenings throwing into relief the golden sunshine of midday. After the heat of summer, some of the most exhilarating weather of the year had set in, as the leaves fell in the forest after turning red and gold. The ancient oaks burned burnished bronze while, amidst the thinning trees, the firs showed darkly green. Slowly the landscape turned more sombre. The husbandmen began sowing their winter grain. Together, the royal honeymooners indulged their favourite sport of hawking. Soon most of the singing birds would be gone; only a few notes were heard now in the woods, though the woodcocks, the snipe and the redwing were among the fresh arrivals of the autumn days. . . . All too quickly the drear month of November, with its leaden skies, would herald in the winter and the cattle would have to be slaughtered and salted down.

Joan delighted in those early mornings when the sound of the dogs whining, the horses stamping in the courtyard, and the voices of the falconers gathering below, woke them before the dawn. Directly the bridal pair got down to them, the old falconers proudly exhibited the falcons in their rough wooden cages for their choice, while stable-boys wiped off the horses and hounds with clean wisps of straw. With much laughter, the hunters chose

21

hooded hawks for their gauntleted wrists and rode off among the beaters and dogs. Joan left the largest falcon to the Black Prince though she herself was also adept at slipping the falcon's hood from his eyes and hurling him, like an arrow from a bow, at the first sight of a quarry. Some of the great falcons flew to tremendous heights in order to plummet like slingshots on their prey to the falconers' swelling chorus of encouragement . . . Sometimes the horses galloped for miles as if this chase were part of a real battle-field – as indeed all life was, thought the Black Prince exultantly, looking at the flushed and laughing woman beside him. A fit mate indeed for a warrior!

So it was here that the Prince and Princess of Wales entertained the whole Royal Family at a five-day house party before they at length departed for their domains in Aquitaine. It was a gay hilarious party; Jean Froissart was never to forget it, owing to a small odd circumstance. Difficult to recognise at the time they occur, those happenings that will, eventually in retrospect, bear most significance.

It had worried Jean Froissart on this visit to Berkhamsted to see a momentary look of sadness rest on Queen Philippa's broad and candid brow. Yes, she was going to mind this more permanent parting with her eldest son. But meeting Jean's eyes, she smiled quite gaily. Once more he marvelled at all the noble unselfish qualities his patroness possessed. Ah, *c'est un coeur d'or*, he thought; whatever she went through was her own private battle and was never allowed to destroy contentment or serenity . . . But this visit was an opportunity. He must not be deflected from gathering material for his chronicles. Nothing passed that he did not wish to witness, nothing escaped his curiosity. Even gossip and the most casual chatter intrigued him so that he never went to bed before he'd written down all he'd heard and seen during the day.

Now, wandering about the castle, he suddenly overheard the sound of merry bantering voices from a group of the Queen's ladies by the arras in the great hall. Why, that was a knight known as Burghersshe centred among them, silencing them now with some more serious tale. Heads pivoted in Jean's direction, then ignored him completely as the old knight's voice sank. Jean hesitated, then, hearing the magic name Merlin, sat down on a nearby bench and listened to an exposition of ancient prophecy made by that famous necromancer eight hundred years ago . . . Naturally enough, the Queen's ladies had been talking wistfully, a little enviously, of this love match in the Royal family, of the

22

radiant resurgence of beauty shown by the new Princess of Wales. Burghersshe, lowering his voice, was saying: 'Never begrudge a man his good fortune – or even consider him fortunate – till he is safely dead.' And, to the twittering questions, continued: 'If you believe in the prophecies of Merlin – and who does not? – you will understand that he foretold this Prince of Wales will never wear the crown of England – nor, for that matter will Lionel, Duke of Clarence, the next surviving son of our good King.' A dramatic pause, punctured by a nervous giggle, preluded Burghersshe's low-voiced conclusion: 'The crown will fall, according to his prophecy, to the House of Lancaster.'

Why, thought Jean confusedly, through all the gasps and exclamations of the circle of ladies, that would mean John of Gaunt, or his descendants. What nonsense – not only was the Prince of Wales the beau ideal of every Englishman, but, since he was just married and violently in love, likely to sire an heir . . . Not that Froissart ignored such prophecies as Merlin's – no, no they had been fulfilled too often to be scoffed at; but he did wonder whether the wording had been more ambiguous than Burghersshe implied. In Jean's experience, all too often the text was vague enough to allow almost any construction to be placed upon it.

Appalled, one of the ladies breathed: "That sounds almost like treason,' and half-laughing, half alarmed, the circle broke up, with the ladies swishing and murmuring down the stone-flagged corridor which echoed to their footsteps . . . I must really look up *Le Brut* again, thought Jean. Or, if I can't find that ancient chronicle, perhaps Geoffrey Monmouth's *Vita Merlin* of two hundred years ago will give me a clue. Impossible to dismiss all divinations as untrue and unreliable, he decided. After all, thousands of people had faith in such forms as sideromancy (divination by red-hot iron); thromancy (by oracles); cleromancy (by dice); palmistry (by reading the hand); sortilege (by drawing lots); oneiromancy (by dreams); necromancy (by questioning the spirits of the dead) – and all the other methods of determining fate, including the universally-known astrology.

Strangely enough, it was to be thirty-eight years before this scene recurred forcibly to Jean Froissart's retentive mind.

CHAPTER FOUR

Ah! how Joan, as Princess of Wales, enjoyed queening it at the gay Court of Bordeaux among her colourful circle of ladies. She knew they were much admired for their delicate colouring – her own complexion was wild-rose fair. And their clothes made even the French women envious. Joan wore her cotehardie more and more exaggeratedly form-fitting and of gold tissue or brilliant silks. She loved the new dagged cloaks and the long trailing sleeves. The soft barbette under her chin disguised the fact that she was a trifle heavier, and her draped and spangled veils were carefully chosen to contrast with her kirtle and to be transparent enough to reveal the jewelled circlet in her hair.

That she became *enceinte* within three months of her arrival in France, of course meant a modification of her style. But she accepted this even though after all these years it seemed odd to start bearing children again. She knew this was her chief duty to the realm, to the Prince of Wales, and to King Edward and Queen Philippa. A bouncing baby was born 17th July, 1364, and inevitably christened Edward. There – she had done her duty. Everyone was satisfied with her. This youngest boy would soon be taken from her to be rigorously trained in all the arts of chivalry and to be a future king; now she could revert to being gay, lovely, admired and, above all, to being the chosen companion and lover of her own Black Prince.

She was unreasonably resentful when she realised she'd conceived another child. It was too much.

Towards the sixth and seventh months, the Black Prince, while still affectionately considerate of her, not unnaturally left her to her ladies for longer and longer periods while he went hunting, hawking, or on one of his forays into the French countryside. He was due now to depart on campaign and was amazed to find her flouncing up and down her small chamber, averting her face from him when he approached.

'What's the matter, my lady?' he asked, frowning quizzically.

'Huh! How free you men are compared with us – no wonder you're all selfish – after all, it's a man's world.'

'Nonsense,' he retorted firmly, 'you know perfectly well how much women's status has improved – vastly improved – in this age of a chivalry born in this poetic south – and especially under the Plantagenet kings. Come, my love, you will have your full share again of hunting, riding, accompanying me almost on to the battlefield. B'our Lady, you can hardly blame me for the fact that it's the women who bear the children!'

She turned her head away sulkily. After a moment she said grudgingly: 'I expect I'm just tired of bearing children – this will be my sixth. Thomas Holland, my first, was seventeen years ago – a lifetime.'

'Ah!' he said tenderly, 'but this will be only *my* second. Edward of Angouléme is a fine boy – but he's two and a half years old. Time indeed we had another.'

Nettled by the implication that she was far more experienced than he, she said sharply: 'Your second by *me*, you mean, my lord.' Then added pitifully: 'I did not expect you to leave me on your campaigns at such an hour. *I* worry day and night about your safety yet you – yet you – can leave me without a qualm.' Tears rolled down her cheeks, but, when he approached her placatingly, she simply screamed with laughter.

He had never seen Joan hysterical before and it alarmed him mightily. If she continued like this he would call the court midwife and the physician. But first to speak harshly enough to bring her to her senses.

'You can hardly expect me to tarry in your chamber just because you are bearing a child. That is women's work just as man's avocation is to make war. Almighty God made the difference between our functions – not I! Joan, you know I am committed to this expedition to Spain to aid Pedro in his war – and you – you are not even near your time.'

Suddenly she put her head down and sobbed. 'What shall I do – what shall I do – if I lose you? You are all the world to me – I care for nothing else – and to the whole world you are the very flower of chivalry.'

At once he was all tenderness, knelt by the bench on which she sat and embraced her thickened figure. 'Come now, my sweetheart, you are not losing me. You are more likely to lose our baby if you carry on like this.'

And suddenly she raised her head and looked at him as if her eyes were blind or only focused inwardly. 'I think – I really think – I'm having the baby now,' she stammered.

Suddenly the whole household was alerted. The stone-flagged corridors echoed with running feet as pages ran hither and yon with ewers of hot water, the physician arrived in haste to administer various calming nostrums, and the court midwife ejected most of the chattering circle of attendant ladies and equably took charge of the situation. Presently she would admit those who must bear witness to the birth of a royal heir – not that, even if a boy he would be in direct line for the throne. Nevertheless, all such important births must be legally attested by those who were officially present.

It was 3 a.m. of 6th January, 1367 that the thin wail of a new-born infant stirred the arras in that room of the Abey at Bordeaux. Yes, it was a boy, a premature child whose life at first hung in the balance. Joan, who had been crying to the Blessed Virgin for succour every time pain racked her body on that great canopied bed, seemed hardly conscious as she turned away and fell into the pit of sleep, a small smile of relief and satisfaction on her tired face. They would not disturb her now, but directly she awoke, her ladies would wash her hands and face with scented water, brush out her tangled hair and tell her once more how beautiful she looked and that her new son, God permitting, would survive.

Presently she woke when the Prince of Wales bent over her under the bed-canopy. She smiled at him, completely herself again, and murmured: 'Tired, tired.' It was bliss just to lie there and know it was all over. 'A boy?' she queried, searching his face with her great eyes, and wondering at his inscrutable expression. 'Why can't I have him here, my lord?'

'Just rest for the moment – you shall have him presently, my love. Yes, a boy – yes, he's correct in every detail! A little premature, shall we say?' And suddenly she was asleep again as if fallen to the bottom of a well. Ah! Jesu, he thought, later will be time enough to break it to her.

Even when she did awaken, it was to lie half-snoozing, dreaming within the soft comfort of the feather-bed. She thought about her recent life and decided she enjoyed queening it here in Bordeaux and seeing her husband ruling a third of France as Prince of the Duchy and Principality of Aquitaine. Whatever opposition may have been felt for them was apparently disarmed by his great reputation and her loveliness, emphasised by the dazzling sumptuousness of her costly dresses. After all, Bordeaux, along with Guienne, had really belonged to the English kings for over two hundred years; not only was it the seat of the brilliant Court, but extensive commerce had sprung up between the merchants of Bordeaux and those of London, Exeter and Bristol. All had benefited.

Thus day-dreaming, she never heard the hastily-stilled murmurs in the corridors, the slithering footsteps of those who came hurriedly to the next chamber dragging a succession of goats whose throats were expertly cut so that the weakly premature babe could be thrust into the warmth of the animals' bellies – into a succession of quivering hot and dying flesh – to compensate for the fact that he had been ejected too soon from his mother's womb. It was a desperate expedient. But it worked. By the Friday when the babe was christened ('Richard' in compliment to the Prince of Wales's Chancellor) it looked as if, with continued cosseting, he would live. And by the following Sunday. the Prince of Wales was off once more to the wars.

Ashamed of her recent hysteria, Joan managed a smiling, loving farewell, as he knelt by her bed and embraced her in *au revoir*. And when her ladies trooped in from the ramparts, some in tears at bidding a husband or a lover farewell, and described to her how gallant and colourful the departing embannered troop had looked in the thin winter sunshine as it clattered across the drawbridge and away, she laughed and chided those who wept. 'Come now – think of the joy and gay celebrations we shall have on their return.' Nevertheless, her heart was weeping with a sad premonition. Perhaps all that saved her from breaking down was the fact that the tactful French nurse, Mundina Danos, chose that moment to bring in tidings of her charge to comfort her Royal Mistress. Yes, she should see him soon; for the moment he needed extra care.

And in his lodgings in the town, the young chronicler, Jean Froissart, who endlessly set down fact, fiction, rumour and conjecture, was puzzling his head over another strange prophecy that one of the Prince's officers had just related to him: that this frail babe, whose life hung by a thread, would one day be King of England. God's blood, thought Froissart crossly, even if he manages to survive at all, he'll never make half the man his elder brother will. Richard of Bordeaux – maybe he'll be dearer to his mother for all the cosseting he'll need. Mothers, royal ones or not, are apt to be that way.

And when at last, Joan did see the babe, holding her hands out formally to receive the thickly swaddled bundle, expertly carried in Mundina's motherly arms, she burst into irrepressible mirth.

'Why – I can't believe it! He's quite ugly . . . How terribly red and wrinkled he is – one would think he was parboiled. And his head – look, Mundina – the shape at the back – isn't it odd?'

Mundina Danos was quite outraged. She held the infant tightly against her abundant bosom and refused to give him over to such a scant welcoming.

'He was born two months too soon,' she said stiffly, 'he's only just growing his skin by virtue of being continuously placed within the throbbing bodies of still-warm animals. His head? I see nothing wrong with that, and when he grows his lovely golden Plantagenet hair he'll be as beautiful as an angel. *We're* glad he's alive,' she added rebukingly.

Joan sobered and took her baby in her arms. Suddenly it was as if her heart turned over in her breast. What is happening to me, she thought angrily, I've never felt this maternal urge so overwhelmingly with any of my other children . . . There are two types of womanhood, and I – I've always been a mate, a wife, a man's ideal lover first and a mother as quite secondary role. I pine now, ceaselessly, God knows, for his father. . . . As for our sons, we lose them so young to the world of pagedom and squiredom, jousts, tournaments and wars – they're little men before they're seven. But this one – he's not my husband's eldest. Edward, a lusty child, will soon be *en train* for eventual Kingship. Maybe, maybe, this one will need me terribly – and I shall turn into a devoted mother. She laughed lightly as if to deny that her strong warm personality had suddenly flowered towards the helpless infant.

And Mundina was indeed proved right. Richard of Bordeaux developed an almost luminous beauty since his skin, translucently fair, glowed as with an inner light. Glancing at him, one was apt to remember that eight hundred years earlier, Pope Gregory, struck by the same angelic fairness of the little English boys in the slave-marts of Rome, had remarked he wished the Angles could qualify as Angels – and had sent St Augustine to England towards that end.

Delicate, beautiful, highly-strung, Richard was surrounded by protecting and admiring women who fostered in him both his father's brilliance and his mother's love of beauty and gaiety. It all seemed to suit well enough with his slightly effeminate appearance – which surely mattered not one whit since his elder brother could carry on the war-like traditions of the Black Prince. And yet – he bore a physical resemblance to his absent father though in a slightly different mould, and Bishop Sudbury often commented on the likeness. Even his violent childish tantrums were suffered as part of the Plantagenet legend – when he occasionally rolled on the floor in a paroxysm of babyish rage it would be to the mixed exasperation and adoration of a circle of women. He early realised that he was only the younger son, the one who didn't really matter; all the more did he make a constant demand for affection from his mother, from Mundina, from the whole court. His great need was to give love and to be loved in return.

Strange how selective are childhood memories. Some happenings, even some scraps of conversation, can be recalled over the years as if they happened yesterday. Richard's grandmother, Queen Philippa, died when he was barely three and somehow, from then, tragic events came thick and fast as the Plantagenet dynasty seemed to disintegrate . . . Thirty years later, shivering in a prison cell, Richard would visualise these happenings as clearly as if pictured in murals on the walls. Yet many of them were merely fabrications of his vivid imagination from snatches of conversations carried on above his head by oblivious adults.

The Queen had been ill of the dropsy and was in bed at Windsor Castle. Forty years she and Edward III had lived together; she was well-beloved by high and low for all she had done, not only for her family, but for England. The Black Prince, absent from her death-bed on campaign, was prostrated with grief; when he returned to England, he found his father a broken man.

In fact, when the Queen's illness took so severe a turn, none of the family was with her at Windsor except her husband and her youngest son, Thomas Woodstock, now fifteen years old. Somehow, at the end, it did not seem to matter. This was how it had been more than forty years ago when as a golden boy with his mother, Edward had visited the homely Court of Hainault and she, the little princess, had sobbed so innocently, so childishly, at his leaving: 'I can't bear to part with you,' – much to the mortifying amusement of the courtiers. . . . Now, turning her waxen face on the pillow to see him stoop his tall head neath the lintel, she felt again – how can I bear to leave him? Ah! but there were tears in his eyes and she must not upset him too terribly. Making a great effort, she took her right hand out from under the coverlet and let him seize it in his muscular fist. For a moment neither spoke. His heart felt as if it had risen to his throat and were choking him.

'Ah! my lord,' she whispered, 'this is our separation. But only for a little while. You know, as positively as I, that we shall meet again in Paradise. . . .' Her voice faltered and broke. As a good Catholic, indeed he was sure; but at the moment it seemed scant recompense for the here and now.

'We should not be sad,' she went on after a moment, 'we

29

have had so many years of happiness together.' Tears ran down into his long forked beard; for a moment she looked at them wonderingly. 'I must – must – manage to ask the rest.'

'What is it, my darling wife? You know I have never been able to refuse you anything at all.'

With her voice getting slower and weaker, she outlined exactly what gifts she wanted made to her ladies-in-waiting, to her friends, her relations, the Churches she loved both here and on the Continent wherein she'd paid her devotions. Then suddenly her voice began hurrying – for this was what mattered more than all: 'Lastly – I intreat you – I beg – when it shall please our Lord to call you hence – wherever you may be at the time of passing – that – that – you will not choose to lie in any other grave than mine – by my side in the cloisters of Westminster Abbey.'

The King put his head down on the bed beside her. 'Of course, it shall be exactly as you say. Everything. Everything.' He felt her hand gently withdrawn as she made the sign of the cross, then blessed him too. . . . It was not for a few moments that he realised that she was gone and he allowed himself to burst into the loud weeping of desolation.

Strange how Richard always felt he'd been present in that small chamber at Windsor Castle on that hot August day of 1369, when actually it was his Uncle Thomas, barely a dozen years his senior – always stressing his superiority and Richard's childishness – who boasted he was there when his Queen mother passed away. Actually, what the impressionable Richard afterwards recalled was doubtless the loving description his own mother gave to him. Holding him within the circle of her arm in far-away Bordeaux, Joan described so clearly how the loved Queen had surrendered her spirit to God – 'caught up by holy angels and carried to the glory of heaven, for she had never done anything by thought or deed that could endanger her losing it,' – that for ever after Richard's mind's-eye saw quite vividly that bevy of beautiful angels ascending with his grandma to the very gates of Paradise.

After that, events in his young life telescoped with lightning rapidity. Later he never could disentangle them. For to a child, each year is an eternity. Will Christmas never come? – How endless the months seem since my last birthday! – but in retrospect, the whole of childhood fuses into a golden summer's afternoon, or a jumbled series of pictures of disaster.

Richard was barely four when his brother died. His memory of that was chiefly of Mundina's face, plain and broad and kindly, leaning close to his own in commiseration.

'Come, come, *mon petit* – don't be a worry to your mother just now. She's very sad. You're all leaving for England as fast as possible. The ship's here in harbour. They say the wind's fair.'

He clutched her hands. 'You too, Mundy? Don't leave me.'

Unexpectedly, she wiped her eyes with the corner of her wimple.

'Nonsense – of course I shan't leave you. You can always count on Mundina.'

He remembered next day by the sound of marching feet: marching, marching over the cobblestones down to Bordeaux Harbour – five hundred combatants and archers to take their places in the fore and aft castles of the ships in port. Richard thought all the masts looked like a forest of trees, except that in their fighting-tops men were stationed with stones and other missiles. For who could tell whether Charles V, Le Sage, the King of France, would intercept them before they reached port at Plymouth or Southampton? But as it happened, the winds satisfactorily filled the bellying sails so that it was unnecessary to use the old-fashioned auxiliary oars . . . How frighteningly sick his father looked, being carried aboard ship in a litter – and who was going to look after the Court and all of Aquitaine? Why? Why? Why?

'Don't ask so many questions,' said Mundina gruffly. But she wasn't really cross, he could tell. She would explain presently as far as she was able. As they embarked she turned to take her last look at Bordeaux – a sad nostalgic glance.

Later, aboard, she talked a little while getting him ready for the night. Yes, his brother Edward had gone to be with God. Yes, his mother and father were naturally upset and sad at God taking him so soon. Why was his father travelling in a kind of bed? Well, he'd picked up some sort of bug on this last disastrous foray into Spain. And he had the Bloody Flux. Pray God he'd get better, for the Princess of Wales loved him passionately and thought he might recover his health in England. No, no, of course they hadn't left Aquitaine to fall into the hands of the King of France; his uncle, John of Gaunt, Duke of Lancaster, ten years younger than his father, had yesterday received *hommage de bouche et des mains* from the barons of Aquitaine, Gascony, Poitou and Saintonge who had sworn loyalty.

What a lot of uncles he had, he thought, drowsily, falling asleep to the pleasant motion of the ship. He couldn't remember the giant one, Lionel of Clarence who'd died when he was a baby. But beside Uncle John there was the easy-going Edmund, Duke of York, whom everybody liked without taking too seriously – and then, just before Richard fell asleep, he remembered the youngest uncle, Thomas Woodstock, much younger than Richard's own half-brothers and openly contemptuous of him as a mere baby. Perhaps now he'd get to know this young uncle better and stop being so afraid of him. . . . These thoughts were only half-formulated – the precocious perceptions which subconsciously influence one's whole fate.

These, and the sight of his father's collapsed and yellowing face, like a disintegrating fragment of a manuscript, glimpsed in the litter, were among Richard's earliest memories. His father had been away so much on wars, campaigns, jousts and tournaments, that he never felt he knew him terribly well.

In the night he'd wakened suddenly to the sound of whispering voices. His beautiful mother was sitting beside him in a thick velvet cotehardie edged with ermine. She sounded sad as she murmured despairingly: 'What will become of him? Everything has fallen to pieces at Court since Queen Philippa died. The poor King – indeed I'm sorry for him – but really! Such a woman as Alys Perrers. It isn't even dignified.'

Mundina made commiserating noises. 'Well – after all she *was* a lady of the bed-chamber to Her Majesty,' she said.

'Huh! d'you realise, Mundina, that he's given her goods, jewels, and chattels that were his Queen Consort's private property – in addition to several manor houses? Ah! he's been such a brilliant King – such a genius among men – and now he's the prey of that harpy.' Joan rose in the cramped ship-board space, and struck her hands together: 'I can't bear the Plantagenets to be brought low. *I* am a Plantagenet by birth as well as marriage.

'Mundina,' she went on, her voice rising in her indignation, 'surely he can't be senile, he's not yet sixty. I can't bear for the Prince of Wales, ill as he is, to return to a Court shorn of its dignity.'

'Hush, Madame,' whispered Mundina composedly, 'We shall wake the boy.'

Indeed, he had turned his head and whimpered a little as the nurse laid her hand gently on his brow.

Joan turned and looked at her. The broad weathered face, the determined mouth, the steadfast eyes held her own. A rare emotion stirred the Princess of Wales. 'Mundina,' she said softly, 'you would give your heart's blood for Richard, wouldn't you? And he's not even your own. Thank you – thank you for coming with us to England. I trust you – I can talk to you as I talk to no other woman.' With a swirl of her voluminous robes she was gone.

Nothing of this remained with Richard. Even had he been wide awake his memory would not have retained so incomprehensible a scene. But one day the faint echo of Dame Alys Perrer's name would recur like the lost phrase of a dream.

CHAPTER FIVE

IT WAS a sad homecoming in that bleak January of 1371. The crowds near Plymouth were eager enough to show their enthusiasm at having their Prince and Princess of Wales back with them once more. But it was difficult to display much joy when one saw the bereaved couple who had just lost their elder son; and the sight of the Prince of Wales – their Black Prince – being painfully landed on a pallet, totally unable once ashore to sit a horse, was a blow for which even rumour had ill prepared them. The Princess of Wales – that still Fair Maid at forty-three – though slightly thickened in figure, still retained her wonderful English complexion which had been the envy of the ladies at the brilliant Court of Bordeaux. Subdued cheers were raised for her as she rode astride her palfrey beside the chariot which accommodated the Black Prince's litter. Behind came the wagon with the four-year-old Prince Richard, clutching one hand of Mundina Danos – and beyond, from other ships, some loot was being unpacked from the wars in France.

Crecy and Poitiers had thrown a glamour of military glory over the age, but, horribly enough, this had been followed by the Black Prince's campaign of sheer pillage, with him leading his freebooters up the Garonne valley to rob the simple innocent inhabitants of that rich peaceful countryside of everything they owned. Consequently, north and central France were ravaged by famine; ruins and uncultivated land lay in the wake of the bandits whose horses could hardly move beneath the weight of looted treasure. Not that the loot did the invading armies much good for beneath its weight they wore and wasted themselves away, finding no sustenance in a countryside they themselves had devastated.

For Charles le Savant (or Le Sage, depending on how you regarded him) – who, in reality, was wily and cunning rather than wise – defeated the English armies in the long run by avoiding and evading pitched battles. He cold-heartedly sacrificed the French countryside – what did the wretched countryfolk matter anyway? – by letting the alien armies drag themselves through the land they'd laid waste, where, eventually they were obliged to abandon not only much of their plunder but some of their own accoutrements. . . . Charles's health had always been wretched: as a youth he suffered from a mysterious malady which involved the loss of his hair and his nails. He had a chronic abscess under his arm and his doctors told him that he would die within two weeks of its closing. (This sign would occur in 1380 when he accepted death.) In the meantime, leading the sedentary life of a sickly man, he turned towards learning. He knew several languages, studied astrology, alchemy and theology, and was popularly credited with practising black magic in the secret chambers of his palace. All this, coupled with his silent unscrupulous life, his cold-hearted successful policy of 'no battles' even to defend his own countryside, led to the revival of French power and the complete bafflement of King Edward III.

And now here was the Black Prince returning to England after a meteoric career, to languish out the sad remainder of his days with the sight etched on his memory of his last act of war – that of being carried slowly on his litter through the smoke and blood of burned and ruined Limoges, past the blackened ruins of homes, the thousands of bloody corpses of women, children and warriors . . . And smelling the hot sweet odour of blood. Yet, it had availed nothing. The English rule in France had become precarious and was drawing to its end.

To the Princess of Wales, seeing her husband now probably doomed to an early death – Ah, Mother Mary have mercy! she kept whispering – the price for all past glory at last seemed exorbitant. Surely this lovely peaceful land of England, unbelievably fair, unravaged and untouched, would restore the Black Prince's health? Oh, it was time they all came home. She shuddered when she remembered her husband's last terrible act of vengeance at Limoges, when he'd ordered his troops to retake the town and massacre three thousand men, women and children. She pushed the nightmare memory to the back of her mind. It was a barren success. In a few years, Bordeaux, Bayonne and Calais alone would remain of the great English possessions in France.

'Where are we going?' the Black Prince asked, turning his head painfully on the pillow. The wax-like pallor of his face struck Joan to the heart. Somehow he looked older and frailer against the tender greens of England where the pale winter sunlight came filtered as through gauze. . . . She smiled down at him, pulling on her scalloped reins. 'Our manor of Berkhamsted will be most restful till you've recovered your strength. I'll ride with you part of the way – and part with Richard. He's right behind you with Mundina.' The rumble of wagons came to his ears mingled with the clatter of men-at-arms.

'We should show ourselves to the Londoners,' said the Black Prince fretfully. 'Then, too, I've never been enough with Richard. He'll need severe training and discipline for his position – if I can manage it.'

'Of course you can, my love,' Joan countered firmly. 'And we'll go through London to Berkhamsted. As for Richard, I know you intend to let your excellent Sir Simon Burley help with his tutoring,' Sir Simon, now in his mid-thirties, was not only a trusted comrade-in-arms of the Black Prince but was a noted scholar, famed for owning a prodigious library of twenty-one manuscript books – an astounding number to be found outside a cloister.

'Yes,' murmured the Prince and closed his eyes wincingly. Joan drew her fur-lined cloak around her shoulders. Her legs, wrapped around with her voluminous skirts and bundled into pouches on the horse's flanks, were warm enough. Her voluptuous mouth drew into a sad line as she considered the future. Not only was she aware that her husband was terribly ill of that dysentery known as Bloody Flux which gave him griping agony, loss of weight, frequent nausea, with evacuations of blood and mucous, but she realised that this was one of the great killing diseases of the world.

Then, too, to complicate their return, Edward III, her father-in-law, who had been so glorious and famed a King, must be declining into his dotage if only a hundredth part were true of all one heard of his involvement with the notorious Dame Alys Perrers. That such a woman, of neither beauty nor grace – and quite middle-aged into the bargain – should dare to flaunt herself as the King's mistress and appropriate Queen Philippa's jewellery was quite unbearable. Better for them to be at quiet Berkhamsted near Oxford than at Westminster or Windsor with all these goings-on – or even within striking distance of Dame Alys's over-clever yet scurrilous tongue.

Then Joan's mind turned anxiously to the child, Richard. His inheritance might all too easily be threatened by the unscrupulous ambitions of the barons, and even of his uncles. And the mere mention of loot from the struggles on the Continent meant that most of them would want to see almost continuous wars. Was it only women who realised the desolation, the starvation and utter misery that wars left in their wake? Of course she exulted in her husband's fame, but even he had deplored the fact that gun-powder had ever been invented, ruefully declaring that victory nowadays was becoming less a matter of personal courage, of trained valour, of noble blood and knightliness, than of possessing enough engines of war. Yes, he declared, half-jokingly half-serious, he'd rather go back to the brave days of single combat than see fortitude entirely mechanised! Thank God, he himself still had his archers to depend upon.

Suddenly the sun broke through the mist, revealing the distant clear blue of the sky, setting spiders' webs a-glitter and tipping the branches of bare trees with light. Everything smelled sharply fresh as if the world were new-made; a stream of faint sunlight struck the distant hills. Nearby, a robin on a bare hawthorn spray burst into song. . . . Joan's spirits soared. She laughed aloud – ah, we shall be happy! My Edward will recover. Richard will learn to know England, his own country. I've had eight years of glory and success at the Court of Aquitaine where I and my ladies entertained the army and the nobility while displaying our fine shot-silks, our gauzy dresses, our bodices trimmed with ermine. But I don't wish any of it back. Here we are in our own country – unspoiled, beautiful, untouched by warfare. Soon the daffodils will be blowing their trumpets on all the banks around the moat at Berkhamsted. Home! How Richard will love it. . . . She fell back far enough to gaze into the second trundling wagon. He was peacefully asleep with Mundina leaning over him, as if on guard.

CHAPTER SIX

ENGLAND WAS fun, Richard decided. There appeared to be more physical activity than in the more indolent south. Timidly at first and then with increasing zest, he took part in outdoor sports that this colder climate seemed to demand. His fair skin flushed easily with the cold breeze that whipped him to a frenzy of often exhausting animation. His mother was almost feverishly gay as if to deny that her husband was not regaining strength. When she could not be with Richard, his father's friend, Sir Simon Burley, encouraged him at junior joustings in the tilt-yard, to learn wrestling and quarter-stick, to sit his pony with courage for the quintain practices, and even to try to emulate his cousin, Henry Bolingbroke – son to his Uncle John of Gaunt, Duke of Lancaster – in all the exercises at which Henry was already becoming most discouragingly and effortlessly adept.

Soon Richard found he could confide anything to Burley's understanding ears – became, indeed, so fond of dear Sir Simon that, in gratitude, he was willing to spend hours over his studies to please him, knowing that in a few years Burley would become his regular tutor. 'I'll never be as good as Cousin Henry,' he'd said one day despairingly as he and Simon came in together from the tilt-yard, 'yet he and I are almost of an age. He – he – called me a French fop when I didn't ride fast enough at the quintain to avoid a blow from the sand-bag.' He rubbed the back of his head ruefully, remembering the mocking laughter. 'I'm English, aren't I, even if I was born in France? Why do he and Uncle Thomas despise me?'

Sir Simon put one arm across his shoulder. 'You will be the most English of us all,' he promised. 'Your cousin Henry – and your Uncle Thomas – are a little jealous of your position. Try to keep in with them – you have a better mind than either – but make your own friends as well.'

My position? Richard wondered. But couldn't bring himself to ask how it was better than theirs. 'Didn't I see you with Robert de Vere the other day, trying out a disarmed lance?' went on Simon easily. 'Well, I know he's older than you and far more frivolous. That'll do you no harm at all,' he added laughing. Robert already had a precocious eye for the wenches and would take Richard's mind off serious matters. Besides, it was as well for him to have a friend outside the royal family. 'Enough lessons for now – let's take a holiday – cross London to see the frozen fen. B'rhh – it's cold!'

Richard loved crossing London with Sir Simon. At this Christmas season the streets looked gay since the houses were decked with ever-green oak, ivy and bays. Even the pipes and posts in the streets were garnished. Richard was amused to see his own breath frozen on the air and drew his fashionable parti-coloured tabard closer about him, pulling his gaily-patterned gauntlet gloves well up over his wrists.

When they reached the great fen which watered the walls of the city on the north, he was surprised to see the number of young men and boys disporting themselves on the ice. Some had tied the leg-bones of animals to their feet with thongs, carried iron-tipped poles, and propelled themselves by striking these against the ice. The velocity they attained was amazing – like bolts discharged from a cross-bow as Sir Simon remarked. Sometimes several of them collided and made mock battle with their staves as if imitating the royal tournaments – whereat some would be hurled down to slide, recumbent and shouting, along the ice. Even young children joined in the tumultuous scene by using the jaw-bones of horses or cows as sleds. And some sat on great blocks of ice, like mill-stones, to slide rapidly along before they melted.

'The people have as much fun as the nobility,' said Sir Simon. 'It helps, heaven knows, to ease their poverty.'

Their clothes are far less colourful than ours, Richard was thinking. It was true that the working people were easily distinguished from the leisured classes in that they wore russet or kersey, and not silk. They wore no ornaments and their materials were of coarse weave. Their plain shapeless woollen kirtles were belted to hold them at knee length when exercising, and their cloth hose were wrinkled. A cloak or hooded cape, by now quite unfashionable for the upper classes, was still worn for extra warmth by the peasants. Although he was still a young boy, Richard was becoming aware of the great gulf between the people as a whole and those at Court. Probably that was how God meant it to be – a kind of Divine Plan. He didn't understand Burley's next remark that the abject state of the lowest classes was bound to debase their minds and their manners. And that sometime they would realise their oppression and would cause social trouble. They lived wretchedly; indeed many of the common people died like flies in times of scarcity. Yet they couldn't be unaware of the waste of food by the Barons in their lavish entertainments – nor of the excessively high living of many of the clergy who yet always preached to them to be content with their lot. And at the same time, the upper classes were beginning, for the first time to indulge in four meals a day: 7 a.m. breakfast, 10 a.m. dinner, 5 p.m. supper, and refreshments in their bedrooms between 8 and 9 p.m. A great gulf increasingly yawned between the classes. No wonder discontent seethed under the placid surface.

'They seem happy enough,' the child Richard objected, a trifle enviously, despite Simon's bare hint of poverty. 'They must be sorry when the ice melts in the spring.' He wished he were with them now.

'These young men? I was talking of the near-starving classes below them. Hundreds of them *do* starve in hard winters. The wars, the taxes, the aftermath of the *magna pestilentia* – ha! life isn't easy for any, but worst of all for them. . . . But these working men and boys have exercise and games for every season: when the ice is gone they fight their mimic battles in boats on the Thames from which they thrust each other overboard; they practise feats of war with disarmed lances and shields – play ball in the fields – wrestle – cast the stone – leap and dance – and delight in cock-fighting, bull-and bear-baiting. As you see, they wear good plain dark worsteds – not the silk, satins and velvets of the Courts – that indeed would not be suitable for these working classes who do well enough and are getting ahead with the weaving of woollens in England.'

Richard was always to remember that outing because it was not long after this that he realised with horror and dismay that his father, the famed Black Prince, was dying. What on earth would his mother do then?

Pale and silent, the Prince of Wales languished in such pitiable suffering that, when he closed his eyes for the last time on 8th June, 1376, even Joan could not have wished him back. He died knowing that, after all his glory, there had been no cash left in the Treasury to reward his mercenaries, that the treasure-ship with the English money to pay the Gascon army had gone to the bottom and, worse yet, that the English fleet had been defeated off La Rochelle in a two-day battle. All, all was lost. Soon the south coast of England and its dependency, the Isle of Wight, would lie open and vulnerable to French attack.

King Edward, senile though he was, became frantic at his heir dying at such a difficult time for a young boy to inherit. After all the years of military success – and there was no denying that a unified England was flowering with joy and confidence – would the young grandson inherit merely the shadow of luxurious living, but in reality a *damnosa hereditas*? Avidly, the once-great King turned back for comfort to his middle-aged mistress. Besotted, he could deny Alys Perrers nothing. Her broad hands were weighted down with Queen Philippa's rings, and her extravagance in dress was flaunted in everybody's face. Once she was seen whispering with a Dominican friar. Gossip ran mad: he was obviously in league with the Devil, brewing strange potions at Alys's behest – how else could she have so enslaved the King? The unfortunate friar was clapped under arrest for sorcery and no one ever learned his fate.

And what did the Princess of Wales do? All marvelled at Joan's sudden unexpected strength. Despite her terrible grief she was determined Richard should not suffer. Christmas and Candlemas were times for celebration and it should be so for him even within seven months of his father's death. Besides, to her own surprise she was finding some comfort in the side of the church exemplified by Wycliffe, now in his fifties, and a spiritual genius who was in revolt against the gross materialism into which his church had fallen. There were about six hundred monasteries in England, owning between them one quarter of the land. Wycliffe endangered himself by castigating their luxury-induced immorality and by declaring that every man should be able to read the Bible in his own language. Joan did not go as far as the extreme followers of that great leader – there was that 'mad priest of Kent' John Ball, for instance, who for fifteen or twenty years had been tramping the rough by-ways preaching that all men were equal, that everyone possessed natural rights, and that the system of inequality that the clergy had always taught, as part of the Divine Plan was just set up by the church and the nobility to keep the downtrodden in serfdom and enforced labour. His favourite text was the old jingle composed half a century earlier by Richard Rolle de Hampole:

> 'When Adam delved and Eve span –
> Who was then the gentleman?'

He added many rhymes of his own, all of which excited the people, and carried his Lollard tenets much further than Wycliffe himself did – one of Ball's most stubbornly expounded theories being that all those born out of wedlock were destined straight for hell fire, and could never enter the Kingdom of God – would not even attain purgatory!

But Joan drew courage from Wycliffe's faith as being more pietistic than that of the more worldly priests. It enabled her to be happy, even gay, for her young son. Richard never forgot that Christmastide – the last of his untrammeled boyhood.

They were at Kennington Palace near Lambeth. Richard, in bed, was suddenly awakened by the most alarming noise. Startled, eyes wide, he sat up just as Joan rustled in, excited as a girl.

'Listen, listen!' she cried, 'the citizens are making a Mummery for you.' In a moment Mundina was there too, and they hustled him into his warmest gippon and thickest hose.

'What is it? What is it?' he kept exclaiming, then, through the slit casement caught the flashing lights of approaching torches. Lines and lines of them danced in the distance against the dark sky as they came over the bridge and were reflected in the water. The noise from the ones already at hand rose in a sharp crescendo from trumpets, sackbuts, cornets, shalmes, and every other instrument they could devise. The champing of horses, the sound of laughter, heralded the entry on foot into the Great Hall of 130 masked citizens. The impassivity of the huge elaborate masks – animals, giants, demons, grotesques – somehow lent a weirdly contrasting effect to the contortions of the elaborately costumed figures which carried them. Some appeared as Popes, Cardinals, Emperors, and all were there to amuse the little boy who soon would be their King.

The Mummers saluted Richard, his mother, his uncle John of Gaunt, and all the other lords who streamed out into the great Hall to share the fun. Richard was enchanted; this was even more exciting than the King's Lord-of-Misrule who had made merry for them earlier in the day. After parading around the Hall, the Mummers insisted on throwing dice with the little Prince. Astounded, he found that, somehow, he won every time he threw: three jewels, a gold bowl, a golden cup, and a ring!

Laughingly, the Princess of Wales gestured for wines and spices to be brought and served. The sprightly deafening music beat on and on till, gay as larks, the prince and the lords all joined in a mad dance with the Mummers. One last stirrup cup – then they had all gone, streaming out into the dark night with their waxen torches flaring. The young prince was carried, already dropping with sleep, to bed.

When Richard woke next morning he would have thought it all had been a dream if he had not found, lying beside the bed, the golden bowl, cup, ring and jewels.

Time began rushing by like the waters of the River. Spring was suddenly upon them with all the wild flowers a-blooming, then June, the lovely month of roses. Suddenly it was a year since his father's death and he himself was beginning to fill out, what with all the manly sport, the feasting, the good fresh sunny air.

Yes, it was June of 1377 – and at last the old King, who had once lived so gloriously, died dishonoured and alone, at lovely Sheen Palace in Surrey. Shocked, the Princess of Wales was told one horrible detail: Alys had crept into his room and stripped the poor flailing dying hands of all their rings. . . . But nothing mattered now but to recall his earlier famous exploits, the shining lustre of his life with Philippa – and to confront the new King with his destiny. And once the corpse had been place in its coffin with the face exposed, it seemed to reassume its old nobility. One

41

could forget the furtive figure of Alys Perrers slinking off down the corridor after her last act of betrayal, and remember the greatness and glory of most of his life. Indeed his children and grandchildren shed bitter tears for him as they followed the sad cortège across London and laid him at rest beside his beloved Philippa in Westminster.

Richard, glancing around at the lovely glades of Sheen, dappled with July sunshine, through which the Thames ran like a silver ribbon, thought he had never seen a more beautiful retreat. Burley had told him that Edward the Confessor gave it the expressive Saxon name to indicate all that was bright and beauteous. Perhaps I can come here again, thought Richard – and then, half-guiltily at such wandering thoughts during the start of this sad funeral procession – after all I am the King, and glanced up at his mother as if she could be aware. Not that he really believed it yet – nor was even sure that he wanted to. He'd said to Sir Simon when the latter had reminded him gently but urgently of the future: 'Ah, it must be a lonely job, being a King. I mean . . .' and fell silent. For by that time his grandfather had had him presented before Parliament.

Sir Simon darted a quick look at him. 'Yes. Much will be expected of you. You will pay for it in loneliness – as does anyone who stands out from the crowd. But don't forget, Richard, you will be anointed with consecrated oil.'

And does something happen then, he wanted to ask urgently, but merely looked searchingly in his tutor's face.

'The answer to the question you would ask me, Richard – it is only the King's touch that can cure the "King's evil", scrofula. The miracle *is* performed – you have seen it happen. You yourself will perform in the future. It is a divine prerogative, belongs only to the anointed King.'

Suddenly the boy felt curiously humble. I am ten years old. I must grow up quickly if so much will be demanded of me. Perhaps I can stand the lonely pinnacle if I have Sir Simon to confide in, my eldest uncle, John of Gaunt Duke of Lancaster to depend upon – and Robert de Vere like an older brother to help me endure Cousin Henry Bolingbroke's superior airs, and Uncle Thomas's hard dislike.

Less than four weeks after Edward III's death, on a hot day half-way through July, Richard rode from his palace at Westminster – whither he had repaired from the Tower a day earlier – to the nearby Abbey for his coronation. The Mayor of London in brave array, the sheriffs, the barons with their retainers in brilliant liveries, heralds with a blare of trumpets, citizens cheering as if they'd split the heavens, the sound of fountains of wine playing in the squares, various city guilds competing in the effectiveness of their display – all added to the unreality of the fantastic scene. And at the heart and centre was the slim ten-year-old boy whose blond and glowing beauty was quite breathtaking.

The day was a long drawn-out ordeal of stamina even though the wine of adulation was heady. The Abbey was alarmingly hot and crowded. The lengthy ceremonial service started with a Mass, included an interminable sermon, and the taking of the royal oath – at which Richard's voice a little faltered – his presentation to the people who wildly accepted him. Then, in a pregnant hush, came the blessing and anointing. The little prince, who was thus becoming a king, tried to keep his mind on the mysticism of this regality – to understand its spiritual and traditional symbolism. Next, he was robed, invested, armed, and found himself at long last upon the throne with the archbishop placing the heavy crown upon his brow and proclaiming him King of England, King of France, Lord of Ireland. Confession, absolution, the offering, the acceptance of the people's devotion – so much ceremony, all of it part of the warp and woof of time-hallowed tradition – he told himself he must remember it all. Tired and confused, he clanged at his Uncle John of Gaunt who ceremoniously bore the sword Curtana which, with its blunted point, symbolised mercy, and felt the reassurance of his presence. Beyond him stood young Robert de Vere, Earl of Oxford, acting as King's Chamberlain. And over there, with the light from a stained-glass window falling on her, and still radiating the fascination that enslaved all who met her, sat Joan the Queen-Mother, keeping an anxious eye upon his now strained exhausted face.

For a few moments he was sunk. Then, to his astonishment, found himself being carried out into the fresh air, through the hushed watching crowds, on the broad shoulders of his beloved Sir Simon. Someone had removed the heavy crown in which a huge ruby given to his father by Pedro the Cruel (who otherwise had defaulted in the expenses of the war undertaken by the Black Prince on his behalf) glowed like a clot of blood. Trust Sir Simon to see that I'm all right thought Richard contentedly, and closed his eyes against the soft velvet of his tutor's tabard. He could have a short rest before the great coronation banquet in Westminster Hall climaxed the stupendous day.

'Tut tut,' said Sir Simon Burley as he put him down, 'we've dropped one of your jewelled velvet slippers! Here, sip this ale – sit still a little while. The Princess of Wales – the Queen-Mother, I should say – will be with you in a few minutes. Tonight's doings will be endless.'

I shall think of all the mysticism of my oaths and of the whole Service tomorrow, thought Richard drowsily. I'm too tired tonight. *Am* I a different peson from what I was when I awoke this morning? I shall never forget today with its bestowal of sanctifying grace. Yes – I believe God's finger was laid on me.

A gargantuan banquet followed with Uncle John of Gaunt as the official carver. Colour and pageantry and all the glory of chivalric heraldry swam before Richard's bemused eyes. But the most dramatic moment was at the commencement of the feast when the clomp-clomp of a well-caparisoned horse was heard riding straight into the Hall bearing the elaborately armoured figure of the King's Champion. Raising his visor, the rider revealed the heavy features of Sir John Dymoke who lifted his gauntlet in challenge while reining in his steed to face the company.

'Oyez! Oyez! Oyez!' shouted a herald, springing to attention at that signal. 'Herewith the hereditary Champion of our Sovereign Lord the King doth challenge to mortal combat any person who dares dispute our Sovereign's title.' The words echoed round the suddenly silent Hall and were followed startlingly by the violent Crash! on the flagstones of the armoured gauntlet flung down by the champion as proof of his defiance of the King's enemies. The whole chamber seemed to ring with sound. Twice more this ceremonious challenge was repeated. It was a great moment in Sir John Dymoke's life; he jealously clung to his right to this inherited office that was only activated at coronations but which carried with it gifts from the Keeper of the Royal Wardrobe of the suit of armour and the well-caparisoned horse, as well as twenty yards of crimson satin.

Richard remembered what he was supposed to do next. A brimming golden cup was handed to him; the young King raised it in toast to the Champion and drank his health, then handed the cup up to Sir John who bowed smilingly to his Sovereign, gulped the remainder as a return toast, and retained the cup as further perquisite.

London, with its 40,000 inhabitants, thriving on the wool trade with the Low Countries, enjoyed to the full all the celebrations of the Coronation. It helped them to ignore the threatening shadow of a third outbreak of the *magna pestilentia*, and the realities of the continuing wars with France with the attacks now on the English coasts.

So, with the navïeté and idealism of adolescence, the boy came into his kingdom and sat upon a throne which his father, or his elder brother, should have inherited. His boyhood ceased before it had begun – he was expected to step from childhood into maturity. Thus, took was the heritage, the background, the moulding and upbringing of Richard Plantagenet – Richard of Bordeaux – who, with a sense of exaltation and dedication felt the leadership of a gloriously-burgeoning country fall upon his shoulders at a time of difficult crises hardly yet realised. The Great Seal, the Privy Seal, the Signet, were his. A Great Council was soon appointed which was, in effect, a Council of Regency. But the powers behind the throne were his beloved Queen-Mother who wielded more personal influence with him than anyone, and his eldest uncle, Gaunt, Duke of Lancaster.

This is the story of his private life, of his two widely-disparate marriages, of their influence upon him and therefore upon his people. For no king is really allowed to have a private life. And Fate has two strokes against those who are naïve enough to believe that goodness is bound to triumph – that right is might – for in cold fact, it is the wicked who flourish as the green bay tree. Richard was eventually to learn, in bitter disillusion, that virtue is its own reward – that indeed it can have no other or it too would be merely a marketable commodity.

And yet, by his shining example, he at first taught everyone to expect such a high standard of rectitude from him, that when, at last, his hand forced by those who attacked him without any of his scruples, he defended himself by opposing them on their own terms and at their own level – he destroyed himself. Virtue must never ask to be victorious. The virtuous are the victims of their own innocence; at the best, their triumph is of a spiritual quality.

Thus life itself, for most, eventually becomes a compromise, or, for the saints, a martyrdom. That Richard himself was not of the stuff that saints are made of, can hardly be counted against him. If he had been less sensitive, less intelligent, less cultured – even wholly wicked – his life would have been more successful, less star-crossed.

But at this stage he was merely an idealistic adolescent, determined to be good. And, in his more exalted moments, he was most uniquely lonely.

CHAPTER SEVEN

THE CHAPEL ROYAL of the Palace of Westminster was trembling with sound that mid-January day of 1382 when the boy-king – one week past his fifteenth birthday – married Anne, eldest daughter of Emperor Charles IV of Bohemia. Blooming with health and excitement, the young bride's complexion and bearing were beyond compare.

The bridegroom, taking the step into matrimony that was expected of him, was almost relieved to find that his bride was no exceptional beauty, but simply appeared to be gentle, kind, intelligent. Richard had relied entirely on Sir Simon's advice that she would make a suitable Queen Consort; Burley had visited Prague last year as Ambassador to make the preliminary arrangements. So little was known there of that distant and perhaps savage country, England, that Princess Anne had been a little nervous at the idea of travelling to such a *terra incognita*. But Sir Simon Burley's suave manners, his impeccable courtesy, not only won Anne's confidence, but, ultimately, her complete affection.

He had assured her that the young King Richard, almost her own age, though sometimes capricious and temperamental – and occasionally wont to indulge in violent Plantagenet rages – was of the most chivalric affection towards his own family, particularly his women-folk. Nothing could exceed his devotion to his mother, which, as Sir Simon saw it, augured well for future relations with a wife. He was also capable of the utmost loyalty to his friends.

Fortified by Burley's advice, the young Princess sent a letter to the English Council, saying she was becoming the wife of their King of her own free will. Even so, she had set out on her perilous journey with some misgivings. Attended by her relatives, the Duke and Duchess of Saxony, in addition to a number of knights and ladies, they travelled as far as Brussels where they stayed a month afraid to cross the Channel. Reports were rife that twelve large armed vessels were cruising off the coast between Calais and Holland anxious to seize her person since the King of France was uneasy at the idea of this German alliance for England. Eventually Charles VI agreed to let her have safe escort but made it clear he gave it out of regard for his cousin Anne – not at all out of consideration for Richard of England. The royal bride then continued on to Bruges, escorted by one hundred spearmen, where great entertainment was afforded her by the Earl of Flanders. At long last, outside Calais, the city which belonged to her betrothed, the Earl of Salisbury awaited her with a guard of honour of five hundred spearmen and as many archers.

At last, one Wednesday morning, the wind was favourable, and she embarked on a swift ship that arrived the same day at Dover. There, ahead, were the white cliffs, gleaming in the thin sunshine of the new year; the young Princess began to feel her long journey was almost over. What kind of life did this strange country hold in store for her? And how would her ladies react to these far different surroundings? Above all – what was Richard really like? In any case, she was prepared to do her duty by him.

The wind had completely dropped. The landing on Dover quay was uneventful – till, amazingly, behind them the ships ran foul of one another, and the one from which Anne had just disembarked, splintered violently against the quay. This phenomenon, doubtless due to a submarine earthquake, remained as an inexplicable omen to the frightened onlookers.

Nothing could have exceeded the grandeur of her reception in London. Was this the city she'd been afraid might be uncouth, uncivilised? Why, minstrels serenaded her through the streets to Cheapside where a pageant was enacted against a mock castle with towers whose walls ran with fountains of wine. Beautiful damsels threw flowers, and counterfeit gold coins glittered under the Queen's horses' feet.

Astonished, the enraptured crowds gazed at these ladies from overseas in their strange head-dresses – the horned caps so fashionable at the time in Hungary and Bohemia. Two feet high, and the same in width, the gauzy fabric was stretched on wire and pasteboard with horns of glittering tissue. 'Monstrous!' 'Outrageous!' laughed some of the crowd, eagerly determining nevertheless to try how such fashions became themselves. It was laughable in any case to see how it diminished the importance of masculine heads!

For this formal occasion, Anne rode in a whirlicote. But later she would often be seen on her favourite white palfrey – and again her foreign style attracted great attention. Her saddle was a kind of short bench with a hanging step for both feet to be on the same side. This entailed having a squire hold her bridle.

A year ago, perhaps, all this ceremony might have seemed overwhelming to the young Richard now serenely solemnising his marriage in the Chapel Royal. But today he knew himself a completely different mortal from what he'd been only a few short months ago. For last year's terrible events had confirmed his faith in his regality. Suddenly he had ruled absolutely as King, when everyone around him had been paralysed with terror.

Even now, here in the Chapel Royal, they were still treating him with some deference, though the priority he had seized with such courage had unfortunately slipped through his fingers.

The music of the lengthy service, the chanting, thundered on, and Richard glanced surreptitiously at his bride. How piqued she would be if she realised that his thoughts were on the Peasants' Revolt, and whether it had been as inevitable as his advisers made out for him to go back on his promises. For a short and heady time I knew I was King of the people and that they trusted me so freely that I could afford to trust them in return. And then I betrayed them – on the advice of all my elders who professed to know better than a mere boy of fourteen, even though a King. Ah well! I suppose they're right to say one cannot give in to mob rule. But . . . Thomas of Woodstock and his crony Arundel – *did* they know better?

He sighed and Anne gave him a tremulous shy smile. Shy, she looks kind and sweet, he thought. Sweet and sound as a good English apple, even if she is Bohemian.

And his mind reverted once more to last summer and its unprecedented happenings. Was this great Peasants' Revolt, that flared across England from sea to sea, the beginning of a social revolution that, even though repressed for a while, would gather force and ultimately alter the whole face of the country? Or was it merely an expression of lawlessness by the lowest classes that had to be kept sternly down lest anarchy result?

He only knew that he'd chafed at the cowardice and cautiousness shown by his own circle, and that the unforgettable moment when Walworth had rashly struck down Wat the Tyler and the mob moved in on them, growling threats, was the high-note so far of Richard's whole existence. A mixture of fear, elation and ecstasy had moved him. Spurring his horse forward as the thousands of rebels fitted arrows to their bows, he, a boy of fourteen, faced them alone.

'What would you?' he shouted clearly, 'let *me* be your leader. I am your King.'

As one man, they lowered their bows in frank admiration, and he, riding alone at the head of the rabble, led them to the meadows of Clerkenwell. Here, quite clearly understanding their plight, he promised them relief from the Poll Tax which had been the last straw to the poorest of them, alleviation of their serfdom, and indemnity for what had happened these past few days. . . And then – the royal retinue, courage regained now the danger was over, planned to massacre the lot of them. Congratulated him on having tricked them! Sick at heart, the young King saved them from that fate, only to have pressure put on him not to encourage anarchy, to forswear all his promises. Perhaps he *had* been wrong to lead them to expect things that would inevitably upset the whole social economy?

Thomas Woodstock even watched with ironical contempt to see how he was standing the sight of John Ball, flushed out of his hiding place amid the ruins of a house, being hanged, drawn and quartered. He forced himself not to flinch, for he knew now that Thomas Woodstock and the Earl of Arundel would never forgive him for showing up their own cowardice, and that the baronage as a whole would make him their scapegoat. After so glorious an interval, he was again in leading-strings. But he realised now what it would be like when he had come of age and was out of their power. It was worth waiting for.

Strangely, one of the small incidents that had enraged Richard *against* the rebels had been their encounter with his mother. When the Kentish faction began their march upon London they had set upon a smart chariot *en route* from Canterbury to West-minster. The startled occupant turned out to be Joan of Kent – the Princess of Wales – their young King's mother. Good-humouredly, they saluted her as such: 'Look who's here – the Lady from our own county,' and had even dared a few gallant kisses before urging her on her way. She had shrunk from their unwashed bodies, their stale malodorous clothes – but, at fifty-three years of age, it had been an excitingly unexpected experience. Later, when the stimulation of adventure had passed, she began shivering with revulsion – especially when the maddened mob invaded the Tower of London.

In six years I shall be twenty-one, he told himself now. In the meantime, with this gentle wife and with his benign mother to be with them both, at least his domestic life would be well-ordered and peaceable.

And the Queen Mother was indeed a kindly mother-in-law. Once she'd realised that Anne was a less vivid character than herself she'd guided the young married children with devoted benignity. Sometime she would be leaving her son, and she felt now he would be in loving hands. Once, over-stepping the barrier between the generations, over a shared strip of tapestry work, Joan had even dared to say:

'Be good to my son when I am gone. He'll need you terribly.'

'Good to him,' Anne had stammered, a bright tide of colour washing her face and neck. Then, after a moment: 'You're – you're – not ill, Madame?'

'As to that – I think my heart is tired – I get so short of breath. . . . But enough of me.' She eyed Anne's flushed face compassionately: 'You're terribly in love with him, are you not, Anne! Don't be too proud to let him know it. His is not a nature which gains from solitude – yet somehow he's often much alone.'

'But I – but I – ' poor Anne stammered, 'I only wish I were beautiful – like you – like so many of the ladies of the Court.' Beauty is so unfair, she thought now violently. It does things to you. Richard's beauty had turned her knees to water since the fitst time she set eyes on him.

And Joan, casting her mind back to a day on which she'd cursed her own loveliness as too superficial a thing to hold the devotion of her Black Prince, went on: 'You are being absurd, *ma petite*. Beauty certainly gives an initial advantage – nothing more.' She tilted Anne's face up with long thin fingers: 'Believe me, you have deeper gifts that could hold him far beyond the Gates of Paradise.' She sighed now and broke off, as a young girl appeared in the doorway carrying spindle and thread. 'Don't speak of my health to anyone – I won't have my son worried.'

'Thank you, *Belle-Mere*,' Anne answered softly. But how, she wondered, could she ever assume the role of mediator and conciliator that this mellowed wise Queen Mother had often had to be for a young King so highly strung and highly tempered? And yet so lovable.

It was with Joan's advice that Anne, as a boon after her coronation, begged Richard to grant a general pardon to all those who were still being hunted down and put to death as taking part in Wat the Tyler's insurrection. Richard, although by now half-convinced that the well-being of society was dependent on the different strata remaining as God had ordained them, was yet glad to have an excuse to halt the wholesale executions of those he had once thought to lead. 'Good' was the adjective now constantly applied to Anne by the common people who sensed her kindness and benevolence.

CHAPTER EIGHT

THE ROYAL Manor House of Sheen lay in a verdant hollow on the right bank of the Thames just nine miles south-west of London. Its tufted groves provided the richest type of English scenery, while, as a background, the river moved past, slowly yet purposefully, endowing the whole landscape with a deep placidity. Anne felt happier here than in any of their palaces, for it was a kind of rural retreat where convention could be relaxed and she feel closer to Richard than at the bustling Courts. For hours on end, all that moved in the landscape were the fallow and red deer, standing about in the bracken or leaping between the dappled tree-trunks, and the swans floating regally by on the placid water.

It could be heaven, she thought now wistfully, if only . . . if only . . . ! Well, perhaps there was always, in every human circumstance, this corrosive supposition. He was a kind, considerate husband, yet somehow she never felt entirely necessary to his happiness. He was not promiscuous, like his friend, Robert de Vere, or coarsely bawdy like Arundel and Uncle Thomas Woodstock, and yet – and yet – she always felt a certain aloofness under his affectionate courtesy. That aloofness held even when Joan, the Queen Mother, had died with a cloud between her and her son a year ago – in 1385 – and for a moment of supreme sympathy, Anne had almost broken down the intangible barrier between them.

That same year, the King had played a man's part in the expedition against Scotland where a French force had landed to invade England. Though he was no war-monger, Richard would never shirk the defence of his beloved country or the settlement and pacification of neighbouring Ireland. And though Thomas Woodstock and the Duke of Arundel were viciously hand-in-glove in opposition to the young King, Richard tried to appease his Uncle Thomas on this foray by making him Duke of Gloucester. But nothing seemed to pacify those of the barons who, more and more stridently, opposed Richard on every possible point and policy. . . . How he must chafe, thought Anne, at still being kept in leading strings. Really, he has enough to worry him without *my* being difficult and temperamental.

She heard the clatter of horses in the courtyard and hurried back into the Great Hall just in time to see him arrive, his favourite greyhound, Math, welcoming him by leaping up to lick his face. Behind Richard came the graceful Robert de Vere, Earl of Oxford, with his easy manners, his laughing handsome face. Anne came forward eagerly to greet them. The greatest rule of her life was to love and welcome everyone whom the King loved. Jealousy must never be entertained for a single moment.

The young men were in the midst of a discussion – Richard quite angrily so. 'They are reducing me to a mere figure-head,' he was saying stormily, 'to curb all my extravagances, forsooth. I shall be told what I can wear, next.'

Robert de Vere merely laughed. 'You'll soon be of age, Sire – patience a little while. Your opponents are mainly your Uncle Gloucester, and his cronies the two Arundels. Perhaps also your cousin, Henry – but your good Uncle Lancaster will keep that son of his in order. And don't put any credence in Gloucester's attempts to make you suspect your Uncle Lancaster of treachery. . . . But this must be boring for the Queen.' He turned to Anne with his most fascinating smile. 'I thought we'd forget affairs of State for a few hours in this blessed retreat.'

'Of course,' said Anne breathlessly. She so longed to have Richard to herself that she was alarmed at how deeply his arrival disturbed her.

But Richard still remained on edge; even his friend Robert could not placate him.

'All very well for you,' he burst out now, 'you'd be astonished at all they make of our friendship – despite your marriages, and your gallantries with the ladies of the Court.'

Robert's face darkened. But he bit back an angry retort and merely said with the suavity of good breeding: 'I can imagine, Sire.'

Distressed, Anne put her arm in Richard's and reminded the two young men that supper was now *en train* and that her ladies were eager to welcome them.

After her tire-woman had undressed her, brushed her hair and made her comfortable for the night, Anne bade her pull back the window-shade that she might listen to the Thames flowing softly by. 'Why, it's moonlight,' Anne said, marvelling at the beauty of the sky, and wondering if Richard would come to her or whether he and Robert would sit up talking into the small hours. She could understand their comradeship; de Vere demanded nothing of the King and gave him an easy frivolous friendship that even an older man like Burley recognised as a safety valve from all the champing ambitions and jealousies of his near relatives. Dear

Sir Simon!

She was drowsing on the edge of sleep when she heard slithering footsteps down the corridor and caught the flickering torchlight rapidly doused outside her chamber. 'Richard?' she whispered.

'You are awake? Too tired, Anne, for me to come in?'

Her heart began beating a wild tattoo. Against the moonlit sky beyond, his face looked a mere shadow, his hair, caught by a moonbeam, almost silver. In the momentary silence, they both listened to the murmuring river. . . . Careful, she told herself now, careful. I long for him to make love to me – but oh, God! I want so much more than his usual perfunctory taking. I want now – *now* – to get through to the essential Richard. Tonight – has something happened? he seems more vulnerable. I want to get through to him so that in future it will always be – he and I – he and I against the world. She felt for one fleeting second as though Joan's unresting spirit stirred in the shadows behind the tester.

Her voice came on a little gasp. 'My sweet! my love!' she said, and felt his weight as he sat on the edge of the bed and pushed back the canopy with his head.

'I won't stay – it's late. I thought – I'd sit here a few moments for the comfort of your presence.' His voice was blurred; for an incredible moment she believed he'd been weeping. What could she say? Apparently he didn't even want the solace of his gentle but all-too-casual love-making.

'Is anything the matter, my King?' she asked after a moment's silence, and saw him shake his head against the moonlit sky. Her heart ached with the pain of his aloofness. How absurd I am, she was thinking, to demand so much from a political marriage like mine – and felt dizzy with unreality. The words burst from her: 'To be Queen Consort of England – what more – what greater role could I expect?' Her voice broke.

He turned her face gently toward him To his dismay two huge tears rolled down her cheeks.

'What is it, Anne?' he asked in a completely different tone. She started twice to speak, swallowed with difficulty, wiped her wet cheek upon the bed-clothes. Instantly he whipped from his sleeve a delicate wisp of cambric and tenderly rubbed the tears away. 'I have discovered the real use for my "unmanly" handkerchief,' laughing gently, 'but tell me now while we are by ourselves.'

How could she tell him? She adored him – felt sick with longing for him – yes, this calmly arranged marriage had become a head-over-heels love match on her side since the first moment she had seen him. His mystic withdrawn expression, the look of shining goodness that radiated at times from his whole personality, his sensitivity to beauty, his feeling of consecration to the great ideal of Kingship -- though she worshipped him for all these attributes, they lay like a drawn sword between them even when he made love to her. . . . She knew, too, with the intuition of love, how terribly vulnerable his high ideals made him – how he would suffer in guilt and remorse when, in his struggles with a brutal world, he fell below his own self-imposed standards. As he was bound to do.

His eyes were very near her own. She gazed into them with the courage of desperation: 'It's just – just that I love you so terribly.' Love! what a stupid word – used too easily to mean too little. It was a word that should be reserved for such overwhelming devotion as she felt for him; or another expression should be coined. But she had released him by the avowal – for he let her see then that he had indeed been weeping. His face crumpled in woe. 'Tell me – tell me,' she cried. 'What is it? What has happened?'

He groaned, putting his head down on her shoulder. 'It isn't fit for your ears, Anne. I – I can't possibly tell you.' She felt him shuddering as she twined her arms around him.

'Tell me, tell me,' she reiterated, 'there is *nothing* we cannot share.'

His voice came muffled from her shoulder. 'That beast Arundel – and Uncle Gloucester – came to me yesterday. They threaten to depose me. Depose *me*. They hate the favours and titles I've given de Vere. Why! he's the only one who never demands anything. They even loathe good Sir Simon – because he was my tutor – and because I often ask his advice.'

She suddenly felt frozen. 'They can't depose you,' she said. Could they? Could they? Could they?

'No – not unless they want Civil War. Robert would stand up to them,' he boasted. Civil war? Her blood ran cold.

She put her hand caressingly on his face. 'You are the anointed King – no one can touch you.'

'So I said and shouted at them. I – I – threw a pewter mug at Gloucester.' After a moment he shuddered again. 'But that isn't the worst.'

'Tell me,' she whispered.

'He said – he said – I was behaving like my great-grandfather, King Edward II. You know of him, Anne?'

'Yes,' she said doubtfully, turning her head in the darkness to stare into his eyes, 'wasn't he murdered in Berkeley Castle? But that's ages ago – and what has that to do with us?'

'Sixty years ago,' he assented. 'But they told me – they stood there and gloated t-t-telling me – he was a pervert in his love for Gaveston – and he – he went into the horrible crude details of the – the murder employing the methods to – to fit the crime. They're blackmailing me to throw de Vere out – they can't *really* believe. . . ."

'No – of course not,' she said in a strongly intense voice.

'Every normal man needs the friendship of men as well as the love of women,' he said.

'Naturally. And didn't Sir Simon say that you showed such sagacity, prudence and courage dealing with the insurgents that your uncles would never forgive you? You must never give in to them again as you were forced to do then. This is part of their revenge.'

Suddenly the pupils of his eyes dilated with emotion till the blue iris looked almost black. 'But Anne – how beautiful you are,' he stammered, 'how dull I've been for you.' He put one hand instinctively as if to still his heart beats. 'Oh Anne – my Queen – how happy we are going to be. I could kn-kneel at your feet. You and I – you will be – my confidante – my – my greatest friend. Kingship is so lonely a job.'

'Your lover,' she said, feeling her pulse leap. Her love had kindled his at a moment when he desperately needed someone to whom to turn. Never again need she bewail her lack of beauty; for him henceforth she would always have the enduring charm of a woman who is passionately adored.

Hours later, after they had made love with ecstasy, with passion, and once again tenderly, peacefully, he talked to her as he had never talked to anyone before: openly, without fear, in the sure knowledge of no ultimate betrayal.

'How fortunate I am in the three women in my life,' he teased her. Seldom had she seen him in this light-hearted mood. She raised herself on one elbow on the feather-bed, gazing at his face, shadowed by the gorgeous canopy.

'*Three?* Is this a confession, my lord?'

'Ah, Anne,' he caught her hand, then pressed it to his lips. 'My mother – the loveliest woman in the kingdom. She was a good mother to me; warm-hearted, devoted, always kind. I suppose I worshipped her as a boy. It was she who made me so aware of beauty – in architecture, in painting, in music, in poetry, in religion – yes, she helped me to be truly civilised.'

'You are the most cultured King in Christendom,' she murmured.

'But of course I was always aware that her whole being was centred on my father. To be quite frank – she was in love with him first – and secondly with herself. Understandable enough I suppose. I came third – and naturally she was always holding my father up to me as an example of what I should be. It wasn't too bad while he was alive – not that I saw much of him, he was always on campaign – but one can talk of a living person with ease . . . He died when I was nine, and somehow the example held up of the dead is more – well – more exacting. How could I say, against such hallowed tradition, that I couldn't emulate a military glory I was beginning to deplore? The timing was wrong for me. You see his early exploits – the ones that were wonderfully glorious and that would fire any boy's blood – happened before I was born. . . . One of my first memories, when I was three or so, was of all the talk over the victorious sack of Limoges. By the time I was older and realised the savagery of that victory – and that war had become an end in itself – well, I was horrified.'

'*Mon pauvre*,' she whispered caressing his cheek. 'But what other women have you?' His face lit up with affectionate laughter.

'Ah! you know Mundina Danos, my old nurse? I pensioned her off years ago. But I still go to see her. I don't know how in my early years I could have lived without her. She was my second mother. Solid, uncritical, undemanding, immovable as a rock. I think she would have given me her heart's blood.'

That old plain woman, thought Anne – how wonderful. 'As would I – as would I,' she cried, 'though I'm just the third woman in your life.' She dimpled provocatively up at him, behaving as a beautiful woman should, she who had never dared be provocative before, but who now dared anything.

'Anne – Anne – Anne!'

'Hush, hush, my lord,' she soothed, 'the whole palace of Sheen will hear you.'

'I care not if the whole world hears. You are the *only* woman I shall ever have. You are my whole world.'

And when, with the dawn, the overwhelming chorus of birdsongs awakened her, Anne's first protective thought was – in two years he will come of age. Then he can assert himself. In the meantime we have each other and can afford to be patient and careful. . . . I suppose it is a pity, she thought next, wickedly, that Gloucester and Arundel could not hear us. *That* would dispose of their malicious innuendos. But then, it is hardly likely they themselves really believe in them.

'And so they both lived happily ever after.' To Anne this was the inevitable corollary to the obvious fact that Richard could hardly bear to be apart from her. She was so suffused with delight that the fairy-tale ending seemed assured. Walking in her privy garden at Sheen she found herself smiling as she plucked the roses and held them protectingly in her arms, and stood dreaming in the sunshine. Sir Simon Burley, coming unexpectedly upon her there, was so struck with her radiance that he wondered, with a hopeful prayer, whether the Queen were pregnant.

'Sir Simon,' she said, 'you remember all you told me – about Richard – long ago – in Prague?'

'Indeed I do,' he said, smiling faintly.

'I've always wanted to thank you for all you did for me. Everything you said of him was so true. So true. . . . How happy I am.'

'He is the better for having you,' he said gallantly, stooping to kiss her fingers. 'You will help to keep him cool when he has reason to be angry.'

'Ah! that is a forgivable lapse in one who has so many virtues. Even his uncles and the barons will appreciate them all in time,' she said equably.

But Burley was thinking ironically that it is often for our virtues that we are most disliked. He knew that Richard's very modern reluctance to repress the labouring classes would estrange all landowners whose whole concept of the set-up of society was based on the condition of the serfs; that the church was extremely critical of his tolerance of the Lollards whose tenets he did not share but whom he refused, on principle, to persecute and that now he was enraging the barons by expressing views on a peace policy – which was the last thing they desired. Well, if the land-owners, the clergy and the baronage were all against him for the good points of his government, they could tear him to pieces for his weaknesses, extravagances, faults and mistakes he would inevitably, being human, make. And those of his own clan who were against him, were actuated mainly by jealousy and spite – but also by the fact that, to them, he was the new type of man: too artistic, too cultured, to endure with equanimity their rough-hewn boorishness. . . . I shall stand by him, thought Burley loyally, but I, and John of Gaunt Duke of Lancaster, for that matter, are becoming the older generation. I should like to see him with a strong circle of younger friends. For social qualities are expressed every day of one's life – the higher virtues, like outstanding courage, can only display themselves occasionally on compulsion.

CHAPTER NINE

It says much for the bliss of the royal couple's private existence that love, acting like a drug prevented Anne from sensing the torture of Richard's public life until at last he was unable to prevent its shock from reaching her and shattering the romantic dream in which she moved. To both of them, their mutual affection expressed the greatest intensity of living; but a King is too much in the public eye to keep outside events from touching those around him.

They were at Westminster Palace when Gloucester, Warwick and Arundel demanded an audience on urgent matters of State. Richard agreed to meet them in Westminster Hall. He had already talked to de Vere as to the stand he would take with Gloucester and his supporters directly he himself came of age, regarding the galling restraints they continually imposed on him. So it was with impatience and anger he faced this forestalling of his intentions.

'How now, my lords?' he demanded as he entered the lofty and imposing building which he had already determined to rebuild and embellish: 'What is it you want of me?' The November day was sharply cold and he retained his cloak.

Warwick gestured to include the three of them. 'We have no evil intentions against yourself but . . .' he hesitated as the King, still young and headstrong broke in angrily.

'Evil intentions? I should say not. After all, I am your King, with a King's *regalitée*.'

Arundel, the most ferocious of the King's enemies and hotly resentful of de Vere's honours, broke in with: 'For how long . . . ?' but Gloucester interrupted more smoothly: 'We are here to lay a formal charge of treason against your advisers – those in the circle nearest to you. We do this in defence of your own good name.' He did not flinch when Richard jumped up, seizing his dagger and flinging the chair on which he sat backwards to the ground. The sound of his shouting reverberated in the empty hall as he reproached them hotly, for always infringing on the royal prerogative.

'It will be better for you, Richard, to listen to the advice of us who are in power,' said Gloucester coolly, 'the Londoners are on our side.' At last, cornered by their disingenuous arguments,

Richard retorted that his circle of loyal advisers would meet the charges at an early Parliament.

That night, at Westminster Palace, Richard was unable entirely to hide his disquiet from Anne who awaited his return so smilingly. Seeing his flushed unhappy face, she faltered in expostulation: 'But Thomas Woodstock, Earl of Gloucester – why he's your uncle. Yes yes, I remember your telling me before some of the dreadful things he implied. But could he possibly be so vile a traitor as to attack Sir Simon – and Suffolk – and de Vere – and *Chaucer*? Why, Chaucer is a poet not a statesman!'

'Ah! I've had to learn that it's our nearest relations who can injure us far more savagely than any avowed enemy. It's only a relative who knows exactly where to place the barb. But I'll circumvent them,' he said with a bitterness she seldom saw in him. 'Arundel, Warwick and Gloucester are so greedy and self-seeking they would stop at nothing. Our gifted Chaucer? He's merely Comptroller of the Petty Customs – but, as you say, he's a poet first! They'll attack anyone who is loyal to us.'

But at first she was quite sure that Richard would indeed be able to out-manoeuvre them. She had been sheltered from so much that led up to this that the shock was all the greater now Richard confided more easily in her since his other friends and advisers were gone.

For de Vere, friend of his youth, routed at Radcot Bridge by the barons, swam his horse across the Thames and escaped to France. Gloucester tried to spread the rumour that Richard was deposed and had every man arrested who had shown loyalty to the throne. In fact, the bloody work of the well-designated Merciless Parliament resulted in death or exile for every one of the King's nearest friends despite his impassioned pleas on their behalf. The longed-for attainment of his majority saw the young King beaten helplessly to his knees, by the men who, ironically, were professing to act in defence of Richard's good name. They also went far beyond the law in forfeiting their victims' estates. Unfortunately, since everything that happened at this time cut the young King profoundly, this illegal forfeiture remained a dreadful precedent that he would, one day, disastrously follow.

Anne realised that he had not, after all, been able to circumvent his enemies or save his friends, by the desperate expression on his face when next he came into her apartments. They held each other in a fierce embrace as if in defiance of a hostile world.

'If only your Uncle John of Gaunt were here,' said Anne, distraught, 'his brother, Gloucester, stands in some awe of him.'

'Ha! yes – he would never have got control of the government if Uncle John hadn't been away on this wild military adventure to make himself King of Castile.' The Duke of Lancaster had been on campaign for the last two years; it was in his absence that Gloucester had begun taunting the young King with the unimaginable details of Edward II's murder.

'When is he likely to be back?' asked Anne.

Richard shook his head. 'Not in time to save Burley, Beauchamp, Berners or Salisbury.' His voice broke: 'They are all condemned to death.'

'No – no – not dear Sir Simon,' Anne cried.

'I begged – *begged* – fought – tried to persuade them – to spare my father's old comrade-in-arms. They told me – Gloucester told me – that all I was doing was risking my throne – and that even that sacrifice wouldn't save any of them.'

The usually gentle Anne suddenly flashed into militancy. '*I* will go to him. He surely will not refuse the Queen. Besides,' she flushed with embarrassment, 'Arundel is supposed to like my sex – he may give in to me – if I entreat him charmingly.'

Richard shook himself violently free of her. 'What! you think I'd allow you to debase yourself by asking favours of that lecher? Not for all the lives in Christendom. Not for your life and mine.'

'Richard, Richard, Richard. I've never gone against your decision in anything before. But we shall be haunted by it all our lives if we let Simon Burley be hanged, drawn, and quartered.' Her voice thickened; she put one hand to her throat. 'I will do anything to rescue him.'

At last, miserably, Richard gave in and watched her go. She went proudly, head up, colour high – a Queen glad to offer propitiation.

Three hours later she crept back. Wordlessly she sat down, staring at the floor. Richard knelt by her, taking her cold hand in his.

'Tell me – tell me,' he said, 'I've been in agony. What happened?' he tilted her face up but she would not meet his eyes. 'Why were you so long?'

'I – I – I knelt at Gloucester and Arundel's feet,' she whispered.

'You *what*?' said the King, recoiling.

'They – they would not see me – unless I knelt. And then – then – they made no reply. I was there three hours.' She shuddered. 'I was determined – I became determined – not to leave till they spoke to me. It was for Sir Simon,' she said faintly, then glanced up hurriedly at Richard's impassioned face and added whisperingly: 'It was – was – no good.'

'What did they *say*?'

'They said – they said – I'd be better advised to plead for my own life and yours, and give up this flimsy request.'

'And you, my Queen, the Queen of England, humbled yourself to the dust for this.' He ground his teeth. 'In the reckoning that will come one day – I shall remember. There is nothing I have forgotten. Thank God I can recall even the smallest incidents with the utmost clarity – and one day my actions will begin to remind my enemies.'

But at least, on that sad May day of 1388, the King still retained enough shadow of influence to commute Burley's sentence to decapitation on Tower Hill. And Chaucer had been spared.

The Queen was a little alarmed at Richard's terrible reaction. She too was enraged and heart-sore. But revenge? What was it Wycliffe preached before his death four years ago? 'Vengeance is Mine, I will repay, saith the Lord.' When, timidly, she tried to say this to Richard, he laughed a little grimly,

'Revenge is a form of justice when other justice fails,' he said. 'Besides, what man knows whether he himself is not being used to enact God's vengeance . . . ? Perhaps revenge is only the dark reverse of justice – but at least it is one face of it.'

To those in the crowds which thronged the streets as for a raree-show, the sights were exciting enough: men who'd been close to the King being hanged, drawn, and quartered! And dignified Sir Simon Burley – at fifty-two years of age when surely he'd earned a little peace – being led through these same streets to Tower Hill for execution with his hands bound behind him, all faces turning inward to observe his passage, the crowds parting to let him pass, then closing in his wake like the waters of a stream. A roar from the ignorantly callous washed against the dazed silence of those who thought – this is done in the King's name, allegedly for his protection against those who misled him. Or is it really against the King himself . . . ? At last, gradually, the crowds dispersed – and presently it was just a sunny May day with the carts, the pedestrians, the chariots, going their way about their usual business, and children playing in the quietened streets.

Richard had learned a horrifying lesson – one impossible ever to forget. Henceforth he would walk warily, seemingly content with the usual round of duties, exercise, hunting. In reality he was simply biding his time.

But sometimes it is not sufficient merely to wait. Richard and Anne were so impatiently anticipating his twenty-first birthday as the date that would free him from the assembled Lords' restrictions, that when the early spring of 1388 passed with him still in their leading-strings, his disappointment was bitter. Well – all their indictments had blamed the royal advisers, had dared throw no direct blame on him; so now, when John of Gaunt who believed implicitly in his regalitée, was almost due back in England from his Spanish expedition, was the time, if ever, for Richard to make a dramatic unexpected move.

It was a bright May morning in 1389. A meeting of the Great Council was assembled in the council chamber at Westminster when Richard made a sweeping spectacular entrance and all eyes focused on his youthfully-glowing countenance. Suddenly he seemed sure of himself – smote the palm of his left hand with a gauntlet held in his right, and asked in a challenging imperious voice: 'How now, my Lords – how old am I?' – as if it were not of much consequence but he would like to know.

Astonished, they glanced at one another. What game was this? Well, of course he must know he was twenty-two almost four months ago. And, guiltily, some of them also realised that the country had become as disillusioned with them and their poor policies at home and abroad as ever they had been with the royal advisers they'd so crushingly and brutally supplanted. And here was a King who seemed all at once to realise their weaknesses – a King mentally alert, at last free from the numbed frustration and despair into which he'd been thrown by the deaths and exile of his friends.

'Well – Sire – you have turned twenty,' conceded a grudging hesitant voice.

Richard grinned. Then, dramatically serious, he raised his voice so that it carried to every quarter of the Chamber.

'Yes – so I have. Therefore I am fully of age to govern myself – my own household – and the whole of my realm.' He shook his head and effectively paused before continuing: 'In fact, the lowliest of my subjects who reaches his twentieth year, his parents dead – is granted the right to conduct his own affairs. The same privilege can hardly be denied to me.'

And, stepping forward, he ordered the Chancellor to surrender the Great Seal, declaring that henceforth he would summon whatever advisers he chose. Gloucester and his minions, unprepared, were utterly defeated. Their former ruthlessness in seizing power from the legal King was now repaid in good earnest by his dramatic initiative, backed by their own guilty awareness of inefficiency.

Now, thought Richard exultantly, the reign of terror of Gloucester and his colleagues is over, no more insurrections and civil war. I shall be able to govern my country as a civilised realm should be governed – in peace and tranquillity. Not that I shall ever forget. No, never, never, never.

At last, emancipated from the thraldom of the confederate lords, he was a King indeed – perhaps the first to realise the glory of his country. That he had been born in Bordeaux merely spurred him to emphasise the fact that he was the most English of England's Kings. Behind the encircling seas, this was an Island Race, born of the fusion of Normans and English, cultured enough to lead the world in progressive enlightenment once they threw off the wanton wastefulness of warfare.

Upheld by the constant devotion of his wife, Richard for some years ruled the land with wisdom and moderation. This was a brilliant epoch. He saw that to advance, a country must substitute pacific for warlike occupations. Hence his interest in the development of the wool trade and the country's growing preoccupation with weaving. And, from his mother, he had inherited so great a sensitivity to beauty that architecture, painting, music, literature, fashion, developed unprecedently. Each man in the Kingdom knew where he stood in the social scheme – and the Church reinforced the acceptance by many even of hardship and privation. Despite the devotion given to the Virgin Mary, it was very much a man's world.

Highly intelligent as he was, it was tragic for Richard himself that he could not also accept that true civilisation demands legal justice taking the place of personal revenge. Perhaps that was too much to expect even of one in advance of his contemporaries in so many other ideals. After all, one lives in the context of one's times. It is only slipping behind that level that is totally unforgivable.

If the proverbial straw shows the direction of the wind, so do small but consistent actions betray the emotion of the human mind behind them. Richard at this time chose to remind his Uncle Gloucester, Cousin Henry Bolingbroke and Arundel, that he'd forgotten nothing of the past. Making quite a ceremony of it – a delightful gesture – he had a pair of red velvet shoes worked with jewels into a floral pattern and presented them to the Abbey of Westminster. They were to replace the pair he had worn, when he was ten years old, at his coronation – for had he not dropped one in the mud while Sir Simon bore him through the surging crowds? You see, I have not forgotten my dear tutor, Richard was saying silently to his enemies. . . . Perhaps his Uncle Gloucester only took the pretty gesture at its face value.

But at any rate, whatever else was happening, Richard and Anne were quite divinely happy in their private life. . . . Thousands have endured their whole lives without ever attaining such a level of bliss; and yet – perhaps the greatest misery man can suffer is to reach the point when he realises he *once* was happy.

CHAPTER TEN

THE VERY motes of dust in Westminster Abbey, struck through with dazzling sunshine from the stained-glass windows, were vibrating with sound on that hot 3rd of August, of 1394. Sweet sexless voices of young choristers echoed back piercingly from the walls, supported by the tenor and bass of the monks and friars.

Requiem aeternam dona eis, Domine, et lux perpetua luceat eis. . . . Kyrie eleison! Christie eleison! Kyrie eleison!

Domine Jesu Christe, Rex Gloriae, libera animas omnium fidelium defunctorum de poenis inferni, et de profundo lacu: libera eas de ore leonis, ne absorbeat eas tartarus, ne cadant in abscurum. . . . Sanctus, sanctus, sanctus, Dominus Deus Saboath, pleni sunt coeli et terra. Osanna in excelsis . . . ! Osanna, Osanna, Osanna!

The Requiem Mass, with its heart-breakingly beautiful theme, thundered on. Richard's face was so terrible in its contorted agony, that all who looked briefly at him hastily averted their eyes. Not that he would have noticed them. Nothing yet penetrated his consciousness but the scent of incense, of the smoke from a thousand tapers, from flaring flambeaux; a blurred sight of many mourners clothed in sombre black topped with black hoods; the sound of those terrible awe inspiring words which conveyed to him only one message: Anne is dead – Anne is dead – Anne is dead.

She has been dead, his dazed thoughts ran, almost two months. Ever since Whitsun-tide. She who was my own true friend. My wife, My Queen. We shared twelve years together – though at first I did not realise my happiness – and they have vanished like one summer day. . . . Never again will anyone call me 'Sweet – my love

64

– my King – my spouse.' Never again shall I embrace my dearest wife. Nevermore. Nevermore.

He stared straight ahead. The flaring torches flickered before his bloodshot eyes. Lord have mercy upon us – yes, indeed. But no need to pray for Anne that her soul should be freed from the pains of Hell and from the bottomless pit – surely her pure soul could never fall into darkness. No – it was she who had entered into rest eternal and light everlasting. He himself was already enduring the torment of Hell.

She had been joyously happy at beloved Sheen. Always reluctant to leave that haven of peace, yet she had willingly accompanied him to junketings at Leicester, to magnificent jousts and tournaments at Smithfield – gorgeous ceremonies which gave the commonality their glimpse of pomp and circumstance, yet sometimes cloaked a more serious purpose: international diplomacy enacted at the highest level with foreign visiting dignitaries. . . . Three years ago an outdoor stage play had been produced by the parish clerks of London to show matter from the creation of the world right up to this modern fourteenth century – an entertainment at the Skinners' Well beside Smithfield that lasted three whole days. He remembered the relief of their return to Sheen and her dear laughing face between the outflung flanks of her absurdly exaggerated head-dress as she commented on the actors and the plays in her endearing turn of speech.

Everyone had learned to love her – even these difficult Londoners whom Gloucester and Arundel had tried so frequently to set against the King; aye, and had managed it at times. There had been the little matter of a loan – a thousand pounds – that he, as King, had asked for from the citizens of his capital city. After all, sometimes he was obliged to ask for an advance to the Exchequer; if they couldn't understand that even diplomacy meant incurring expenses, he was at their mercy. Not only did they peremptorily refuse, but when an Italian merchant offered to lend the whole sum personally, a riot ensued in which the unlucky would-be money-lender was torn to pieces. . . . Richard had effectually punished them by resuming their charters, removing the law-courts to York, and deposing the Mayor. This five-month ban was only eventually removed by the intercession of the gentle Queen, implored by the Londoners to use her good offices to patch up the quarrel in which, by all feudal standards, Richard was undoubtedly in the right. But sometimes it is unfortunate to be entirely justified – it is a folly one cannot always afford.

Entreated to speak in London's favour, Anne coaxed Richard

to make a state procession through the city. She herself followed in a second parade, wearing her crown which blazed with gems under the August sun, a dress sparkling with precious stones and a jewelled collar. She was determined to show the citizens that she regarded the occasion as momentous. Yet her benign face assumed an air of such humility that the guild-members and artificers were enheartened by her expression.

London Bridge, encumbered by fortifications guarding the gate towers at each end, was a narrow thoroughfare by which to enter the city. And here some in the Queen's procession met disaster as multitudes rushed out of London to catch a sight of their Queen and her train, and collided with the crowds coming in. One of the benched wagons, gaily ornamented with scarlet, containing the Queen's maids of honour, was capsized on the bridge – to the extreme discomfiture of the ladies in their great horned caps, who literally stood on their heads (to the ribald and unrestrained merriment of the crowds) when the charette overturned.

Richard remembered now that by the time the Queen had arrived at Westminster Palace, he was already seated on his throne, sceptre in hand. She advanced with her maidens and knelt modestly at his feet. Hurriedly, the King took her hands and raised her.

'Anne, what do you wish? *Whatever* you ask shall be granted.'

Confidently, she replied that she was begging him to put the Londoners' offences far from his mind, to forgive all their former behaviour by restoring their ancient charters and liberties – especially in view of all the honour and reverence they'd paid him that day.

'Like us,' she bravely reminded him, 'they are but mortal and liable to frailty.'

At the time, did either Richard or Anne recall the last time she had knelt at a man's feet – and been so rudely repulsed? If so, his behaviour was again a reminder by its contrast. He placed her beside him on the wide throne while he told the Londoners he was restoring royal favours to them entirely because of the Queen's prayers on their behalf.

As a drowning man is supposed to visualise all the scenes of his life in a flashing sequence while he himself sinks, so that poor widower, who, for once, felt his Kingship an unimportant accident compared with his love for his dead wife, lived fleetingly through their past together while the sonorous Latin phrases echoed on. *Agnus Dei, qui tollis peccata mundi, dona eis requiem sempiternam.*

Eternal rest? Yes – but surely Anne didn't need that yet? Not as he needed her.

There had been the moment when news came that his boyhood friend and idol was dead. Robert de Vere had escaped the vengeance of Richard's enemies, and Richard had hoped, when he himself got the upper hand, to recall him to England. Both Anne and he would have gladly welcomed him. But he was killed, senselessly, uselessly, in a boar hunt on the Continent. Anne had comforted him as only she could. . . . Now all was lost – friend, wife, the meaning of life itself. But at least he must live in such a manner that he could be sure of rejoining her in heaven.

Dies illa, dies irae calamitatis et miseriae, dies magna et amara valde . . . day of calamity and woe, a great and bitter day indeed. The sublimely awful words struck him to the heart. They reminded him too of the series of terrible plagues that stil! sporadically rent England and brought such famine in their train that thousands of poor persons had to be fed and looked after daily at the royal courts. Less than fifty years earlier, infected rats had brought a newly imported strain of disease from Asia ashore at European ports; the population of Europe had proved so damnably susceptible to a disease from which they had no immunity, that twenty-five million persons died in that first wave of bubonic plague. . . . Perhaps people lived the more intensely when they felt the hounds of death yapping at their heels. Besides, each man considered himself immune until the dread blow actually struck; without such ill-founded optimism life would be impossibly grim. So the successive waves of 1361, 1362, 1369, 1372, 1382 and 1388 – Richard could only remember the last three – shook the basis of society without bringing all joustings and merrymaking to a halt. Perhaps they even intensified the sense of frenzied enjoyment of the passing hour. Eat, drink, and be merry. . . .

'You look tired, my sweet,' Richard had murmured as he and Anne started homeward from a long day's jousting. Anne reined her palfrey and looked a little wildly around her. 'I – I – don't know,' she stammered, 'it's never seemed so far.' Then laughed: 'I must be getting old.'

He noticed that her face was unwontedly flushed. Her eyes glittered. 'You? You'll never be old,' he said, 'twenty-seven may be middle-aged for some – never for you . . . But look – let's turn aside and stay the night at Westminster, my love.' After all, Sheen was only one of many palaces, a pleasant retreat from a busy life. But Anne seemed to regard it specifically as home.

'No, no – I want to lie in bed at Sheen,' she said. 'Sheen is the

67

loveliest place on earth – where you and I learned happiness. Let's spend Whitsun-tide there. Early June among those glades is heaven.'

Libera me, Domine. . . . Against the vibrating music of the Requiem, the King's involuntary groan went unheard. He was violently relegating the thought of those dreadful days at Sheen to the back of his mind. For they were utterly unendurable. Against his will, a series of disconnected faces swam into his view: Mundina taking charge of the Queen's bedroom and pushing him out, her plain old face creased with anxiety.

'Go, go – there's nothing you can do. Go away for a little while, Richard,' – she had forgotten all ceremony 'this is woman's work.'

'But what is the matter, Mundy? Anne is never ill. Besides, she must want me.'

Mundina was staring him straight in the face. 'She's asleep. I won't have you disturb her,' she lied, willing to endanger her immortal soul to ensure her Richard's safety. She even managed a smile, pushing one capable hand against his chest. 'I'll call you when she's bet . . . awake.'

And then – the doctor's face. Robert Waldby looking graver than Richard had ever seen him.

'Sir, you owe it to yourself and the country to keep away. It's the plague.'

And Gloucester's face – mocking and hateful, doubtless hoping he'd go in and be infected. But this time there was no opposing Gloucester's wish: for once, their hopes were identical.

Richard thrust Waldby aside. This time even Mundina did not resist him.

Last of all – Anne's face – a parchment white – her eyes great glowing coals – her voice a croak which yet called his name, over and over. He threw himself down on the bed and held her tightly in his straining arms. . . . I should have died then too, thought Richard.

The distorted faces faded as if peopling a sinister inferno.

And for the last two months, since that terrible Whit Sunday in early June when her soul had fied to God, all Richard's thoughts had been towards this, the great day of her magnificent funeral. He knew that this was only her beloved body – an empty cage – but it *was* beloved, and it was not only that of the daughter of an Emperor but of the Consort of England's King, lamented by all both great and humble, whose welfare she'd always sought. The bitterness of Richard's grief as yet knew no moderation:

the wing of lovely Sheen in which she died had been razed to the ground by his impassioned orders. And he had only been able to exist through these last eight weeks by using every waking moment to plan these grandiose reverent ceremonies: and in feeling to some small extent the very real supporting grief of Geoffrey Chaucer, of Uncle John Lancaster, and Uncle Edmund of York, of dear faithful Mundina (standing now among the weeping household servants), and of nearly everyone who had ever come in contact with Anne's shining spirit.

The Archbishop's voice continued to intone. The monks and choristers still sang . . . *in Paradisum deducant te Angeli, in tuo adventu suscipiant te martyres* . . . indeed, indeed the angels must be leading her to Paradise, the martyrs receiving her. Suddenly there were tears on Richard's ashy face. He was aware at last how many around him were openly weeping. How exhausted they all looked. He reminded himself that for several days ceremonies had been continuing: last Wednesday all Peers of the realm had been invited – by Royal Command – to be in attendance in London with their wives and to join in the funeral procession yesterday that brought the embalmed body from Sheen to Westminster. All along the way the flambeaux, of wax purposely imported from Flanders, enlivened the dead black of the mourning multitudes.

Only one had failed to join in even the last short stage from St. Paul's to Westminster Abbey. The turbulent Earl of Arundel, Uncle Thomas of Gloucester's crony, couldn't have failed to receive Richard's carefully-worded letter written individually to every English peer, and dated 10th June, 1394.

'Inasmuch as our beloved companion, the Queen (whom God has hence commanded) will be buried at Westminster on Monday the third of August next, we earnestly entreat that you (setting aside all excuses) will repair to our City of London the Wednesday previous to the same day, bringing with you your consort at the same time. We desire that you will, the preceding day, accompany the corpse of our dear consort from our Manor of Sheen to Westminster . . .' and so on, with full particulars. The King would at least have the memory of a magnificent gesture in her memory to afford some small comfort in his joyless future.

Arundel had not even bothered with an excuse. He simply had absented himself. In his numbed state of agonised grief, Richard might not have noticed the empty space beside Gloucester. But Arundel was brutally determined that Richard should know exactly what his attitude was: he chose his moment with savage precision.

The slithering of sandals, the mounting crescendo of the 'In Paradisum' – *Chorus Angelorum te suscipiat, et cum Lazaro quondam paupere aeternam habeas requiem* – warned Richard that the climax of the service was near. He found himself at the edge of the vault wherein, in a moment, the coffin would be lowered. Then a sudden diminuendo of sound accentuated the breathless intensity of feeling.

Crash! against the solemnly reverent hush, the sound of the Abbey doors being flung to, reverberated like an obscenity. Suddenly the impossible, the unbelievable was happening. Arundel, noisily jangling his spurs and armour, swaggered down the aisle and took his allotted place beside Gloucester – flourishing the King's letter of command in his hands to emphasise the point that his belated arrival was not due to any error of communication.

After a moment's ghastly pause, the interrupted service was resumed. But Arundel, with a smirk of complicity at Gloucester – who at least had the grace to hang his head – continued with inconceivable insolence to bait his victim. After a few moments he approached the King, exclaiming: 'Sire – my regrets, but urgent business calls me elsewhere. May I have your permission to retire?'

This – this was the man who had spoken impudently to Anne during her life and was now desecrating her funeral. It was he who had said with incredible familiarity to the kneeling Queen: 'M'amie, you'd much better pray for yourself and for your husband,' when she'd interceded for Burley... Now with uncontrollable Plantagenet fury – but what man in his senses could do less? – Richard awoke to full awareness of his surroundings. The shocked gasp that ran through the ranks of mourners at Arundel's brutality was broken by the King's instantaneous reaction: oblivious of time and place he hit Arundel hard across the mouth. Blood spurted. The earl fell heavily, his skull striking the flagstones with a resounding crash. Gloucester knelt beside him to staunch the flow of blood, glancing up once furtively at the King, his nephew. 'They both deserved death long ago,' thought Richard, 'if we are ever to have harmony within my Kingdom. Even my private sorrows are not respected by such insensate brutes. Ah! Anne – even this sacred occasion is spoiled for me.'

CHAPTER ELEVEN

THAT SADDEST of all French kings, Charles VI, known as Le
Bien-Aimé, (though also, pathetically, as Le Fou) was wandering
forlornly through the fair chambers of the Parisian Royal Palace,
the Louvre, where his father, Charles Le Savant, had deposited
nine hundred manuscript books thus laying the foundations of
the great library of Paris.

Not that Charles VI was particularly interested in his surroundings on that cool early spring day of 1396; he was merely
restless and impatient, expecting, as he was, a visit from his wife,
Isabeau of Bavaria, resident in the Palace de St. Pol on the banks of
the Seine. With her would be their adored infant daughter, Isabella.

Charles had now been King for sixteen years, ever since the
death of his sickly father when he himself was eleven years old – so
handsome, good natured and gentle that high hopes had been
entertained of him by the commonality. But he was also fickle-
minded, self-indulgent; and his uncles had encouraged him in
excesses that weakened his mind and left more power to them. . . .
When he was sixteen he had been married to a fair innocent child
two years his junior, Isabeau of Bavaria. She was destined to be
the scourge not only of her royal husband but of France itself,
notorious for her debauchery. But that time was not yet; at
present she was merely pleasure-loving, idle, amoral – sowing
the seeds of the future.

Four years ago, when only twenty-three, Charles had been
frappé de folie, as his pitying subjects expressed it, when on a
punitive expedition in that torrid August of 1392. . . . Dozing
on their horses in the heat of the day, his companions in arms had
suddenly been aroused by the King's voice shrieking; 'Treason!'
treason!' as if awakening from a bad dream. Drawing his sword,
he fell on his astounded escort and slaughtered four of them before
falling senseless to the ground, where he lay as if dead. When
he came to himself, he gaped up at his men in astonishment.

'Who are you? And you . . . ? Where am I?'

'Sire – Your Majesty – ' they stammered.

'You make mock at me,' he raged, 'one would think I was a
King . . . *Who am I*? . . . Where are you taking me . . . ? Who are
you . . . ? *Who am I*?' The faint repetitive voice went on and on.

71

Inevitably the news leaked out and the common people bewailed the harmless young man who was their King. 'Who can have bewitched him?' was the question whispered throughout the French countryside. It was then that the luckless Charles was deserted by the Dukes of Burgundy and Orleans and left at the mercy of his trivial hedonistic wife.

The common people prayed that their young King would recover his sanity. They hailed his every half-lucid interval with hopeful joy. Unfortunately, not only was his madness recurrent, but he himself always seemed aware when he approached the brink of the precipice down which he would make another hurtling descent into lunacy. Suddenly he would stare at the courtiers around him, crying piteously: 'Who is bewitching me? In Christ's name, put me to death sooner.' Or: 'Ah! take this knife away. . . . I might attack somebody – or even do myself a mischief.'

But today – today he was feeling better. He would soon be seeing that darling of the Court, his six-year-old daughter, Isabella, and would return to his apartment at St Pol.

Yes – the door had slammed down below. Footsteps approached along the flagged corridor. His eyes blurred with happiness. A page flung the door open and stammered:

'Queen Isabeau and the Princess Isabella.'

They stood silhouetted against the tapestry: the Queen, her beautiful but hardened eyes sweeping the room imperiously as if demanding acknowledgement of her luxurious attire and of her beauty. And beside her, like a snowdrop, like the buds of spring, the darling fragile child who so innocently aped the grown-ups in her precocious seriousness and dignity, and who would never even begin to comprehend the evil of the world . . . Isabella of Valois had inherited her mother's beauty and her father's gentleness without the weakness that accompanied both.

Seriously intent, she dropped him a curtsey. Then, forgetting her childishly-assumed stateliness, the infant gathered her long skirts and ran across the smooth floor to embrace her father's knees. 'Pa-pa, pa-pa! How are you? I love you,' she said, all in one breathless sentence.

'Ah! *ma petite. Je t'adore.*' He stroked her smooth fair curls, and pinched the pale cheeks to make her laugh. Her large dark eyes sparkled as she gurgled adorably. That 'French beauty' of dark eyes contrasted with flaxen hair was her combined heritage from her mother's parents: a blond German prince and a brunette Italian princess. He wished, fleetingly, that her colouring were as brilliant as her mother's, for sometimes his heart sank at the thought of her babyish fragility. There were younger brothers and sisters, but none so dear to his heart as this, their first-born to survive, slim, with skin of a delicate velvety smoothness and those hauntingly expressive eyes.

'You are coming back to St Pol today?' the Queen asked. 'You're looking much better, Charles. There are several things we have to discuss with you – Orleans and I.'

The attacks of inflammation of the brain had, at this time, yielded for a while to medical treatment. Charles knew that he must indeed assume the reins of power or Isabeau and his brother, Orleans, would rule, and ignore him utterly. He knew she sometimes said carelessly of him, as if half-joking: 'His Majesty? Oh, he's mad as a March hare!' Now that he was well again was the time to show his authority and revel in his undoubted popularity.

But what was this the Queen was saying to him?

'King Richard of England has been advised to marry again. His subjects expect it of him. After all, Queen Anne died two years ago.'

'What has that to do with us?' he demanded harshly. Then, seeing her great eyes flicker towards their daughter, he added: 'No – no – nonsense.'

'But why? Your Counsellors will tell you otherwise,' she said.

'She's but a baby.'

'Royalties have been married younger,' she said smoothly. 'We shall have – several others – to place to advantage – eventually. Lucky if we can do as well for them.'

'Royal children are married young – yes. But not, usually, to a bridegroom twenty years their senior – and a widower at that.' He spoke violently. 'Why, he must be as old as I am.' Even as he fought down the rising tide of anguish, he knew that he was being absurd.

'Hush! don't upset yourself. It's bad for you. Think what it would mean for France. A truce from all these cursed endless wars. Richard seems a pacific-minded King. . . . Well,' she went on, gathering up the skirts of her gorgeously-brocaded houppe-land, with it newly-fashionable high waist, in one practised hand, 'I only thought I'd remind you before your advisers speak of it.'

As a matter of fact, the preliminary steps had already been taken as Charles now recollected. Yes, he supposed, while Isabella slipped her tiny warm hand into his, and smiled enchantingly up at him as she pulled towards the door, that really no higher position could be found for her than that of Queen of England. After sixty years of this indecisive war, surely a Royal Marriage would mean that peace could be declared? Or, at the very least, the breathing space of a long truce?

'I'm coming, *ma petite*,' he said. 'What have you been doing with yourself the last few days?'

'Oh, playing games with Cousin Charles – doing lessons – learning a little English. I'd rather have you to play with than even Charles,' she added coaxingly. Charles, son of Louis, Duke of Orleans, slightly younger than herself and a sensitive intelligent child, was her chosen playmate, so her father felt suitably complimented. Yes, it would be agonising parting with this apple-of-his-eye, but already he knew he must resign himself. Everyone had to use his own offspring as pawns in a game of diplomacy, power, position or finance.

And across La Manche in England, Richard, still sadly remembering that Whitsun-tide of two years earlier when his beloved Anne had died of plague, hardly listened at first to the growing suggestions that he should marry again. His mind still winced at the thought of lovely Sheen lying abandoned and partially destroyed by his own frantic orders immediately after her death. He had no wish whatever to remarry. Hers had been the kind of spiritual beauty that holds a man long beyond the grave. He knew with the certainty of a firm religious faith that they would be re-united in Paradise. Anne! After her, a *mariage de convenance* would be distasteful in the extreme. But then, he knew he was being absurd – marriages hardly ever were made for liking, let alone for love. To regard such sentiments as a prerequisite was ridiculous. He'd simply been astoundingly fortunate that he and Anne – but no! better to forget that now.

But his Uncle Thomas of Gloucester, as ever his chief enemy, and Gloucester's friend Arundel, sneered openly at his lack of interest in sexual matters – hinted at impotence. Slowly his mind turned the matter over, rejecting one by one the various brides suggested to him by Parliament. Yes, he was the consecrated King. The holy oil of that consecration reminded him that even in the question of marriage he had a duty towards his country – *his* England. Gloucester now even suggested his own daughter, a grown-up girl and would no doubt be delighted that she, Richard's first cousin, would thus be Queen Consort and any son of theirs reign one day as King. . . . Such of the barons as did not want to see the rapacious Gloucester become even more overwhelmingly powerful mentioned the King of Navarre's sisters or daughters as giving a suitable choice.

Richard laughed to himself. Well – any marriage of his should certainly involve diplomatic negotiations and advantages. As far as the succession was concerned, that was safely vested in Roger Mortimer, Earl of March, heir, through his mother, to the throne. As for himself – well, his heart was not yet divorced from Anne. And so the brilliant idea had flashed into his mind – he would espouse the tiny daughter of Charles-Le-Bien-Aimé of France.

As things were, the negotiations for peace had dragged on and on; such an alliance would help give pause to a wasteful war. And that such a marriage could not be consummated for years, was all to his liking. After all, he was only twenty-nine, plenty of time ahead if any of that side of life meant anything to him again – and if not, when the little bride reached puberty, the marriage could always be annulled. In the meantime, culture and the arts of peace would have a chance to flourish. For Richard was too intelligent and sensitive not to realise how much true civilisation was evolving during his years on the throne. Despite great struggles and difficulties – perhaps partly because of them – it had become a glad and brilliant period with men like Chaucer and Gower expressing the new flowering in their poetry, Henry Yevele's architectural masterpieces promising to endure for centuries, gifted sculptors and brass-engravers working as if for eternity, Wycliffe and his English Bible affecting religious thought, and a difficult social awakening that was yet annihilating serfdom.

Richard almost collided with Gloucester in the corridors at Eltham Palace. The latter was in a fury, slapping the palm of his hand with his gauntlet as he spoke: 'What's this bee in your bonnet about marriage with a child? Have you taken leave of your senses, nephew?' He always boasted that *he* wasn't afraid to give Richard the rough edge of his tongue – he was less boastful of the fact that he never hesitated to demand favours and position.

The doors were open to the pleasant terraces and Richard was aware of the vagrant breeze wafting the scent of flowers. 'Not at all,' he said smoothly, 'perhaps I should be allowed some small say in my own marriage arrangements.'

'Parliament is to debate your suggestion here in the Gothic Hall?' asked Gloucester. 'I warn you, I shall oppose it.'

'Doubtless. But perhaps the Archbishop of Canterbury, the Earl of Rutland and the Earl Marshal will see advantages – concealed from you, dear Uncle – in the prospect of peace with France.'

'Faugh! Peace? When much rich loot is still to be had? Our English archers will not love you the better for it, no – nor the nobles either.'

Neither will you, thought Richard, goaded as you are by ruthless ambition and insensate greed, as well as by jealousy of, and hatred for, myself.

'My Uncle Gaunt of Lancaster – your eldest surviving brother need I remind you? agrees with me.'

'He seems nowadays to be in your pocket. B'our Lady, it's as well events keep him out of England for long periods.' A sneering note crept into Gloucester's rough voice: 'Maybe he sees some hope of the succession for his son, Henry Bolingbroke. Ha!' Gloucester passed on, scowling.

Richard gazed after him thoughtfully. Difficult to remember now that long ago Gloucester had sown seeds of distrust in his mind against John of Gaunt, always implying he meant to seize the throne for the House of Lancaster. Later, Richard realised that this was Gloucester's own devious mind, stirring up trouble in case eventually it could turn to his own advantage. Yet gradually Richard had been able to rely on his eldest uncle – indeed, felt safer these days, had more courage to stand up for what he believed in, and against Gloucester's machinations, when John of Gaunt, Duke of Lancaster, was in the kingdom. . . . Richard had never been able to forget the terrible affront his nerves had suffered when, as a lonely sensitive boy, he had been taunted by Gloucester for his friendship with Robert de Vere and threatened with a similar fate as his great-grandfather – allegedly for the same offence. Even now he shuddered at the memory. The Fates might spin the thread of life yet inevitably the end would come – and how much should he be expected to endure from this evil man (who had made his Anne suffer and even dared affront the consecrated King) before the thread was snapped?

Gloucester, bursting with venom after this encounter, sought his own quarters at Eltham where his squire, Sir John Lackingay, awaited him, and shouted so violently against the King that even his squire expostulated.

Gloucester ignored him, rushing on at full torrent: 'Why have any truces with the French? Can you tell me that? *Now* – while the flower of French chivalry is either slain or in captivity – is the time to annihilate them, root and branch. To men at arms like us, idleness is death. Look at the way they've deprived us of

Aquitaine – stolen our rightful inheritance from us. If the King of England had any sense he'd find a hundred thousand archers and six thousand men-at-arms itching to cross the sea and plunder the French. The people of England are always eager to fight those richer than themselves. I myself would be the first to renew the wars.'

When he stopped for a moment to draw breath, Lackingay murmured that he'd heard, as doubtless Gloucester knew, that after the truces between England and France were signed, Richard planned to make a second expedition to Ireland and employ his archers and men-at-arms in settling that country.

'Ireland?' shouted Gloucester, 'a poor and wicked people. Not worth conquering. To raise taxes for that would indeed cause a rebellion here.' He smiled savagely: 'I would foment one myself if necessary.'

'Come now,' said Lackingay daringly, 'the King is generous to a fault. Your two brothers, Lancaster and York, usually live with him – as you yourself could if you wished – and he often sends for you. Not that you always bother to go.'

'My brothers? You are right, they are far too much of an expense to the King. I make no secret of my opinion. And I come and go as I choose. I prefer to live at my castle at Pleshy in Essex, thirty miles from London, where I'm independent of everybody.' He laughed now. 'I never allow myself to be contradicted. After all, am I not Duke of Gloucester, Earl of Essex and Buckingham, and Constable of England? Even the King is usually submissive to me, gives in to my demands. . . . If he is not in this matter, it will be the worse for him.'

And to whom do you owe all those honours thought his squire derisively. But Lackingay knew better than to dare oppose him. Nevertheless he could not help thinking that for the last seven years or so Richard had reason to feel satisfied with what he had achieved in the face of a brutal world. In spite of such as Gloucester and Arundel, he had managed to get the weight of Gaunt's experience on his side, and together they were building up an instrument of government around the kingship and towards the full regality of that sacred office for which Richard wistfully yearned. As far as his own personality was concerned, he was at last turning his passionate grief for Anne into a serene faith.

If he could but consolidate his position by this truce with France he might well appear what in truth he was – England's most sensitively civilised King, patron of those arts that were composing a brilliant culture. Could he keep the ruthless power of the barons in check? Sometimes, thought Lackingay darkly, he must wish to strike back at them. Revenge on those who had deprived him of his friends, struck at him through them, insulted his Queen, his sacred office and himself, might begin to appear within his powers. But no – surely that would be seen by the King himself as a tactical error? Besides, Richard was an idealist. His problem must be how to deal with such men as Gloucester and Arundel – who recognised no holds as barred – without descending to their level. To do that would finish him, for not only did he demand better of himself but had taught others to expect the best of him. It was the ancient dilemma facing those of the highest standards in any era: do I oppose my enemy on his terms or my own? To be too hard on oneself is perhaps a form of conceit.

Well, Gloucester had been right to some extent. At first there was a storm of protest at the projected royal marriage. However, it was easy for Gloucester to be proved correct since he himself stirred up some of the disaffection. . . . Everyone appeared eager to advise the King that the lady was far too young – that even in half a dozen years she would not be the proper age for a wife. And why, in heaven's name, should he wish to marry the daughter of England's greatest foe? He would simply be misunderstood or hated for it.

Once upon a time Richard would have flown into one of the famous Plantagenet rages at so much gratuitous advice. Now he was self-confident enough to smile pleasantly – a smile that irradiated his still youthfully-glowing face – and reply with the greatest affability.

'Yes, indeed, it's extremely fortunate that she's so very young. One has only to pause for a moment to be struck by all the advantages of that fact: every day will remedy the deficiency of age – for if it be a deficiency, it is certainly one that time inevitably cures. And then – her youthfulness is one of my chief reasons for preferring her above all others; I shall be able to educate her myself, not only to my way of thinking, but to the manners and customs of the English.' He did not always present his other reasons – that of wishing for peace instead of war – and never mentioned the great personal one of remaining true to his dead love. Richard was learning subterfuge.

And when his listeners hesitated at such frank argument, he merely laughed and drove the point home with: 'As for myself, I'm still young enough to wait for her.'

Biding his time, Gloucester thought: doesn't the young fool

realise he'll still need to impose taxes to run the realm, and that it's easier to extort them for invading the enemy than for the less tangible blessings of peace? Unless he makes it worth my while, I need only remind the Londoners that the motto *n'impose qui ne veut* ('no taxation without consent') is becoming firmly established, to enlist them solidly on my side. . . . However, we'll see first what this deal with France brings forth.

And it was true that there were better men than Thomas of Gloucester who yet saw war as the great flashing adventure, the highest test of personal valour, and whose love of their country was expressed in that ultimate brilliant clash of forces in which they were willing to sacrifice even their own joyous lusty lives. To them, art, fashion, poetry, style in architecture – in fact all so-called art – was the beginning of decay. And when a nation – or a man for that matter – began to brood on beauty, they considered it a sign of fatal degeneracy and effeminacy!

Richard's restlessness drove him to a perpetual round of his castles, palaces, and manor houses. Sometimes he was at Windsor, or the Tower of London, again he would return to Eltham seven miles south-east of London, then to Havering-atte-Bower in Essex where his grandfather had invested him, long ago, as his successor, next to fairy-like Leeds Castle in Kent, and back to Westminster Palace – but never Sheen, never any more.

Sometimes when he retreated to rural Eltham for peace and quiet, he grumbled smilingly that he was persecuted even there by his councillors. After the long debate on his marriage, he stayed late in his apartment one Sunday morning when all of them but his Uncle Edmund of York had at last returned to the capital. It was here, in bed and yawning prodigiously, that he was advised of a very unexpected visitor.

'What? Who?' Richard demanded incredulously, 'Jean Froissart? Sir John you call him? I thought he was dead.'

Jean Froissart, in the corridor outside the King's bed-chamber, grinned to himself at the embarrassment in old Sir Richard Sturry's voice as he whispered in reply. Froissart had remembered Sir Richard Sturry from the days when he had been squire of the bed-chamber to King Edward; apparently he now held the same office to this grandson, King Richard. It was a relief to Froissart to find *someone* he knew still alive, as it was twenty-eight years since he'd left England and he was beginning to feel that he was only meeting the descendants of those he'd once known so well. It was a disconcerting experience. (And now they'd thought *him* dead!)

'The Duke of York remembers him,' said another voice within the Chamber, 'and he has brought letters from the Count of Hainault, and Lord de Gomegines. Actually, I had promised to present him to you at Leeds Castle – he did indeed come there but you were about to leave, Sire.' Surely, thought Froissart, that was the voice of Sir Thomas Percy, High Steward of England?

'I suppose we'd better see him,' came Richard's voice, 'my Uncle Edmund of York always spoke of his attachment to my grandmother, Queen Philippa.'

A moment later, Froissart found himself bending his knee beside the King's bed.

'Welcome, Sir John,' said Richard easily, his fair skin flushed, his long golden locks somewhat tousled. 'When did you get back to England?'

'Renowned sovereign,' said Froissart formally, 'I apologise for intruding on your rest. But – but – ' he stammered a little, 'I might say I was educated at the Court of your Grandsire of happy memory, and Queen Philippa was my gracious patroness. England – the Court – your Grandparents – all treated me with honour, courtesy and liberality. In all my travels, I have always wanted to come back. How long have I been here? I crossed from Calais to Dover on 12th July.'

'You wear your years lightly,' said Richard, looking at him keenly. 'I am glad to have the pleasure of setting eyes on you after all the years I had heard of you.'

Froissart smiled faintly. 'I am fifty-eight – a great age no doubt to you, Sire, but I was seven years younger than your lamented Father, the Prince of Wales, whom I knew very well. May I venture to contradict you? You set eyes on me once, long ago.'

Richard leaned up on one elbow. 'I was only three years old when my grandmother died.'

'Yes – but I was present at your christening in the Cathedral Church of Bordeaux. I hardly expect you to recollect the occasion, Sire . . . ! Actually, I had intended to accompany the Prince of Wales, your Father, on his expedition to Spain. But he decreed otherwise – he sent me back to the Queen, his Mother, in England.'

'It sounds like ancient history,' commented Richard, kicking the bedclothes back, 'but in remembrance of your past affection for our family you are very welcome to remain in our households as often as you please – not that I remain long in the same place . . . I have been wondering what made you return?'

'Ah, I have never forgotten my youthful years here. For twenty-seven years I've been promising myself I'd return one day – absurd, I suppose, but it ran in my imagination that if I once saw England again – I should live the longer.'

'Sturry tells me you're an historian. You must notice huge changes here in more than quarter of a century.'

'Indeed, Sire. That, too, encouraged me to come – I've been seeing people who can help me in the verification of my manuscript.'

Sir Richard Sturry came forward with the King's robe. Froissart realised it was his signal for departure. But he was still anxious to make a little ceremony out of the presentation of his offering.

So now he carefully took from out of the folds of his cote-hardie his most precious possession: a book bound in rich crimson velvet, with ten silver-gilt studs, a rose pattern in silver-gilt in the centre, and two large ornamental silver-gilt clasps. As he laid it on the bed, Jean Froissart felt as if he were parting with his heart's blood. These were all the poems on love and morality that he had composed over the last quarter of a century; he had had them painstakingly and handsomely penned, and adorned with coloured lettering and illustrations. Any book was a unique creation – this one was, in addition, a work of art.

'If you will graciously accept this gift, Sire.'

The King sat up and shot him an appreciative look, carefully opening the large clasps, and stroking the crimson velvet with loving fingers. His face, often now sadly drooping when in repose lit up with pleasure.

'Aha! – and of what does your book treat?'

'Of love!' replied Jean – and at once remembered that Anne had died and that Richard was inconsolable. But now he seemed quite delighted with that answer, and dipped into the book in several places, reading parts of it, here and there, aloud with, as Jean Froissart instantly noted, an excellent French accent.

'Ah, ecoutez!' he kept saying, and everyone turned and listened to that lightly musical voice reading of the raptures of infatuation, the delights of *amour*. Then, 'Credon,' he called, and when Sir Richard Credon hurried forward, he handed him the precious volume with, 'take that – carefully now! – to my oratory. Please put it away safely. I shall always treasure it.'

As he returned to the Inn, Froissart felt for a moment a keen sense of loss. That making a book took so many years, represented such an infinity of loving care with every stroke of brush or pen, meant they were rare and precious. Pehaps, he dreamed, one day a method would be invented of making several copies at once? Pah! he was being absurd. . . . But that the King of England spoke such fluent French, appreciated Gallic poetry – surely augured well for the success of this projected French alliance? Have I, in some small measure, repaid part of the debt of gratitude and affection owed for so long to my great benefactress? It was a comforting thought.

But before even such pleasant matters as the French alliance could be concluded, Richard very carefully in 1395 gave a second signal to his enemies, Arundel and Gloucester, that his memory of past injuries was still active. Had they understood the message of the red velvet slippers? If not, perhaps they would get this far more obvious reminder of the great injustice done to that friend of his youth, Robert de Vere, news of whose death in 1392 near Louvaine had grieved both him and Anne. Now, three years later, peace with France in sight, Richard felt sure enough of his position to make a second gesture of reminder. A strange and macabre gesture this – he had his friend's body brought back from France to be re-interred, with magnificent ceremonials, in the de Vere vault at Earls Colne, Essex.

Richard spared neither trouble nor expense in arranging the ceremony. But even the Archbishop, priest and barons who attended were quite unprepared for the extraordinary drama with which he invested the affair. The King, bareheaded, clothed in black, slowly approached the bier whereon lay the embalmed body of the friend of his youth.

'Open the coffin,' he ordered calmly.

In a deep hush, the bearers broke the casket. After one glance at Richard's face, they partially unwound the shroud. With bent head he stood gazing down at the face he had not seen for eight long years.

'What is he doing?' whispered someone in the crowd.

For Richard had stepped still closer to the bier. Suddenly he took the dankly cold hand in his own warm vital clasp as if renewing a pledge. After a moment he took a ring from his own hand and carefully placed it on one of the dead fingers. There – that is both an acknowledgement of the past and a vow for the future, Richard was thinking and turned slowly away. . . . He was well aware that neither Arundel nor Gloucester had attended – nor even his cousin, Henry Bolingbroke, Earl of Derby. Yet surely they could hardly miss the significance of this strange theatrical ceremony?

What a brilliant autumn that was of 1396! In France it still seemed more like mid-summer than sad autumn days, when the two kings, those of France and England, met for a four-day interview to end with the handing-over to Richard of his new little Queen.

The marriage treaty had been arranged the previous March by Rutland, Nottingham and William le Scrope, and was accompanied by an extension of the Truce with France for twenty-eight years. In reality it secured substantial advantages to England, but Gloucester, stressing the fact that it did not restore lost territory, minimised its popularity. He and Arundel carefully fanned any embers of discontent. There had been two embassies preparing the way for the marriage; the first, headed by Mowbray as Earl-Marshal, came back with the report that the tiny child had replied quite spontaneously to their questionings: 'Yes − I would like to be Queen of England, if it is God's will, and my lord and father's, for then, I am told, I shall be a great lady.' Richard had laughed aloud at this delicious absurdity when he was told of it. It pleased him very much.

And now, since the marriage contract had been signed in Paris on 9th March, 1396, Richard had come over in October to take delivery of his little bride, a month before her seventh birthday. Ever since that espousal in March with the Earl-Marshal as proxy for Richard she had been styled Queen of England. It was time indeed for Richard to fetch her in person for their formal marriage in Calais on 4th November.

So here, half-way between Guisnes and Andres, for four days in that gorgeous October, the two kings met with all the flamboyancy and ostentation of the age. By now, Charles le Bien Aimé was in a satisfied mood about the whole affair. He was in one of the more lucid optimistic remissions of his mental malady, and talked at length on how he would show his son-in-law, by the magnificence of their meeting-place, just how rich a country France still was. When Richard arrived, as arranged, bareheaded and on foot, to meet Charles, also on foot and similarly attired, his eyes swept the plain, noticing how thickly it was dotted with gay tents and pavilions housing the French and English nobility and men-at-arms. Richard had taken with him, in addition to the four hundred English knights to balance the number of French awaiting them, his eldest and his youngest uncles: John of Gaunt, Duke of Lancaster, and Thomas, Duke of Gloucester. Gloucester's inclusion was a matter of appeasement. Conciliation of this rapacious relative had also included the promise of an earldom for his son and immense monetary bribes to both of them.

Acceptance of such gifts never sweetened Gloucester's manners. Richard was angered to hear him now, on seeing the gorgeous gold and silver plate, the cloth of gold of the more important tents and all the magnificence of preparation, mutter: 'Looks as if France is still a very rich country – a great mistake to make peace with her.' He sounds more like a freebooter than a royal guest, thought Richard resentfully. But he himself must not allow anything to spoil this moment for him – after all he had spent £200,000 in splendid extravagances and presents to prepare for it and had different gorgeous outfits to war on each day. By a quirk, personal costuming on this occasion was Charles's only economy – he neatly made personal ostentation seem rather vulgar by wearing the same outfit throughout the ceremonies.

King Richard and King Charles thus met bareheaded under the blue vault of the morning sky while the four hundred English knights faced their French counterparts in serried ranks, looking each other over good-humouredly! King Charles smiled, took Richard by the hand and led him into the gorgeous tent prepared in his honour where they could talk freely. Wine, spices and comfits were presented to them by French and English dukes in attendance.

Presently the dinner tables were set out with great formality. The Duke of Burbon, waiting upon the two monarchs, was the wit of the occasion and kept the conversational ball juggling with light dexterity. The laughter that became almost incessant spurred Burbon to more and more audacity. At last, on the fourth day, primed with wine, he dared to say, addressing the King of England directly across the laden board: 'My lord King of England you *ought* to make good cheer, for you've had all your wishes gratified. You have a wife – or shall have one, for she will speedily be delivered to you.'

Before Richard could reply, Charles had glanced at his face and broken tactfully in: 'That's as may be, Bourbonnois. But we could wish our little daughter were as old as our cousin of St Pol,' (Richard had already glimpsed this neice of his, the belle of the festival) 'for then,' went on poor Charles wistfully, 'she would be of an age to love our son-in-law of England properly.'

Richard sprang to his feet, knocking over a goblet whose wine ran to the table's edge and dropped to the floor like gouts of blood. Formally, he bowed to the King of France, raising a beaker to his lips in gallant salute: 'Good father-in-law – the age of our wife is exactly perfect and pleases us right well. What does the mere count of years signify after all? What matters is that our two countries will from henceforth be so strongly united in love that no King in Christendom can harm either of us.'

Charles bowed in acknowledgement, raising his own goblet. The cloths were being removed, tables carried away by scuttling pages, and more wines and spices circulated. At this point Richard was thinking – now I shall at last see my little bride. All I have to do is to be sure she lives in happiness and honour, and is educated as befits her position. This is no relationship that need even remind me of my Anne.

Sunlight suddenly flooded the tent as the flaps were raised by two pages; immediately a scattered procession of ladies, damsels and young children surged in, giving a kaleidoscopic effect of brilliant colours and rapid movement. A child headed this feminine bevy. Slim, delicate, with a touching fragility that yet held an appeal of childish dignity, she gave the effect of perfection in not only her face, her figure, but in every unstudied gesture and pose. Obviously she hadn't expected to face such a crowd, and for a moment shrank back, discomfited. Then she recollected herself, gathered her long skirt in one tiny hand, and assumed the dignity of a court lady. One could hardly imagine her formed of the same common clay as ordinary folks.

King Charles, altogether unable to prolong leave-taking with his darling, sprang roughly up and took her by the hand. Then led her straight across to the English King. Startled, Richard thought – so this is she – why! she's *petite* indeed – merely a child. It's as if I'm taking delivery of a present. . . . Behind her, a small boy, her cousin and play mate, Charles d'Orleans, pulled at her surcoat.

'Can't I come with you, Bella?'

She looked up at Richard questioningly but with a child's complete trust and put her hand in his. His face, smooth and rosy between the fair curls, looked down at her from his six-foot height as benevolently and gently as a woman's. Why, she thought, he'll be kind to me as is my Papa. Then she half-turned to her little cousin.

'No, I'm afraid you can't come, Chas – I'm going to England to be Queen.' It sounded like a continuation of their games of make-believe.

This was no sport for Richard to indulge in. He immediately took his ceremonious leave of the whole company. Outside was the rich litter reserved for the accommodation of the Queen-consort of England who soon became universally referred to as The Little Queen.

The French ladies wept at parting and the Lady de Coucy was selected to remain with her. The circle of English ladies exclaimed with admiration and affection in their greetings. It was better for the child to be surrounded by ladies who usually talked in English, Richard considered carefully, though he didn't want her to be too homesick. But he frowned absently at a remark he overheard Lady de Coucy make to her intimates: 'We can rejoice that *this* little Queen Isabella will end the wars between France and England which that she-wolf Queen Isabella began.' Ah! so they still recalled his great-grandfather's tragic times and that other Isabella, also a Princess of France and a Queen of England, and rejoiced that the new Isabella was instrumental in reversing that terrible trend.

It was on this thought, that Richard vaulted on to his favourite roan horse, Barbary, and headed the cavalcade into the town that still remained to the English – Calais – where the formal marriage took place at the beginning of November – on All Saints' Day.

If Richard had been at all uneasy as to how he would feel in that Church of St. Nicholas being married for the second time, he need not have worried. Although the Archbishop of Canterbury was there to tie the knot nothing in the service reminded him painfully of Anne; rather, it was as if he were adopting this child in both their names. The service itself satisfied the aesthetic sense, since beauty of carving, of architecture, of stained glass windows always delighted him. Then, too, his love of sumptuous dress, of colour, was stirred by the gorgeous silks, satins, velvets, furs and jewellery. And the music of the portable organs, of guitars, of eleven-string harps in gilded frames, of the rebecks with their sensual strains, of the chanting of the monks and friars – and of one boy-soloist with heart-twisting treble – was only broken by the occasional jangle of a spur.

And at the centre of this brilliant scene of pomp and heraldry, the tiny bride, by some stroke of genius, wore instead of a jewelled circlet, crown or coronet – a little wreath of real flowers.

She is the child Anne and I did not have, thought Richard.

And he himself was the inevitable product of all these earlier years. Though the thought never crossed his mind, the infant Richard had been father to this man.

CHAPTER TWELVE

WHAT JOY it was to have an English *papa*. Well – almost like papa over again, though of course Richard was really entirely different. But he treated her, thought Isabella happily, as if she were a little kitten to be cosseted and yet trained. And here, at beautiful Windsor Castle she had her own apartments – known as those of *La Petite Reine* – as if she were continuing her babyish games in a more realistic dimension.

Sometimes she ran blithely down the sloping greensward towards the Thames and watched its silver-ribbon eddy, its clear reflection of skimming clouds, the proud swans and cygnets sailing by each doubled by its mirrored image in the water. Why did everyone call it *the* River as if it were totally unique? Didn't they know of the Seine? But when she asked Richard about this on one of his visits (why, oh, why didn't he come more often? Lady de Coucy told her he was too busy being King, and that all she, Isabella, could do to please him was to get on with her lessons) he stooped his tall head down towards her with: 'Are you homesick, then, my poppet?' sat down and took her on his knee. Math came and circled them both, pushing his wet muzzle into Richard's hand, looking up at them with adoring doggy eyes.

'Good dog!' said Richard, fondling him with his free hand, 'see, he's jealous of you, ma petite.'

'You are as fond of me as of Math?' the child persisted, and, satisfied, cuddled against the soft velvet of Richard's tunic when he admitted, surprising himself by the warmth of his feeling: 'Far more fond.'

At such times, amazed, he found himself less restless, more content. Surprisingly, sometimes he still looked as if the world hadn't touched him. Perhaps that effect was due to his idealist's mystical eyes, his still translucent skin, and his air of ecstatic dedication. At other times, recently, he'd shown traces of tension in the lines from nose to chin, in shadows beneath the eyes that gave him an appearance of pathos, even of tragedy – but not yet a look of maturity. It was only gradually that he'd been able to harden his nature, and that only in defence of his regality, rather than of himself, or of his women-folk with whom he was always gentle and tender.

'Are you happy here at Windsor?' pursued the King, 'or would you rather be in the Royal Apartments at the Tower – or at Westminster Palace?' Actually he preferred her to be here at Windsor, or at Eltham, or Leeds Castle in Kent, all within easy reach of London and yet quietly rural. Here her apartments were richly hung with red and white satin heavily embroidered in patterns of grapevines and shepherdesses. 'In any case, you'll be coming to Westminster for your coronation in January,' he promised.

She looked up at him artfully, under her heavy eyelashes: 'It's lovely here,' she conceded, 'if only you could visit me more often.'

'Come now, Lady de Coucy says I interrupt the routine of your education too much already. You have to speak perfect English by – well, let's say, by the time of your coronation. You mustn't lapse into French all the time, he said, pulling her ear.

Presently he sang to her in his clear musical tenor, while she, cuddled in his arms, half-listened and half-thought of the alternative homes he'd offered her. Of her crossing to England in November she had confused kaleidoscopic memories. She remembered arriving, dead tired, at Eltham, and the next day being conducted in great pomp from Kennington through Southwark to the Tower of London. Here she could smell the open sea again on the cold east wind. But what she most vividly recalled was the multitude that rushed, shouting, laughing, pushing, to see her when she entered the capital. 'Ah look – what a tiny darling! No wonder they're calling her The Little Queen!'. . . 'Ah-h-h-h,' the voices rolled along beside her, suddenly broken by screams from the bottle-neck of London Bridge. Involuntarily she'd turned her head, in its hood of miniver fur, at the hubbub on the Bridge, then, recollecting herself, had smoothed down her robe of red velvet lined with ermine and embossed with birds, of goldsmiths' work, perched upon branches of pearls and emeralds: then pulled her miniver cape snugly around her. . . It wasn't till later that she learned nine persons had been crushed to death on that 900-foot bridge that gave entrance to the city and where, on the gate at its northern end, heads of executed traitors withered in the breeze. . . . That night she slept at the Tower and the next day continued her triumphal journey to Westminster Palace, where Richard was awaiting to receive her amid the plaudits of the crowds. Yes, it had all been an intoxicating game to play. And now she was settled here at Windsor, working hard at her lessons with Madame de Coucy entirely to please Richard who arrived, unannounced, hurriedly, in sumptuous dress, merely to stay a short while from time to time and to see how she was progressing. She was beginning to speak English with a clear but almost too perfect enunciation that Richard found enchanting.

Once when he arrived unexpectedly, he heard the plaintive notes of the citole and her childish voice raised in song. So! she was going to be musical as well! He stood unnoticed, listening, as she plucked plaintively at the strings, her blonde hair luminously outlined against a window beyond. What a sad folk-song for a child to choose he thought, listening to her.

'Blow, blow thou northern wind,
Send thou me my sweeting –
Blow, northern wind, blow, blow, blow!'

As her voice died away into a wistful pathos, the guitar trailed from one hand. Suddenly, from behind her, his light tenor broke into the silence that still trembled from the citole strings:

'Fils d'or ne gette tel luur
Cum si chevel cuntre li jur.'

She whirled round. 'Mon cher mari! Ah, Richard!' And dropped the citole in a crash of musical discord.

That was a new expression from her, he thought consideringly – did it mean that she was outgrowing her childhood? – and stood looking at her glowing face. She faltered for words – for the first time felt shy with him, and so pretended to scold.

'Why – you keep telling *me* not to lapse into French – and here you are setting a bad example in song.' Grinning, he improvised gaily to the same popular tune:

'No golden thread shines quite so bright
As *your* fair hair against daylight.'

'Not bad for an improvised translation,' he teased her – and for the first time wondered what he should talk to her about. Absurdly enough, he began discoursing on Ireland, that strange foreign country inhabited by savages, far more alien to Englishmen than was France which, after all, was almost a part of their own country. 'They don't even wear breeches,' he told her laughingly, referred to his earlier Irish expedition of 1394, and outlined his well-thought-out policy for the pacification and administration of Ireland which would have to be implemented almost immediately. Oddly, he found himself thinking aloud along these lines as if talking to an equal.

Not that it mattered to Isabella *what* he discussed. She sat, entranced, eyes avidly fixed on Richard in innocent devotion, perfectly content that he was talking to her alone.

But his visits were erratically spaced. She could have no idea of all that was happening in his life since she considered herself only living when he was there. . . . Sometimes when he sat silent, preoccupied, she wondered, what is he doing, what is he thinking? Is he remote in the world of his past – the world I cannot share? Or can he have worries today. . . .? She could hardly be aware that his Uncle of Gloucester, who, as long ago as December of 1387 had plotted with Arundel to capture and depose him, remained his implacable enemy. And that Richard had just learned that he was now plotting to imprison him and his little bride in separate castles – had indeed confided the whole plan to a shocked Earl of March. . . . Richard was being forced to the ultimate revenges which, though he'd long considered, he'd hoped, in his happier hours, to be able to forego. Sometimes life offered little choice to those who had dependants to defend.

She looked at him with anxiety when his face saddened and lengthened in repose. 'Why doesn't he look happy all the time?' she'd asked Lady de Coucy who glanced at her speculatively before replying: 'He still misses his wife, I expect.' Isabella frowned childishly: 'But I'm his wife.' Lady de Coucy laughed unkindly: 'Not really, ma petite Reine.'

'I am – I am,' she protested tearfully.

'Lady de Coucy says I'm not a real wife to you – or you would look happier,' Isabella told Richard the moment she saw him next. A look of anger crossed his face, quickly suppressed. After that, he was careful only to share with Isabella his sunnier hours, to wipe from his face the tensions caused by the struggle he was having to liquidate the debts incurred by the Royal Progress to France and the ceremonials in England for the Little Queen.

In great anguish, Richard had even confided in Uncle John of Gaunt, Duke of Lancaster, and easy-going Uncle Edmund of York, that he'd been informed of Gloucester's dastardly plot. As it turned out, they'd both already heard this wild talk but could scarcely credit that Gloucester would carry it through. 'You know, my lord King,' they said to Richard, 'our brother is apt to say all these things when in one of his frantic rages – but his bark is worse than his bite.' However, the very next day, Richard had secret confirmation of this terrible plot and that Gloucester had ranged the Londoners on his side by pretending that costs of government should be practically nil now that the wars with France were in abeyance, and that, in imposing taxes, Richard was merely being wantonly extravagant.

Richard groaned. His hands were forced. He couldn't bear even to sit peacefully in little Isabella's presence while this threat hung over them both. He would be no man – let alone a King – if he couldn't protect his own. Besides, each time he saw the Little Queen he became increasingly aware of how rapidly she was developing – and that her intuition regarding him was becoming more acute.

He had no choice, then, but to destroy his uncle before he himself and Isabella were seized. He realised now that in always being submissive to Gloucester, in attempting appeasement, he had simply been submitting to a blackmail that would be endless since it had led Gloucester to feel he had him at his mercy.

So now, on that summer day of 1397, the time had come. On the pretext of going deer hunting, Richard went to his palace at Havering-atte-Bower in Essex. The heat was so intense that the deerhounds were dozing in the paved yards and the hooded falcons sat blinking on their perches. Undeterred, Richard set out from there in the hot afternoon with a few attendants to ride to Pleshy Castle, Gloucester's seat, twenty miles further on, in the centre of Essex.

As they jogged along the sun-scorched dusty roads, Richard's thoughts were sombre. He remembered Anne and her reminder that vengeance lay with God. But how long he had held his hand from being God's instrument. Eleven long years ago, this fierce unscrupulous uncle of his had, with the even more malicious Arundel, headed a movement to dethrone him, had removed or murdered all his friends, and enriched himself by blackmailing his nephew. And now Gloucester was publicly heading another revolt.

At last, there above the trees, the great oval fortress, Pleshy Castle, loomed out against the heat-hazed sky. The waters of the moat shimmered in the afternoon sun. As they cantered across the drawbridge, the clatter of their horses warned the porter of their approach; they heard him calling, 'Here's the King!' and a surprised Gloucester came out into the castle courtyard to meet them, followed by the duchess and their children.

'My liege,' said Gloucester, eyeing him obliquely (what had he come for?), 'I've already supped as it's now five o'clock. Had

I known of your coming, we would have waited.'

The duchess, with a warning glance, hustled her maids to re-set the table in the apartment off the Great Hall for the King to sup. Richard was asking his uncle to saddle his horses and accompany him back to London that evening where there was to be a meeting on the morrow of leading citizens – 'at which, good uncle, your advice will be most acceptable.'

Directly the King had risen from table, the cortège set out, the Dutchess and her children calling and waving their good-byes. Now it was getting cooler, the horsemen rode hard, the King and Gloucester chatting amicably all along the way.

At Stratford, in a lane that led down to the Thames, Gloucester suddenly drew up doubtfully: 'Are we going in the right direction?' It was now between ten and eleven o'clock at night; the moon was up though not clear of the trees. The sudden sound of a large body of men galloping to overtake them shattered the quiet air, and Gloucester, glancing behind him, was astounded to see the Earl-Marshal immediately behind him. Unbelievably, he was shouting: 'I arrest you in the name of the King.'

'Richard! My liege!' shouted the panic-stricken Gloucester, realising, too late, that this was an ambuscade. Immediately he knew, too, that it was Richard, now disappearing into the darkness far ahead, who had led him into it. All his years of plotting had led at last to this; Nemesis had overtaken him when he had become increasingly over confident that the King, his junior by eleven years, would never dare stand out against him.

Fighting every inch of the way, and calling for help to the very man he had been plotting to betray, Gloucester was forced down the rutty lane towards the Thames and into a boat. Two men rowed them out to a vessel anchored nearby and soon they were falling down the river on a favourable tide. The next evening, the ship arrived at Calais where Gloucester was imprisoned in the castle. The wretched man, convinced at last that his time was short, made full confession of treason to a priest, then prayed before the altar for the mercy of God. That very night he was smothered with pillows by four ruffians just before he was to have sat down to dinner. Re-entering the Hall, they announced that unhappily the Duke had succumbed to a fit of apoplexy while washing his hands before the meal. The news was made public, and the Earl Marshal went into mourning.

As the French people had always resented Gloucester's attitude towards France and to the marriage of their Princess Isabella, they considered his death no loss. His widow, Eleanor de Bohun, heiress of the Earls of Hereford, was terribly distressed when her husband's body was returned to England; she spent her months of widowhood at a Barking convent. She was further alarmed when she heard that the King had seized her uncle, the Earl of Arundel, Gloucester's crony, and had had him publicly beheaded in Cheapside.

Now, at long last, Anne's unspeakable humiliation was fully avenged.

For the first time, the King felt that he had absolute power. His two surviving uncles were grieved about Gloucester; however evil his ambitions, yet he was their brother.

And now, heady with the sweet wine of success after his years of subjection, the unfortunate King committed his final folly in September of 1398. It was as if each step led to the next, more perilous and more tempting – and yet, almost inevitable, given the circumstances and the responsibilities. For he was handed the opportunity to rid himself of the last remaining threats – his cousin Henry Bolingbroke, his exact contemporary, and Thomas Mowbray, Duke of Norfolk. Charges and counter-charges of treason had been bandied between them. One would think they were courting destruction as much as had Gloucester and Arundel, who, in a cruel age, had only received their deserts. Bolingbroke and Mowbray were less severely treated – to Richard's ultimate undoing. Encouraged to fight it out to the death in the lists – and before a huge concourse from all over England – at the last moment Richard flung down his baton, cried 'Hold!' to an incredulous audience, and banished both the combatants, his cousin Henry for ten years – later remitted to six – and Norfolk for 'a hundred wynters'.

Now, now he had the Kingdom safe at last; total security for himself and the Little Queen. And all Anne's wrongs avenged; her spirit would forgive him in the hereafter. Yet somehow he found it difficult to face Isabella's clear eyes as easily as in the past before his Uncle Gloucester's death, for he realised he'd had to sink his scruples to the level of his enemies'. Perhaps, he thought mournfully, nothing is ever really settled, solved, finished? And he was finding it difficult to live with himself even though he knew that Gloucester's was a long overdue punishment; that his contemporaries never suffered any pangs of conscience for far more brutal deeds, indulged in with far less excuse. Richard's nights became restless and tormented; he was wrought of too fine and sensitive a metal to sustain such stress.

There remained his well-conceived policy for Ireland to put into execution. Now, in 1399, when he decided it must be settled, it was already five years since his first honest attempt to grapple with the Irish question – an Ireland relapsing into barbarism, where his heir, the Earl of March, had been murdered the previous year.

Perhaps he could allow himself the indulgence of a peaceful interlude with his child – his child and Anne's as he still thought of her – before he left England on this imperatively necessary expedition? Richard was actually on his way to Ireland on that May day when he turned aside at Windsor *en route* to the western coast to embark for Ireland. The countryside was sheeted with hawthorn blossoms whose fragrance filled the air, the trees vibrated with the incessant singing of birds, butterflies revelled in their short day in the sun, all nature seemed to outbreak into beauty. Sweet music ushered in this month of flowers.

And Isabella herself? How long, how very long, she had been wistfully wondering why he never came. Had she offended him? Was he tired of her devotion? Did he realise how quickly she was growing up to please him? Were his heart and mind, as Lady de Coucy always hinted, so engrossed still with the thought of the dead Anne that he had no room for her? Isabella's thoughts ran backwards and forwards and in futile circles like rats in a trap.

At last one of her ladies told her that she had heard that Richard would be arriving at Windsor in a few hours for a short visit. Immediately it was as if her feet took charge of her; she couldn't keep still, she wanted to run and jump. Suddenly she felt gay as a parroquet.

There was a wild sky that night and somehow it comforted her. When Richard arrived, she heard him dismount in the courtyard, the jangle of his spurs. Forsaking all formality, she ran towards him as if the wind were carrying her on its wings – surely the chaos of nature was at one with the new wildness of her heart? I'm changing to someone different, she thought frantically. What is happening to me? In a whirl of giddiness she ran into his arms; but, deep within herself she realised that she was apeing the innocence of childhood to allow herself the babyish pleasure of pursuing him. The complexity of her emotions confused her.

As Richard turned towards those running footsteps, he was taken aback with the almost womanly appearance, the graceful burgeoning figure in its tender budding of early adolescence, of this creature who was nominally his wife. For a moment he felt almost tricked. Then, taking her by both arms, he held her away

94

to survey her with the greatest appreciation.

'Isabella! How tall you've grown! And how beautiful,' he added truthfully. A scarlet tide ran up her face. She laughed with sheer joy. Suddenly he realised that, this time, it was going to be more difficult to part with her. Perhaps, after all, there was to be a real future for them now that he'd insured the safety of the crown, and once he'd controlled the Irish situation. Perhaps even Anne, cognisant of events as she must be in Paradise, would understand his sudden awareness of his need for love as she had once bestowed it. A little more time and even emotional needs could turn out ideally.

Isabella never forgot the next few hours. This time he found himself able to talk quite seriously to her, not only of the high ideals he'd formed for this Irish expedition, but of a future they'd really share together.

How could she know the cold reality behind all the romance? Even this chivalrous foray, royal in its conception, was unsupported financially by the grasping barons. How else could Richard finance it than by confiscating the Lancastrian revenues when his Uncle John of Gaunt, died, and by telling himself that, after all, this was a means to a praiseworthy end? But his cousin, Henry Bolingbroke, now the new Duke of Lancaster and still in exile at the time of his father's death, was driven desperate by this corollary to Richard's recent actions. . . . As far as the King was concerned even taken in the context of the times, this sequestration was more fatal than a crime – it was a blunder for which he was to pay dear. Yet, judged by the standards of his day, Richard would have been justified in putting Bolingbroke and Norfolk to death.

All the time he was talking, his fair head outlined against the blazing colours of the arras, she had an inexplicable innocent urge to touch his face. It was like a thirst on her lips. The pain of wanting spread from her mouth to her small budding breasts. When at last the time came for him to go, suddenly she couldn't bear for him to move away from her. Her heart was throbbing so fast, she involuntarily spread one slim hand above it. What was the matter with her? She was trembling all over. Breathless, she could settle to nothing. At times she had resented and been jealous of his past; now she knew that part of her attraction for him lay in the fact that she wasn't part of his past history, of his humiliating subjections, of his belittlement by his relations. No, she was sharing this high-water-mark of his self-confidence, and all the future would be theirs.

Richard stood up and took her hands in his. 'I would not leave you now,' he was saying, 'if this Irish expedition were not long overdue. O'Neill and MacMurrough are in open rebellion – March was ambushed and killed last July – it's a desperate case of taking immediate action or abandoning Ireland altogether – which would be unthinkable. The sooner I land my army of archers at Waterford the sooner I shall return.'

'When do you expect to get there?' Isabella asked through stiffened lips.

'We sail on May 29th. If this marvellously fine weather holds a two day crossing should suffice.' He was telling her all this now so that their parting words should be in a brighter vein. For his last gesture was to go with her to Windsor Church. Together they attended a solemn Mass, and for the first time she really felt she was his Queen. She noted proudly, as she listened to him chanting the collect, that her head would soon almost reach up to his shoulder. The scent of incense mingled with that of the roses on the altar. She found herself praying to the Christ looking down from the cross that Richard would return to her safely.

As they went down the aisle after the service, Isabella heard the horses champing in the yard. She glanced up at him tearfully. So – they were leaving immediately. She didn't guess that the King had arranged everything so that the parting could not be prolonged – could not, indeed, be too private. Better this way, he'd decided, sensing her emotionalism.

Two of his squires were waiting in the porch with wine and comfits. For the first time she was able to laugh, heading that cavalcade towards the door to have an alfresco meal in the sunshine. 'What a funny place to have a meal,' she stammered. A lock of her fair hair had tumbled out of its crestine, making her look childlike and appealing. For a moment he cursed himself that they were *not* alone.

Now the moment of parting had come. Oblivious of the squires, the pages, the ladies-in-waiting, they gazed at each other intently as if discovering each other for the first time. He tilted her chin to look straight into her eyes, immense, dilated.

'Ah!' he murmured as if recognising her, 'my little girl is growing up.'

'Yes,' she said in a whisper.

'Will you be waiting here for me?' he asked in a voice he hardly knew as his own. Her anwering; 'Yes,' – just that – was almost inaudible, but the look that accompanied it was so heart-rending that he pressed her head against his breast, unable to bear its poignancy. He'd never forget Anne. Yet the adoration of this child was very sweet.

'When do you really go, my lord?' she asked.

'Now. In a few seconds.'

She glanced away. He put his arms around her and felt her tremble.

'Look up at me, *ma cherie*.'

'I wish I were as tall as you. Perhaps then you'd stop treating me as a child.'

'Ah! *ma petite* – I like you as you are. Don't change.' He lifted her by her elbows till her face was in line with his. 'You're beautiful.'

'Am I? But I'm your wife – not your little girl, Richard. I want to catch up with you – I want to go on campaigns with you.' Her face fell against his. 'Kiss me.'

'You make it hard for me to go, my Queen.' He smiled. 'I shall come back to you – you'll see.'

'Promise?'

'Of course. Only don't grow up too fast,' Then, smiling determinedly, he lifted her up in his arms, kissing her repeatedly. 'Adieu, Madame! Adieu, till we meet again,' he said more formally, and noticed that some of her ladies were weeping. But not Isabella. Holding her head high, she was smiling bravely so that he would remember her thus. He had promised to return, or, even, if he were away too long, that she should follow him. She gazed at him now with total trust, as he added, 'I'm going now.'

'Hold me tightly one moment first. There! now I'll shut my eyes. Go – go while I'm not looking.'

He walked unsteadily away, not daring to look back.

'Good-bye – good-bye,' she called after him in the English of heartbreak. 'You will be back soon.'

They never met again.

CHAPTER THIRTEEN

PERHAPS HAPPINESS is either a sense of yearning expectation or a wistful memory. Certainly in the next few days Isabella was ecstatically happy. She was as positive that Richard would return as she was sure of God in heaven. Her feet were never still and yet she seemed hardly to touch the ground. She found herself laughing upon the slightest provocation. Her face glowed till she held her cheeks between her hands thinking, 'I am aflame – I shall burn myself up with joy.' She felt kindly towards everyone, even to Lady de Coucy who was angrily packing to leave since the King had arranged for her dismissal. He had discovered, to his aston-ishment, that she kept a stable of eighteen horses, two or three goldsmiths and several furriers constantly employed for her own sole benefit. In fact her extravagances were boundless – and this at a time when he himself was being bedevilled for every groat he spent on government, or on the archers he'd taken with him to Ireland. No wonder he'd been obliged to sequester the Lancastrian estates in order to carry on at all.

The June days flowed past like one sunny summer hour. All the trees around the mount of Windsor were heavy with green drapery, the reeds and grasses grew high right down to the river banks, and tall foxgloves blazed their reflection across the water. Above all, it was the time of roses; their fragrance never failed to remind Isabella of that last Mass she had attended with Richard when roses lay upon the altar.

Sometimes, in the early morning, she would lean at the deep embrasure of a lancet window and watch the mist upon the river which would surely dispel by mid-morning. What was it Richard had quoted to her?

> 'For I have seen, full many a misty morn
> Followed full oft by merry summer's day'

– well, something like that – Richard said Chaucer had written – dear old-fashioned Chaucer wearing his long sedate cotehardie, but with serene face and good-humoured twinkling eyes belying his age.

Soon – soon – the outer door would open on the main court-yard, she would hear once more the jangle of spurs, the champing and neighing of horses, swift footsteps on the flagstones, and it would be he – the King!

How could she know that Henry Bolingbroke, an astute op-portunist of the first water, had chosen the moment of his cousin Richard's absence in Ireland to break his sentence of banishment and to land on 4th July with a few followers on a lonely spot on the Yorkshire coast, near the little village of Ravenspur south of Bridlington?

How could she imagine the popular enthusiasm he at first

aroused by appealing to the sense of fair play in Englishmen – saying that his estates had been confiscated in his absence?

How could she visualise those few ragged stragglers in Henry's wake turning into a turbulent swollen river of an army by the time they triumphantly entered London?

How could she understand that the cupidity of his listeners would lead them to swallow any fabrications as to Richard's alleged intentions to give back Calais to the French in order to please her, Isabella, the Little Queen? And that they'd even been told that vast new taxes were about to be imposed.

She only knew that early in July the weather broke. Heavy clouds seemed to rest almost on the round tower itself. Raindrops bounced on the smooth surface of the river like miniature balloons thrown by a jester. Suddenly the days seemed to Isabella to go slowly, to drag their weight timelessly along. When would she have news of the King?

Soon she noticed covert glances of pity thrown in her direction: that conversation ceased when she entered a room, or took a newly frivolous turn; that even the maids chattering in French quietened themselves when she came by. *What* was happening? What were they hiding from her? Mary Mother, what shall I do if anything has befallen my lord, the King?

Suddenly she was overcome with lassitude. And when she fell on to her bed, she astounded herself by breaking into a passion of weeping. It was as if she could never stop, as if every fibre of her body had melted and was leaving her. For two whole weeks she lay inert, only taking a little nourishment when it was placed within her lips, then weeping again till an alarming hiccuping took over.

And then one night when she was better an owl hooting in the beeches wakened her. The moon had just arisen making a pattern of the branches. She sat up at the sound of hurried slithering footsteps across the flagstones, and was aware her heart was pounding. Hist! that was the longed-for sound of horses champing beneath her windows – the reverberating clang of the great door – surely here was the climax to all her longing. . . . She could hardly summon breath enough to answer the stealthy tapping on her door.

It was indeed a Plantagenet face that peered round the aperture. But it was old Uncle Edmund of York, the only surviving son of Edward III now that John of Gaunt was dead. The one colourless and easy-going man among the passionately brilliant Plantagenets, he was now Regent of England while Richard was abroad. Sick with disappointment, Isabella bestirred herself to welcome him; and, after all, perhaps he had news to bring of the King.

York's surcoat was mud-splashed from hard riding, and rainwater dripped from it on to the strewn rushes. His usually goodnatured rubicund face was creased into lines of anxious woe. 'My Lady,' he panted, stooping to kiss her extended fingertips, 'I've come to escort you – we must away at once to Wallingford – the fortifications there are much more adequate than they are here at Windsor – which we might not be able to hold.' Yes, it was true, for Edward III had turned Windsor from a fortress into a palace.

'To *hold*?' she repeated incredulously, her eyes wide and dark in her pale face. '*To hold?* Against *whom*? I am the Queen of England . . . and where, where is the King?'

'Hah! I sent him a messenger across to Waterford,' he babbled, 'but Richard may be bogged down in Ireland – even when he gets back to the coast I doubt whether he can get his archers across until this unseasonable storm blows over. They say the seas are mountainous. My Lady, I beg you – let your ladies help you get ready to come at once. This way you'll see him the sooner.'

She found herself feverishly packing a few essentials while he broke the news of Bolingbroke's – Lancaster's – fateful landing. 'Why – he was banished as a traitor,' she said derisively. 'It was legal justice for his estates to be confiscated – and actually the King has seen to it that he's had sufficient income from them for all his needs on the Continent . . . Ha! you wait till the King gets over to Milford Haven. He'll soon put Cousin Henry in his place!'

She was as youthfully confident as Richard himself had been. Kindly York hadn't the heart to disillusion her.

In those five short weeks, the kingdom had virtually been lost.

Directly Isabella saw the great high donjon of Wallingford in Berkshire sticking up from a rising above the River Thames, and then, approaching, realised the might of the embattled walls behind its great moat, she thought it looked more like a prison than a pleasant palace – but then, palaces needed to be fortresses. And surely this, like Windsor, a royal but not a baronial castle, would be a safe retreat, if indeed retreat were needed, until Richard triumphantly rejoined her? The river's frequent double channels, and the sodden swamped meadows, made the Thames banks unapproachable for long reaches. Indeed, this great strategic fortress had been built on its green mound by the Conqueror

expressly to command the most important ford on the river . . .
Here the Little Queen settled down to await the arrival of her
husband, steeling herself to a patience she was far from feeling.
Once, desperately, she wrote a long letter to her father in far-away
France and entrusted it to one of her household; it was many a
long day before she knew that he had never received it.

Perhaps it was just as well that Isabella knew nothing of the
frightful happenings of the next few weeks: that, on reaching
Milford Haven in the last week of July, Richard (in face of his
rapidly disintegrating army, among whom the fainthearted were
tearing his white hart badge from their sleeves) with a few loyal
friends made a desperate effort to hasten along a hundred and
sixty miles of wild Welsh coast to reach the north where faithful
Salisbury was struggling to hold the rest of his army together.
That in those loyal but poverty-stricken Welsh castles he and his
followers existed on bread and water and dossed down at night
on straw. That between Conway and Rhuddlan the luckless
King entered upon the beginning of his doom. That his cousin,
Henry of Bolingbroke, lay at Flint Castle awaiting him with an
army of sixty-thousand Londoners. That Northumberland met
Richard at Conway in the guise of a peaceful emissary, swore to
him upon the Bread and Wine of the Body of Christ in the ruined
Conway Chapel that no harm was intended to one hair of his
head – and then, unbelievably and foully, on 19th August, turned
him over to Henry Bolingbroke at Flint Castle. No – no one, least
of all the Little Queen, could have imagined the baseness of that
betrayal after such an oath.

There followed the long indignity of Richard's ride to London,
each stage on a sorry nag, as a prisoner in Bolingbroke's train.
At Lichfield the unfortunate King, encouraged by the fact that
bands of wild Welshmen kept following to attack the rearguard
in an attempt at rescue, dropped from a window of the tower
where he slept; but he was quickly retaken and forced back into
the castle. At last he found himself in the Royal Apartments in the
Tower of London.

All that Isabella knew was that Uncle Edmund of York, the
Regent, had for some reason weakly yielded to Henry Bolingbroke. In fact, the garrisons of both Windsor and Wallingford
went over to the usurper. Isabella at last knew herself in his power.
She could not bear the thought that he, and his young son Henry,
only a year her senior, had the use of her beautiful apartment at
Windsor – she clenched her fists in impotent fury at the very idea.

And what of Richard in the Tower?

Thoughts of his plight and of Isabella circled in his mind in a wearying crescendo. . . . Perhaps the world was not yet ready for the kind of civilisation he'd envisaged? Sometimes, indeed, frustrated at his inability to attain it, he'd indulged in passions and injustices he shuddered to remember. But wasn't *that* the kind of kingship the people hankered for?

Hist! what was that?

The door in the shadowed corner creaked as it swung open. Henry Bolingbroke, Earl of Lancaster, his first cousin, stood framed against the lintel. Difficult to remember now that as children they'd been playmates, that they were exactly of an age, that sometimes in childhood he'd been aware of whispered comments on the contrast between the swaggering infant and the gentler beauty-loving one; had even caught his fathers wry look, his mother's protective love, when unguarded caustic remarks had reached them as to the desirability in this case of swopping sires!

'Welcome, cousin,' said the King, who at least towered over his cousin in height.

'I came as soon as I received your message. My barge was ready on the Thames,' replied Henry Bolingbroke, gesturing towards the slit window and the river beneath, 'I trust you are fairly comfortable in these – apartments.' His keen gaze travelled swiftly around what in effect was now the state gaol. To be back in England after his uncertainty as to the duration of his banishment was wonderful to him. At thirty-three years of age, the handsome face and figure of this royal widower were at their apogee. He had always resented his shorter stature, yet, beside him, Richard's face appeared almost too smooth and effeminate, and cast now in a mould of despondency. Gazing at Henry, Richard envied the virility, the assurance, that were evidenced in every motion of this cousin who was his enemy. Rumour had it that even in exile he'd taken the first steps towards a rich rewarding second marriage. And, here was another bitter pill to swallow: Henry Bolingbroke already had four sons, the eldest now eleven years old – while he himself – but no; it did not bear considering. Anne, he thought remorsefully, you were all I wanted.

(Life had not yet taught Richard to hesitate in considering a man supremely fortunate until he was beyond the reach of fate. Impossible yet to imagine that Henry, later repentedly to confess to excessive pride in his own masculine good looks, would, within a few brief years, begin suffering from a loathsome skin disease accompanied by bouts of fever, which blurred and ate into his features to such an extent that his many enemies – and popular feeling had indeed by then swung against him – declared that he had leprosy. Legend invested his death with the ultimate horror – though what he suffered from was probably Herpes Labialis with complications.)

For a moment, Richard couldn't remember why he'd consented to see Henry. His mind had flashed vividly back to the last time they'd stood alone together in the courtyard at Flint. As he swung down from his horse, he'd listened eagerly for the accustomed wild rush towards him of that perfect greyhound, Math, beautiful beyond measure and his devoted slave. Math had never followed any but the King and always greeted him by putting his forepaws on his shoulders and licking his face. . . . But now, astoundingly, Math had rushed at Henry Bolingbroke, Duke of Lancaster, and caressed him as lovingly as till then he had done his master, whom, this time, he totally ignored. To Richard it was unbelievable. Dogs, he thought despairingly, are easily won to fawn on any man – and yet, I had not thought it of my Math. An omen? Was this to show that everyone deserted him? But surely – there could be no thought of putting Henry in *his* place? Unless the genealogy was cooked there could be little thought of that. Cousin Henry had no hereditary claim as long as there were descendants of Edward III's second son, the gentle giant Lionel, alive. He himself, of course, was son of the eldest, the Black Prince. . . . What, then, did this stern-visaged man want with him? Perhaps, thought Richard piteously, all would be different if Anne and I had had a son? But no – he put the thought violently away. We were so happy as we were. Anne.

And with the thought, a dark surge of blood rose in his face. Any paternal feeling he had had, was expended on his little Isabella. He had guarded, caressed and loved her with the utmost devoted purity. She represented all that was good and loving left to him in his desolate life. He must see to it at least that she was safe. And if he had any future – he remembered now – towards the end – he'd even thought of the possibility of the two of them sharing a real marriage – since she'd innocently yet clearly shown him such devotion. Suddenly he knew exactly what he wished of Henry Lancaster. Alone together, surely he'd be reasonable where yesterday the assembled lords had been obdurate?

'Let me have my wife,' he said now, his voice tired and broken.

'The Council has forbidden that you should see Queen Isabella.'

'I am the King. I demand. . . . '

But Henry broke in furiously: 'It's time, sirrah, you heard some home truths.' His voice thickened with cruelty always provoked by the sight of this blond cousin whose fair hair hung in heavy curled swathes each side of his smooth cheeks. Henry's own physique was excellent, his body well proportioned and compact, his teeth white and regular against the deep russet of his thick-matted beard – but still, he had to look up to face Richard's six-foot height. Once Henry had heard himself – unfairly – described as 'of mean stature' and he had never forgotten it. Personal slights rankle longer than even such wrongs as banishment.

'Let me have my wife,' Richard repeated, his face somehow appearing tragic despite its mask-like lack of planes and angles, 'I demand. . . . '

'You can demand nothing,' Henry retorted, his face flushing angrily, 'don't you realise yet how little right you have to the crown of England, and how much the people prefer me to you?'

Richard had paled. Yes, he could understand that this type of battle-loving masculinity could be admired as his own father had been. And for the same reasons. That he himself had nurtured the arts of peace, of progress, of civilisation, and that he'd only failed when he'd attempted to live at the level he thought more popular – all this was counted a weakness in him. But 'little right to the Crown of England'. What remark could be more absurd?

Amazed, stunned, incredulous, he now heard Cousin Henry attempting to prove his point.

'When my grandfather, King Edward III of happy memory, educated you and had you publicly acknowledged heir to the throne – well, it was simply because of the great love he bore his eldest son, the Prince of Wales. But even the great King, though he shut his eyes to it, must have realised that your mother, the beautiful amorous Joan, often aroused the Prince's jealousy by her conduct. You know, there are many young handsome priests in the Prince of Wales's household at Bordeaux. And as you grew up so unlike your martial forebears – unwilling even to prosecute war against our natural enemies, the French – the rumour has been generally accepted in England and elsewhere that your true father was one of those. . . . '

'Stop it!' shouted Richard, beside himself with rage. 'Leave my mother, the Princess of Wales, out of this. She has been in her g-g-g-grave fourteen years and cannot d-d-defend herself against your calumny. . . . Not that she would need to. Theirs was a love match as everybody knew.'

'Yes,' sneered his cousin, 'she had with great subtlety enticed the

Prince of Wales to marry her. But when she had no sons by him, fearful of being divorced for want of heirs, she cleverly got connected with someone by whom she had two boys – you and your elder brother. . . . Hah! your very manners, disposition, mode of acting, temperament, are as different from your reputed father's as chalk from cheese.' He ignored the obvious fact, once remarked on by Archbishop Sudbury, that Richard and the Black Prince were, at one stage of their lives, physically as alike as two peas in a pod.

Richard had gone even more deathly white. He leaned down towards his cousin's flushed face and said, with loathing and despair: 'Lies and gossip! Are you really so low as to listen to, and accept, a tithe of the stories that always circulate about us among the riff-raff? Besides, as a boy, I was the living image of my father.' And, at that moment, there flashed into his mind the old story told of his virtuous grandmother, Queen Philippa: that, at the hour of her death she confessed to a priest that John of Gaunt, father of this cousin now before him, was not the son of her husband, the great Edward III whom she'd adored. That, having over-laid her baby, and dreading to disappoint her lord, she'd exchanged the dead body for the off-spring of a waiting woman. Hah! if one believed the story for a second, that would make Cousin Henry of low birth on both sides. . . . ! But Richard couldn't bring himself to use it even as a taunt. It was a palpable lie – as was this one about himself.

No – a struggle for dominance was an ugly factor in every human relationship, and that struggle was inevitably won by the more ruthless and unscrupulous who would use gossip, lies, and twisted history.

Suddenly, remembering all the errors of his reign, he wondered when things had begun to go wrong, and, at the thought, his hands started to tremble so that he instinctively clasped them behind his back. He despised himself for feeling momentarily afraid. Was this the end for him? If so, he must save his little girl – his still untouched Queen. For an instant, his thoughts flew back to Anne, his one true friend. If she had lived none of this would have happened. But as a good Catholic he knew he would meet her again one day amidst a chorus of angels. But not yet, not yet.

The thought steadied him and helped cool the Plantagenet rage he felt rising in his veins. He knew now what he must say if he was to save the child Queen and, perhaps, himself. Crossing to the narrow slit of window he looked down on the silver highway that was the Thames. It had been a hot day for September and, with the approach of evening, a little mist was lying on the water; a sudden welcome breeze ruffled its mirror-surface as boats shuttled along bearing passengers home. A line of ducks crossed his narrow vision, drawing bright pencil-slits across the water. As he turned in profile to Henry Bolingbroke, the latter noted once again the slight but strange distortion of the back of Richard's head – almost a deformity.

'Cousin,' Richard was saying, forcing himself to an unwonted humility for one who fervently believed in his divinely-sanctified regality, 'I have been thinking things over and considering my – my situation.' He stammered a little and his very white skin now showed a thin flush on the high cheek-bones. 'I could almost wish that I were already dead – a natural death – and that King Charles of France had his little daughter back. I quite realise that England regards France as her natural enemy – and resents the truces that alone have broken the almost continuous wars for the last sixty-two years between us – wars that now can go on for a millennium for all I care! But you can't take revenge on a young girl, and that is all she is. If the people of England have grown to hate me as you say, it is partly because of my attempts at peace.'

But in his mind he was still arguing that war could surely never be an end in itself? Even my father, he thought – and, whatever Henry Bolingbroke pretends to believe, he was most indubitably my sire – could not at the end envisage to what a whole lifetime of war was tending.

Turning again to face this cousin, his life-long rival, he felt black rage welling up in him; once he let it get beyond a certain point, he knew he'd lose all control. Not now – not at this moment – he must give in just far enough to save the lives of his Little Queen and their few faithful followers. But a royal prisoner is helpless to prevent risings in his favour that may turn out fatally for them all – so Isabella's path to France must be assured.

Henry was looking at him curiously. 'Next Monday, a committee of lords and barons will visit you here, to accept, if you wish, your resignation. For at the moment, as you must realise, England is really without an effective Head of State.' He bowed himself out.

So now here he was, alone, in the Fortress of the Tower, and though Henry had at first declared he only wished to share in forming a stable government, Richard knew definitely at last that what was being demanded of him was abdication. Personally he was convinced he could only resign his throne to God – never to Henry Bolingbroke. But if that was forced upon him, doubtless the chroniclers, feeling the new Lancastrians breathing down their necks as they wrote, would hasten to record for general consumption – and for posterity – that his renunciation was made joyfully out of affection for his cousin! There were just a few who would be loyal in writing about him – perhaps Froissart, though he was getting old, certainly Creton his French squire who'd sailed so merrily with him on this last Irish adventure – more as a minstrel and a poet than a soldier – and who'd sung of his love and admiration for his king, and impassioned rage at his betrayal; and, just as certainly, the musician-poet, Owen Glendower.

Richard found incarceration very hard to take. Now and then he suffered nightmares of prodigious horror. Sometimes they attacked him as phantasmagoric images which exploded into his consciousness like one of those modern cannons – waking him into an agony of terrified wonder as to *what* he'd been dreaming. At other times, many of the hallucinations were all too clear: he saw again his Uncle Thomas's face at the moment he realised nemesis had caught up with him; Norfolk and Henry Bolingbroke when he condemned them to banishment; even his Uncle John of Gaunt, whom eventually he'd come to trust utterly, distraught with unhappiness that his son had indeed been exiled. And Arundel? Yes – but if treason were allowed to riot unpunished, the whole kingdom would sink in chaos. Actually, he'd not been hard enough with them at the start of disaffection – but then he'd only been an over-sensitive boy – so that all this had eventually been forced upon him.

Forcing himself awake slowly, he was able to think of the eight good years of his reign and at last, by an act of will, visualise Anne's smiling benignant face in place of the horrifying images he'd imagined all too vividly upon the walls. Ah, Anne, he thought, if only I'd been strong enough to prevent the ideal from being defeated by the real! *Tout passe, tout lasse, tout casse.* Strange that things went wrong when, in reality, I had such a mystical ideal of my dedication, my consecration; this is my first punishment – that the verdict of one's own heart shows each as having a share in universal guilt. . . . But to keep sane in this terrible world where one can never foresee the consequence of acts performed in darkness and ignorance, one has to forgive oneself in the end. Anne would have understood and forgiven me anything. Surely God is not less compassionate?

But though he knew he would be rejoining Anne in the hereafter, it was the Little Queen he was concerned about now, for she was alive and defenceless. Mercurial, temperamental Isabella – as different from Anne as chalk from cheese; yet each had loved him devotedly in her own fashion. His heart seemed to swell with affection at the thought of the brilliant child till he found himself talking aloud to the empty air: 'My fair sister, my lady, and my sole desire, since I am robbed of the pleasure of beholding thee, such pain and affliction oppress my heart, I am oft-times near despair.' Ah, surely, after he'd given in to the forced abdication, he would be allowed to see her who was his joy, his solace, and his consort, once again?

CHAPTER FOURTEEN

AH! SHE could see, she could understand at last how men found their only reality in war. She'd never been anything but a petted child, so that when she and Cousin Charles d'Orleans used to play at 'going on crusades', she'd liked to pretend to be a young page, to be wounded, hungry, uncomfortable, all the things she'd never been allowed to feel at all. And now– and now – all her make-belief, her fairy stories, her fantasies were coming true. Richard! Richard! Richard! Richard!

She'd heard three months ago that he'd been forced to give up the throne, that upstart Henry had been magnificently crowned in October – and had had the gall to ride Richard's loved steed Barbary on the way to the ceremony. And she herself had been tricked by Henry's partisans, taken from place to place as a state prisoner, and now was here at Sonning with the regalia and the badges of the Lancastrians all about her.

But now – he'd escaped them. She'd always known he would. He was so strong and valiant. Besides, he was the consecrated King – a status he'd always assured her it was impossible to forfeit. And tonight, 4th January, of the new year 1400, the Earls of Kent, Huntingdon and Salisbury, had arrived triumphantly with four hundred lances they'd collected at Kingston, to make her the rallying point of their assault on Windsor. Before dawn tomorrow morning, one of the posterns of Windsor would be opened by confederates within the castle, and Henry of Lancaster, who was celebrating the festival of Christmas – Twelfth Night – with military force to protect him, would be seized and slain.

The Duke of Kent, flushed and breathless, stooping before her in exultant salutation, told her that he had heard that her husband had escaped from the Tower and was now in full march to come to her at the head of a hundred thousand men. Kent had come to warn her.

To herself, Isabella was saying: I can't wait, I can't wait. She would ride, dressed as a page, this very night to meet him. If he were here, he wouldn't let her endanger herself – he thought her a fragile child. And perhaps this wild ride through the dark would be her last chance of headlong adventure – just as the young men had it – before she settled down to being, as he had promised her, his proper Queen. Sedate, correct the way she'd always acted – but a woman at last, and a Queen. But tonight oh, Mary Mother of God, I'll have the kind of frenzied experience that youths can live for and take for granted. I can't wait to see the expression on his face when he, unexpectedly, catches sight of me; after this he won't be able to treat me any more as a child.

The pages, the squires, the men-at-arms were streaming through the great hall to follow the Earls of Kent and Salisbury, buckling on their swords and – with great exuberant laughs – scrabbling at the insignia of Henry Bolingbroke, tearing it off tabards and uniforms of Isabella's retinue. Laughing exultantly, she seized a dagger and began hacking at them herself with feverish abandon. On tiptoe, she stretched up to them, till some of the younger men knelt down to make her task the easier, looking up at her with adoration as if taking a vow again that she was indeed their liege lady, and would once more be their Queen. This was better than any game she'd ever played with Charles d'Orleans, a fantastic reality, precious beyond all imaginings. No one should stop her now Kent and Salisbury had come to enhearten her. She'd play this game through to the end.

Joyfully – indeed, overjoyed – she subscribed to a Proclamation saying that she did not recognise Henry Bolingbroke, Duke of Lancaster, as King. Hastily, she had her royal husband's badge of the white hart put up where the insignia of the 'So-called Henry IV' had recently blazed.

The stampede of footsteps died away, the night air cleared the stifling room. Stars showed beyond the open door. The draw-bridge once more rattled down. 'Wait,' she whispered to Walter, the young page, 'lace me into a suit of your clothes.'

'But – but – my lady,' he stammered. She stamped her foot imperiously and shrugged herself furiously into the unaccustomed garments with the awed help of Walter. 'Here – how does one tie the points?' she stammered, half in French and half in execrable

English; whereat they both giggled irrepressibly in that moment of near-hysteria.

Perhaps she had to impress him with her ability to cope with affairs of state, for she chose that moment to boast:

'It was I, Walter, who had the spiked mace concealed in Henry Bolingbroke's bed at Windsor Castle. I thought he'd wound himself almost to death when he threw himself on his bed at night – but someone must have noticed it. At least I hear that it depressed him mightily to think we had our spies within the castle!' Suddenly she was no longer smiling; her eyes were distended, grave, anxious.

Now they too were on their way. The cold wintery night air stung her cheeks and flowed past her in exciting eddies. Just ahead rode her brother-in-law, the Duke of Kent. Her hair, tucked neatly under coif and hat, her parti-coloured hose and surcoat, gave her the air of a gallant slender boy. A page rode each side of her. At first they cast doubtful glances at each other across her but soon they shared her youthful excited assurance and that sense of wonderful comradeship that is engendered by shared dangers. Jean Creton rode close behind as if on guard for Richard's sake.

For a moment she was to marvel at how unerringly she'd disposed of each of her attendant ladies on some well-fabricated errand during the hurried crucial moments of metamorphosis and flight. Then she dismissed the past from her mind in the wild unreality of present adventure.

She became aware that behind her someone was humming a tune. Softly, softly, so as not to attract too much attention, a melodious Welsh voice had started on a tuneful melody. Soon, the pervasive music flowed around them as one after another joined gently in. Tears stung Isabella's eyes as she recognised the melody that Owen Glendower, Richard's minstrel, had composed as a tribute of regret to the rightful King – a tune which, under the title of 'Sweet Richard', had swiftly become almost a call to arms.

At the next cross-tracks more followers were assembling under the bare wintry trees which creaked dismally in the breeze. On – on – on, was the cry, as they planned for the advance guard to reach Windsor and seize the false King. And Richard himself must surely be somewhere ahead leading the way to his usurping rival. Her horse's hoofbeats seemed to Isabella no louder than her own heart pounding furiously in her breast with joy, excitement, hope. In the thick darkness and in her boyish disguise, no one recognised the Little Queen, as she so recently had been.

Presently they found themselves in boggy country. The horses slowed down, jangling beneath the weight they carried. The night became even darker, stars hidden by heavy clouds. Here and there a torch flared into bloom, illuminating some floating pennant, a visored face, a horse's sweating flanks. The night began to seem endless to the young girl who travelled in such wild expectation. At one time she found herself dozing in the saddle. Afterwards she could not remember when it was they changed horses.

Suddenly she was wide awake at the sound of angry and dismayed voices all around. A man nearby muttered, 'I'd flay the traitor alive who betrayed our purpose to that bastard, Henry Bolingbroke.' Another cried loudly, 'Who says he's gone – and where? If to the Tower – forward, I say, and drag him out.' Horses were rearing nervously as some of the advance party crowded back to bring dismaying news. When the postern had been opened at Windsor by their confederates to let them in – they found the bird had flown a few scant hours earlier. Warned by a traitor to Richard's cause, Henry and his sons had ridden off to London through this dark night and by now were doubtless safely in the Tower – an almost impregnable fortress. No – no – the loyal insurgents had made no attempt to hold Windsor – what, under the circumstances, could be the use? Best swerve off, then, and retreat westward.

Was it only a rumour, then, that Richard himself had escaped, Isabella wondered in horrified apprehension? How impossible it always was to know what to believe. If he were still incarcerated – all was lost as far as she was concerned. . . . And then she heard it – a swelling cry on the night breeze: 'Richard!' . . . 'The King' . . . and suddenly saw, just ahead of her, the beloved form, shrouded by darkness. Ah! it was true then! He had escaped and would lead them to victory against the usurper. Her still-childish voice calling, 'Richard! Richard!' was lost in the tumult. Nevertheless her exultation at being there nearly choked her with happiness. Tomorrow would be his thirty-third birthday – after all, they would be able to celebrate it together. What joy!

And then – he turned to glance at his crowding followers. Her palfrey reared as she stared at him like a child who has been viciously struck in the face. Numbed with shock, *she* knew, even by that poor flickering torchlight, that that was never Richard. Why – why – it must be Maudelyn his squire and chaplain, the double of his master, arrayed in the King's royal robes. How often they'd joked that Richard's devoted chaplain resembled him so closely that it seemed likely he was an illegitimate son of one of

111

the royal family. . . . Now his eyes met hers, and he too registered shock at seeing her.

It was as if Isabella's numbed mind were a clock that had missed a beat. Then it took over once again, wondering frantically whether the loyalist nobles had arranged for this impersonation in order to rally Richard's followers? And was *he* still a prisoner in the Tower or elsewhere? Was this a ruse to make Henry betray himself by denying Richard was free . . .? Ah! anyone else might be deceived by this psuedo-Richard, but never she.

Clattering hoofs approached. A voice shouted: '*Qui va la?*' and a sweating messenger brought confirmation of the dismaying rumour that Henry and his son had indeed been saved from them by a few scant hours. The usurper was within the shelter of the stout walls of the Tower of London.

The pseudo-Richard wheeled, and, with Kent and Salisbury, began beating a hasty retreat to the still loyal city of Cirencester. By now Isabella could have dropped with fatigue. Time ceased to have any meaning – one just rode on for ever in a stunned state of endurance.

Nearby a cock crowed. Far on the distant horizon the false dawn started to streak the sky as they approached the city. Then – sudden noises were all around them – struggling bodies fell from horses – a blow on the head finished the page on Isabella's right, who slithered on the ground and lay, his body twitching, in the mud.

Her hat with its absurd liripipe had fallen off long ago. Now her too-hastily-wound coif unfastened, and a long fair strand of hair fell to her shoulders. A man's hand seized her reins – an astonished voice said: 'Why it's a girl!' as she fainted for the first time in her young life.

When, filled with desolation, she found herself once more on her feet, she was between two guards on the ground floor of an inn in Cirencester. It was day. The room was crowded. She recognised with relief that Walter, the second page, was still alive. His face was streaked with blood and dirt. He met her gaze by turning his head aside; was he afraid, she wondered, of betraying her? But she would be proud to declare herself.

The noise outside was deafening. Blinking her tired eyes against the morning light, she felt sweat starting out cold and prickly on her body at the unbelievable sight outside in the Market Place: two gory heads stuck up on pikes, blood still dripping from the severed necks. Could that be – yes – indeed it was – Kent – and Salisbury. A wave of faintness threatened to engulf her. But this was not – *could* not be – reality. It was a nightmare from which she must soon awaken.

A rough arm held her up. A gruff, but not unkindly, voice said: 'Here you are, wench. A sip of ale and you'll soon feel the better,' and a mug was thrust into her cold hand. The man looked down at her: 'Should be to home with your parents, girl. Childer should not be where there are armed mobs.' She shuddered as the ale stung her gullet.

His eyes followed hers to the scene outside. 'They both went bravely to their ends,' he said consideringly, 'Salisbury, Lollard as he was, preferred to commend himself to God rather than accept the ministrations of the priest. Brave men both, though woefully mistaken. Didn't have a chance – at dawn this Inn was surrounded by an armed mob – they two was forced to surrender.' He seemed to be thinking things out for himself rather than talking to the damsel in his grasp. With unwonted delicacy for so rough a man he did not add, as he might well have done: 'It's planned to send their heads, with several others, in two panniers – as fish is carried – by a varlet on horseback to rejoice the Londoners.' No sense in giving this child another shock – she looked pale enough already.

The ale gave her tongue courage as she thought of Sir John Montague, Earl of Salisbury – poet, scholar, soldier, loyal friend to the King – coming to this brutal end.

'Not mistaken, true and loyal,' she said in childishly obstinate voice, 'and I – *I* am the Queen.'

He started to laugh at so amusing a quip. 'You are – *what*?' Then, suddenly sobered, he gazed at her in consternation: 'The Little Queen,' he said slowly. Indeed, there was no other.

She found herself before her captors in another room, her numbed senses barely taking in the fact that corpses lay around the floors and blood dripped through the boards. Someone had draped a man's surcoat around her shoulders; it was clumsily large and reached in grotesque folds to the floor, edging itself in the ruddy tide . . . If Maudelyn had been slain too, she thought dully, at least it might mean that Richard had escaped, and that was all that really mattered. Or, did it matter that she should not stain her soft shoes with the seeping blood? She stepped delicately around pools of it, and held up the dagged cloak with two small hands, covering her boy's attire.

Time had ceased to have any meaning. Later, she could never remember when it was that Henry Bolingbroke (Henry IV, forsooth!) himself was there, staring at her consideringly, and with him his son, another Henry, only a year older than herself, who, for one unguarded moment, threw her a look of undisguised admiration as if he'd thought a girl incapable of such exploits.

But *she* was a Queen.

She turned her back on them indifferently, denying the kinghood. She had begun to realise none better, that Richard's humanity was outstanding, and that in getting rid of Arundel and Gloucester he had done what was necessary for England's peace. The realm was well rid of them. If he had been equally stern with this traitor, Henry, nothing could have come to the present terrible pass. But, though he had cautiously planned retribution, he had not been able to cope entirely with the brutalities of his peers. No wonder he'd been thrown, at times into a futile rage. For, after all, he had attempted to turn this into a golden age of English culture – and had partially succeeded despite their animosity.

When next Isabella really became aware of her surroundings, she found herself at the Royal Palace of Havering-atte-Bower in south-west Essex – a pleasant place for queens to retire to when their kings were hunting in the near-by forests. The terraced walks led down by easy stages to fragrant royal gardens. At first, to those around her, she appeared to be in a stupor, to walk as if in a trance, to be desperately ill with grief. All who approached her were amazed at such unswerving constancy in one who till now they'd regarded as merely a delicious unawakened child; they became afraid of startling her from this state of frozen immobility into a life of acute suffering. She did not weep – simply sat staring, by the hour, across the terraces and trees down to the forests. It was uncanny, frightening, to watch her. She had even ceased invoking the Blessed Virgin in her prayers.

Her slow awakening was like recovering, in agonised pain, the use of a frozen limb. All she wanted to know was – where was Richard? Was he well? What had happened to him? When would she see him next?

She realised now how closely guarded and under what restraint she'd been put. Everyone in the palace, of all ranks, had been carefully instructed never to answer her questions, not to mention Richard of Bordeaux, as he was now styled, to her, or simply to misinform her. In all other respects, everyone was infinitely kind and pitiful . . . Her own role gradually become that of the silent listener to distant whispered gossip, of attempting to interpret facial contortions and grimaces, of pretending to understand nothing of the hushed confidences going on around her.

And then one day she heard the whisper: 'Pontefract – if one can believe the rumour. . . .' Were they speaking of Richard?

She stilled herself with a hand upon a heart frantically beating like a captured thrush. If she kept quiet enough, pretending no further interest in their oblique glances and softly mouthed remarks, more news might drift her way in time, even without the mention of Richard's name.

Days later, over her tapestry work, with languid fingers moving slowly and aimlessly, she caught another stray sentence that yet might be relevant: 'Well – forcibly disguised as a forester, 'tis said.' And another voice: 'When? About the end of October, so I heard.' Why! if that were true, Richard had been imprisoned within the impenetrable grim walls of that Plantagenet castle of the north, securely behind a ditch, towers and barbican, at the very time when she and Salisbury and Kent set out so hopefully, so high-heartedly, on their revolt and intended rescue. And, let me see now, that was over three months ago. How they had all been deceived! She would never trust report again. Perhaps this report too was false? But what was happening to him now?

Towards the end of February, when primroses were beginning to push their palely fragrant blossoms through the slushy earth, and the hawthorn began bursting once again into that faint delightful first flush of spring, Isabella had an unexpected visitor.

One of her ladies burst in to tell her: 'Madame, here's the Prince of Wales waiting to pay his respects to you.'

'Who?' asked Isabella incredulously.

'H-H-Henry of Monmouth,' stammered her lady doubtfully and added: 'Actually he's been here several times to see you. We thought perhaps you were not quite–quite up to visitors.'

'I'm *not* receiving Henry of Monmouth,' replied Isabella with cold dignity.

Three days later he was back again. This time, with a catch at her throat, Isabella heard the deep barking of a dog in the great hall. Ah! may the Virgin Mary help me, she thought desperately, that is Math. I'd give the world to see him.

But when her lady-in-waiting again brought her the message, she managed to answer calmly: 'Next time Henry of Monmouth comes, you need not have the drawbridge lowered for him,' – even if it is his father's castle, her rebellious mind added furiously. As he rode reluctantly away – ardently attracted by her high-spirited refusal – she leaned against the lancet window to catch sight of Richard's greyhound, murmuring: 'Forgive me, dear Math – I had to refuse to see you.'

That night, when the moonlight spread a little pattern on her coverlet under the bed canopy, she woke and stared at it, carefully considering. Why was Henry of Monmouth courting her with such pertinacity – and his father doubtless aware and probably treating with France for her? If so – did they believe Richard dead? – or even *know* that he was so? How otherwise explain their conduct?

But she refused absolutely to believe this without proof positive. She'd been tricked too many times, Richard had promised to come back. The pain would be unendurable if she accepted every rumour to the contrary. . . . If only she were at home, in France, no one would hide the truth from her – when Richard escaped as he was bound to do, he would know where to come in search of her. After all, her parents were his in-laws and would be loyal to him. And this horrible pressure that was being put on her to marry Henry of Monmouth – well, her father could deal with that better than she could; he would understand her inflexible rejection of the Lancastrians. . . . At the back of her mind, unacknowledged because unsupportable, was a tiny tentative fear that – perhaps – maybe possibly – they had had Richard – put – to – death. Ah, God not that! Yet she only knew she had a horror of them, and a strange wish to wear mourning – till Richard should return. Or was that expectation simply a sign of her extreme confusion?

At last she slept.

CHAPTER FIFTEEN

ON THAT late July day of 1401, all France seemed to the little Isabella to be one vast carillon of reverberating sound. Ah! how one's country tugged at the heart-strings. She had imagined this home-coming so many many times – but never quite like this. In every French town she passed through on her way to Paris the crowds went mad with joy; they threw blossoms, bouquets, called blessings on the petite reine, set the church bells ringing. All that was even more fervent than her imaginings had envisaged. But she had always pictured returning on a royal visit with Richard at her side. Here she was, without him, clad in deep black.

Perhaps the black was a mistake? She wondered this quite violently while the enthusiastic crowds surged through the streets to welcome her. For, despite everything, she still regarded herself as Queen of England, and, furthermore, her heart did not even recognise that Richard was dead. Proof? What proof was there? Considering all the tricks and subterfuges employed by the Lancastrians, how could she be sure – why should she believe – that it was indeed Richard's body that had been displayed to the people?

And this was how she had dressed a month ago when Sir Thomas Percy was ordered to conduct her with all ceremony to Westminster to appear before the usurper and his son; the two Henrys, as she lumped them together in her mind, childishly, spitefully. The mourning black seemed suitable then, merely to show whose side she was on, and how beyond the bounds of possibility was the thought of marriage with this Prince Henry – Prince of Wales, forsooth! – a year older than herself, who eyed her so hungrily.

She had sat in their presence, slim and frail yet spirited, her pale face half-averted, making no reply to their remarks and questionings. She had determined not to speak at all, to remain sullen and morose. Only once did she almost break-down; there was the sound of scratching on the door and the young Prince himself jumped up and let in – Richard's loved greyhound, Math.

'Math!' she said brokenly, and the old hound came and nuzzled his head on her knees and gazed at her with puzzled faithful eyes. She turned her head violently away that none should sense the tears pricking beneath her eyelids. I won't beg even for him, she thought desperately. Nothing. Nothing. They have stripped me of my dowry and my jewellery, despite all bonds to the contrary. If I give in an inch they may manage to hold me in England till 9th November of this year – when I shall be twelve years old. A year ago, the French ambassadors whispered to me not to involve myself in any matrimonial engagement, as, by my twelfth birthday I could contract another legal marriage. No – I must be back in France before then. And it passed fleetingly through her mind that she'd been just six years old when Richard offered for her – and she would be back, alone, broken-hearted, before her twelfth birthday. Had any other female child ever lived through so strange a half a dozen years?

Sir Thomas Percy had been kindness itself as he conducted her, the day following her one-sided interview at Westminster, through the subdued and silent crowds of Londoners on their way to the coast. Seven Maids-of-Honour accompanied her, as well as the Duchess of Ireland, the Countess of Hereford, Eleanor Holland her governess, Lady Poynings and Lady Mowbray. . . . Had

Isabella but realised it, the awed silence of the English crowds, their immobility, was in reality a far greater tribute to their Little Queen, than had been the frenzied scenes of welcome on her arrival. Even those who'd sided against Richard, admired the constancy, the faithfulness of his young consort. . . . Soon, indeed, English ballads and songs of tribute would be popularly sung in her favour. Whistled and hummed from street to street, these ditties would help eventually to keep Richard's memory green and to rouse the countryside against the usurper, who would find his crown a sorry crown of thorns.

With Sir Thomas Percy and her entourage, Isabella could allow herself to show the sweetness of her real nature. Three balingers – used originally as whaleboats but now converted into excellent light pinnaces – and two armed barges had been appointed to take her and her suite from Dover to Calais. By the time they reached Leulinghen, between Boulogne and Calais, where the English were to deliver Isabella back to the French, Sir Thomas was in tears at parting from her. All the English ladies who'd accompanied her wept quite piteously as they watched Sir Thomas deliver their little Queen into the hands of Waleran the Righteous, Count St Pol, who gave Percy a formal receipt for her delivery. Like a bale of merchandise, thought Isabella hysterically.

'She is exactly in the same condition as when she was received,' said Sir Percy bluntly, 'and I challenge to Mortal combat anyone who shall assert the contrary.' But no one, no one, no one would dispute it.

Yes, I never saw him again after his promise to return from Ireland and really make me his Queen, thought Isabella now forlornly, her eyes on the far horizon. I could have made him so happy that perhaps he would have forgotten Anne. And for the first time for many months, Isabella herself managed to smile with unaccustomed lips as she looked round at her kindly escorts – little realising how her own innocent beauty and her sweet temper tore at people's hearts.

And here at last she was back at the Louvre – that was the Seine glimmering nearby under the summer sun – and a host of child-hood memories of this Gothic palace where she had been born rose up to choke her utterances. All her early experiences centred round this vast building (begun two hundred years ago as a feudal fortress but made luxurious and comfortable far more recently by Charles V), and also round the Hôtel de St Pol used as a place of retirement from this more formal palace, by the Royal family. She hesitated on the threshold, glancing around nostalgically at these lower floors crowded by guards and domestics, but her retinue urged her ceremoniously upward towards the rooms where dwelt the family in its palace of vaulted ceilings, frescoed walls and large stone fireplaces. Oriental silks, gold and silver vessels, floors strewn with handsome rugs above the fresh rushes – all struck a note of dear familiarity. But suddenly shyness and nervousness engulfed her.

Yes – this must be her mother approaching. It was a difficult moment for both of them, beneath all the appraising eyes of courtiers and ladies-in-waiting.

Isabeau of Bavaria, Queen of the Mode, looked magnificently handsome in her sumptuously cut houppeland with its deeply-jagged edges sweeping the floor. This houppeland, taking the place of a surcoat and revealing the brilliant silken cotehardie beneath, boasted a long serpent train, carried obsequiously by a small page; it was superbly designed in wyverns, griffins, unicorns and dragons. The aumôniere attached to her girdle glistened with jewels. As she rustled forward to embrace her daughter, Isabella heard the tiny tinkle of the little bells on the absurdly pointed slippers *à la poulaine* (like the spur of a ship).

And the variety of head-dresses was breath-taking. Isabeau herself, when not wearing a crown, still favoured the great hennin – a tall conic brocaded tube tightly fixed over the hair. In front a short veil softened the face, and from the spiring apex a cloud of fine muslin floated in charming mystery about the figure. A flattering fashion which Isabeau preferred to the newer ascoffions with their great horns either side of the face from which streamers fell to the shoulders. Many of the ladies were wearing this newer style, others the little hennin, or turbans, or a heart-shaped cap, or the soft nebulae net head-dress that framed the face. But no one excelled the Queen in the height and brilliance of her great hennin whose long floating veil somehow lent nobility to her beauty.

'Welcome home, my daughter,' said the Queen, stooping to envelop Isabella in her arms. For a moment, dismayed, the mother had thought: What have they done to her? My poor child – how frail she looks. But the moment passed. Not to be too serious before all these on-lookers. Queen Isabeau laughed and displayed the gewgaw in her hand: a model puppet designed most carefully to preview the changing fashions.

Fleetingly, Isabella realised they were all anxious to impress her with the gorgeous smartness of the French Court. How strange, when that was exactly the kind of thing for which her Richard

119

had been most bitterly criticised! But now she pushed that intrusive thought aside with the words:

'Merci, Madame. But where – where is the King – where is my pa-pa?' For a moment her eyes had dwelt fleetingly on the gorgeous male figure beside her mother – but no! only a small resemblance – this was his brother, Louis Duke d'Orleans. Her innocent mind deduced nothing else from the juxtaposition.

Isabeau and Orleans exchanged glances, and the Queen said easily: 'He is longing to see you, my daughter. But his anxieties and worries about you – well, to be frank – threw him into a frenzy. He has not been himself. . . .I must see you alone presently to exchange all family news and gossip.'

And perhaps I should break it to her then, thought Isabeau, that in less than three months I expect to be brought to bed of another infant – these houppelands cover a multitude of imperfections – otherwise I should still be wearing the figure-hugging cotehardie, with huge extravagant sleeves, laced tightly back and front and with a brilliant sleeveless surcoat slit to display the under-dress. At thirty years of age, Queen Isabeau was still triumphantly handsome.

(Happily, Isabella would not live to see this expected baby sister, Katherine, married to the very suitor she herself was so contemptuously spurning. . . . Fortunate indeed is humankind in being denied that gift of precognition it so ardently desires; otherwise the ironies of history would be quite unsupportable.)

Presently Isabeau drew her daughter in to her own bed-and-sitting-room. Though guests and family often slept in one large room partitioned off by curtains, Isabeau usually managed to keep this chamber to herself – the palace was large enough, heaven knew. Even in daytime, the slits of windows provided little light, but here there was the luxury of a few windows with small panes set in lead. In winter, the thick stone walls meant that the rooms were bitterly cold although provided with large fireplaces. Even on this hot summer day, the indoor air struck dankly cool. But it was quieter here where the scurrying feet of pages, esquires, musicians and waiting-women ceased their distraction.

How well Isabella remembered this room with its walls hung lavishly with textiles of madonna-blue patterned with fleur-de-lys in gold, its chests and stools, the armoire built into the wall, the Prie-Dieu with its high back and low devotional seat, the bed's scarlet covering and tester decorated with Bavarian arms, the gaily-painted ceiling beams, the luxury of a biscuit-coloured carpet – and the gilded cradle where she herself had lain. Even the lap-dog and the greyhound made it seem like home. . . . Isabeau watched her daughter reassembling early memories and said smilingly: 'Ah, – you remember my *étuves de bois*? I take them with me even when we retire to the Hôtel de St Pol; I couldn't do without my vapour-baths,' – and gestured to the wooden tubs specially equipped for that purpose, set in an alcove.

But Isabella was intent on other things than trivialities. 'Tell me,' she said urgently, 'how is le Roi? I understood from Count d'Albret when he came to see me last year at Havering-atte-Bower that it was pa-pa who sent to ask how I, as a prisoner, was being treated. I talked then to several of the French embassy – about you both – oh! for quite a time.' She hesitated, then went on more rapidly: 'In fact, I was greatly surprised that Henry Boling-broke allowed them to see me at all. They'd had to visit him at Eltham first to get permission. Oh, Maman – I asked so many questions of them – it was far better than any letter. Besides, sometimes my letters seem to have been intercepted.'

'Henry Bolingbroke?' repeated Queen Isabeau, leaning forward from the chest on which she sat and placing a mittened hand on her daughter's lap: 'You don't refer to him as King Henry IV – or his son as Prince of Wales?'

'Never – never,' said Isabella passionately. She flushed a deep red and her dark eyes flashed.

'Ah!' murmured Isabeau with satisfaction, 'then will you be willing to issue a declaration that you've never acknowledged Henry as your husband's ' – she hesitated delicately – 'successor?'

'Yes – yes – yes,' cried Isabella, 'the sooner the better. A Royal Declaration.' She smiled gratefully at her mother, and Isabeau thought, why, she is quite beautiful when she lights up like that.

'I shall sign too in support of you. France will never recognise Henry IV,' promised Isabeau warmly.

'You are Regent now?' Isabella sounded distressed: 'My father is really ill again?'

By now her mother had been Regent on several occasions and was practically living apart from her unfortunate husband—with his brother, Orleans, if rumour was to be credited. But such a thought could never touch Isabella's uncorrupted mind.

'No, not at the moment. You shall see him later, daughter. To be truthful with you – he became quite frantic – frenzied – at all the dreadful news of your and Richard's sufferings. Perhaps seeing you will bring him to himself. He always loved you very much,' she added generously. After a moment's silence she asked:

'Naturally it was a great relief to you seeing Count d'Albret and the French Ambassadors – we were overjoyed to get direct news of you on their return – but Isabella – didn't you ask them anything about your Richard?' (How much, Isabeau was wondering, does she *know*?)

The child went very pale. 'If you saw them subsequently – you must know I did. They never replied to that – nor even once mentioned King Richard's name. But to all my eager questions about you – and Pa-pa – and France – they answered at great length, and carefully.' Her voice broke. 'I was so glad to hear of you.'

'Well, ma cherie – you might have surmised the reason. Henry made them promise on oath never to mention "Richard of Bordeaux" (as he referred to him) to you in any way whatever. "Richard of Bordeaux" indeed,' Isabeau went on tartly, 'to hear the turn-coats talk you'd think he'd invented the Plague, the Black Death and the Peasants' Revolt!' After a pause she went on more calmly, 'Those were the conditions on which they were allowed access to you. The forfeit for breaking their oath would have been death.'

Isabella thought this over gravely and accepted it. Then, just as her mother was about to say what was, at the moment, nearest to her heart: We must arrange a marriage for you – after all, you are nearly twelve and have never really been married at all – Isabella took the wind entirely out of her sails.

'Of course, I'm not at all convinced that King Richard is dead,' Isabella confided. She put one pathetically thin hand to her heart. 'I am sure I should have felt it *here* if he were. He – he – promised to come back for me.' She managed a tremulous smile. 'And don't just tell me to be sensible. The heart has its reasons.'

Queen Isabeau threw her an almost frightened glance. Dear God, don't let anyone else in this family have hallucinations, she thought. And then for the first time, she felt a little shame for her own way of life. Such constancy, such purity in the midst of frivolous corruption almost defeated her. Did I conceive this, she wondered.

Abruptly she got up. 'We'll leave serious talks like this for when we are alone again. You look worn out, my child, and no wonder. May I suggest you see the King in the morning when you both are fresh and rested? And now – we'll go to the Banqueting Hall, have supper and be festive. Then you can retire early. But remember – to all my ladies – to all the Court, in fact – it's a great occasion to have you back. We must be gay for their sakes tonight.'

Although it was still broad daylight outside, the Great Hall needed lighting – was indeed flickering with hundreds of candles. The long main table glittered with gold and silver vessels, and, at Queen Isabeau's place, a rare goblet and ewer in white glass. Two important seats had canopies, and a few benches – settles – had backs, but most of the seating was plain backless benching. But there were ornamental chests; and Love Seats at the windows. The credence and dressoirs were crowded with food ready to be served to the main table.

And the talk was gay. It swirled about Isabella's tired head among the torch-lights, the baubles, the scent of food, the coming and going of squires and pages, and the ravishing taste of French wines. The conversation, light as foam, seemed designed tonight to entertain, and perhaps impress, the young visiting Queen. To please her mother she had donned a crimson sleeveless surcoat, opened at the side from shoulder to hip to display the slim golden cotehardie beneath, whose long sleeves dripped to the floor. An ermine garde corps adorned the top of the surcoat, but was cut low to reveal her tenderly-budding bosom. Her fair hair, with its jewelled circlet, shone through the gay crestine.

Neither the King nor his immediate retainers appeared, so, inevitably it seemed, the talk ran mainly on frivolous topics and fashions. Some of it amused Isabella, though much of it she'd already heard. Did she know, they gaily asked her, complimenting her on her becoming gown against the pallor of her skin, that in France the priests, monks and friars were loudly denouncing modern dress, not only from the pulpits, but from platforms erected in the town squares? They wanted all women to wear simple coifs once more, declaring that little hennins, great hennins and escoffions were the direct invention of the Devil. One preacher, giggled a lady-in-waiting, declared that escoffions were inspired by the likeness of the Great Horned Beast, Satan himself, and that the wearers thereof would be cast directly into Hell without even an interim in Purgatory.

As for those enticing slits in the surcoats that allowed tempting glimpses of the cotehardie, did the Little Queen realise that preachers were referring to these as 'doorways to Hell'? And that to distort the shape of one's body – even merely to the extent of sporting the absurd but amusing long-spurred shoes – was 'an outrage against the Creator'? The Black Death was ascribed as the result of Divine Wrath at their introduction.

Louis, Duke d'Orleans was heard to remark dryly that he'd always understood that that particular fashion was simply invented by an unfortunate noble who suffered from corns, bunions, and in-growing toenails! Of course new fashions had always been railed against by moralists in every generation; but as long as new designs were amusing and enticing, they would be eagerly followed despite an army of preachers.

Presently the talk grew more and more bawdy. Guessing-games began, only half-subdued, as to who would spend the night with whom; Isabella sat frozen in her place. She was accustomed to brutal frankness of speech, but stark lewdness was another story – a desecration of the idea of love. Suddenly, the need to leave was like a nausea. The Duke d'Orleans spoke pleasantly across the board: 'Our fair guest, the English Queen, is drooping with fatigue.' He signalled to the musicians in the gallery to play softly, and whispered to Queen Isabeau, who immediately arose to conduct her daughter to her sleeping-chamber. It was a small room in the thickness of the walls, but at least she would have it to herself – an unwonted privilege.

'Good night, Isabella. Everything will look better in the morning. There's much we must discuss. Oh – and by the way, do you remember Louis d'Orleans's son, the young Charles d'Orleans? He used to be your playmate.'

'Charles d'Orleans? No – I don't think so. Oh! you mean Charles. Why yes. Wasn't he here tonight? How long long ago all that seems.'

'No – he didn't somehow want to come. I think he was with the King. Ah! – ' she broke off abruptly, 'here comes the faithful Creton.' A sturdy masculine figure was hastening towards them down the long corridor. He went down on one knee before the little Queen to hide the tears that coursed down his cheeks at sight of her.

'Creton,' she said brokenly and laid one hand caressingly on his head. Thank God that at least he had survived the slaughter at Cirencester and escaped to France.

After they both had left her, Isabella did not go straight to bed. Despite the Prie-Dieu in her room, it seemed fitting at this crucial moment to creep into the Oratory to give thanks to the Virgin for having succoured her thus far. The familiar chapel was dark and empty at this hour, but to her mind it was peopled by the spirits of the past. Since the public churches had neither seats nor benches, it was convenient and comfortable for chateaux to have their own oratories. She knelt, than sat gazing at the light before the altar until her tempestuous spirit felt a little calmed. . . . Later, falling mother-naked – as was customary – into her comfortable feather bed which in winter would be piled high with heavy covers and fur rugs but now boasted merely a flimsy silken sheet, Creton's figure was the last in the kaleidoscope of colour that whirled before her tired eyes as she fell into the pit of sleep.

Queen Isabeau herself came to her daughter's chamber in the morning. The sun threw narrow slit patterns of gold across the flagged floors and lit up unexpected streaks of tapestry into sudden brilliance. The tire-woman was dressing Isabella's smooth fair hair! The Queen frowned slightly as she watched.

'I want to warn you, ma petite, not to excite His Majesty. He keeps mainly to his own apartments – either here or in the Hôtel de St Pol which is quieter and more retired. He knows you're coming, but be placid with him.'

'You don't mean . . . he's not in bed all the time, is he? I understood that . . . he was better – sometimes.' Her voice trembled. 'What do his medical men say?'

'Oh, Master William de Harseley has been most attentive – really performed an astounding cure – says he may live another twenty years. Bed-ridden? Oh, no. He's allowed to ride, hunt and hawk on his good days. But, Isabella, his nerves have never really recovered. You must be prepared for a great change in him.'

And it was indeed a pitiful figure Isabella visited that morning in his apartments. He sprang up at her entry.

'Is it – ' he peered at her, 'my little daughter?' His voice held a plaintive gentleness, almost as if he were forgiving her for some neglect or misdemeanour. He was but a shadow King.

She knelt at his feet as she had in childhood, then sprang up and embraced him in eager arms. 'Yes, dear Pa-pa, I am back with you.'

His tragic eyes searched hers as he said softly: 'You must only kneel to God now, my child. All I ask for is never to harm anyone and to be able always to give alms to heaven. That's not much to pray for when you've been King for twenty years, is it?' Abruptly he began weeping: 'You stayed away a long time, ma petite. Everyone leaves me. Yet I'm told my people love me.'

Impossible to visualise, seeing this poor wraith in his half-world of delusion, that he could reign another twenty years as a figure of crazy unreality, a voice that seemed to echo sadly from a tomb.

No sooner were they alone together once more than Isabeau brought up with Isabella the subject of her projected marriage. Perhaps, Isabeau thought, this talk would help to break the shock

125

of seeing the poor King so changed. The two had seated themselves at one long strip of tapestry-work over which Isabella sat with sadly bent head while her mother sorted through the coloured skeins, and threw sharp glances at her daughter's averted cheek.

'Look, Isabella – you don't intend to spend your life in a cloister?'

'No – perhaps not,' murmured Isabella softly.

Her mother, suddenly feeling old and experienced, hardly knew how to deal with a creature so impractical as to attempt to hold a farthing candle to the sun. She burst out at that averted face: 'There are no guarantees of happiness for any of us, child. You're still living in a fairy-tale world where there are good and bad angels always around you. That's just a romantic unreal conception. Life isn't like that. We women have to face the brutal facts of hard reality and come to practical decisions. If we're clever, we pretend to accept some illusions, and even clothe the hardest events with grace – diversion – amusement. That's partly what we're *for* . . . . I still think you would do best to get married.' And she thought to herself – poor girl, she has had a *désenchantment* with life and it has moulded her character. Perhaps if we could find her a young *parti* with as romantic ideals as her own, it might work. 'Yes,' she repeated, 'you must marry again.' Even that 'again' she felt to be a concession to unreality, since the poor child in cold fact had no experience.

Isabella's head came up. 'I *am* married,' she said calmly, 'I am the Queen of England.'

'Isabella – how much have you heard of – of Richard's death – or *alleged* death, if you wish to put it that way?'

'Very little,' said Isabella evenly, intent on threading a needle, 'everyone seems to have been forbidden to mention his name to me.' A sob thickened her voice, but she forced it down: 'I'm waiting for you to tell me.'

Even the wordly-wise Isabeau felt sharp compassion. 'Can you bear to talk about him yet, my dear child?'

'Yes – since I think of very little else.'

'You have heard for a fact that King Richard was imprisoned at Pontefract in Yorkshire . . . ? You accept that as true?' asked Queen Isabeau abruptly. There must be some basis of agreement between them to make this conversation possible.

'Yes,' whispered Isabella, her mind's eye flashing to that white-walled castle crowning a bold rocky hill in the West Riding, where, Richard once told her, Wycliffe had preached before John of Gaunt, and Chaucer had read his poems. 'Yes.'

Isabeau dropped the skeins of bright silk and placed her hands over her eyes. Better not to watch her daughter's face. Easier this way to visualise the vividly-imagined scene that had haunted her dreams since she'd been told of it by Creton who'd pieced together all the fast-gathering legends, surmises, half-truths and fables of the countryside, about the young King who had disappeared so completely into that grim battlemented fortress. That such a thing could happen in this brilliant modern age to an anointed monarch was frightening to such as Isabeau. She'd thought about it so incessantly, made such a complete story of it – even down to what thoughts must have passed through the luck-less Monarch's mind if half that Creton hinted at were true – that by now she could hardly disentangle her own imaginings from the wild speculations of others, founded on the bits and pieces of evidence of the few who'd seen him. She must remember it all once more – though only the barest expurgated story could be passed on to Isabella.

As if they were scenes on a tapestry, Isabeau clearly envisaged a muffled figure being hustled across a drawbridge, under a raised portcullis, through the grim and battered walls, down a narrow curving stairway, into a thick-walled dank dark cell. Here, he must have fretted away the long and lonely hours waiting in vain for news of the outer world – in particular as to what was happening to the innocent little Queen. The cold of that bitter winter couldn't fail to penetrate to his bones. Doubtless he paced restlessly from side to side of his cell in order to restore some circulation to his clammy feet and to keep fit to the limited extent left possible to him.

Some of the gaolers had whisperingly reported that whenever a guard approached him with his meagre fare, this gaunt shadow of a King would stammer a few words – as if dying to communicate with another human being even though his tongue was stiffening with disuse. Poor broken words that meant nothing very much: 'Are the marshes north of London frozen hard this year?' A tremulous attempted smile would flit across his face: 'How the young men loved to skate there on polished bones strapped to their feet!' And then, inevitably, piteously: 'Tell me – does anyone know where I am?' – though he must have realised that such questions never drew any reply.

And gradually, too, he must have become inured to the idea that this was the end. Sooner or later Henry would have him murdered – all the more surely if there *had* been any revolts in his favour – and if not he would merely rot there. A stealthy footstep could raise the gooseflesh on his skin and make his heart hammer. Pst! there was someone coming now.

Miraculously, it was one of the grooms of his stable. 'Why, B-b-ben,' he stammered incredulously.

'I'm to fetch these,' said the groom wretchedly, clearing the remnants of the last poor meal, 'quite a change of job from tending horses.'

'Ah! you groomed Barbary!' exclaimed Richard. 'How is my favourite roan?' Surely there could be no harm in asking such pathetically innocuous questions?

'Bestride by the usurper on his coronation day, Sire,' the groom said angrily, 'to think any horse I currycombed could fall so low,' and he snatched up the few poor utensils, passing close enough to Richard to whisper: 'You are not forgotten, Sire. King Henry is not so happy with his crown of thorns, 'tis said his health is suffering.' Absurd to think how light-hearted this short contact must have rendered the poor prisoner.

The next day's doings would have been all the more unexpected. Such a plentiful dinner was set before him that Richard's mouth obviously watered as he looked at it, waiting for his gaoler to to taste it first as proof the viands were not poisoned. 'Oh – we're omitting that ceremony by the King's orders,' said the man insolently. Whereat Richard shouted, 'The devil take Henry of Lancaster and thee together.' At once, it seemed, the cell was crowded. A partisan of Henry, Sir Piers Exton, had rushed in with several followers, carrying bare weapons in their hands.

By the various accounts that later circulated, it was almost joyously that Richard rose to meet the challenge – as if he were less afraid than exhilarated. He pushed the heavy table in front of him as a barrier and, as the panting breaths of desperately struggling men filled the cell, managed to wrest a brown-bill from the astonished man confronting him. Swinging it above his head, he decapitated the first, thrust the heavy table against his companion's legs, then ran him through. At that, Richard's laughter filled the chamber, maddening Sir Piers who'd been convinced the prisoner would cravenly give in and beg for mercy at the first sight of such overwhelming odds.

But now, Richard was once more swinging the brownbill and chasing another ruffian across the room. Sir Piers took the chance to leap up on to the heavy carved stone seat, and, as Richard rushed after his quarry, a blow from Sir Piers's pole-axe felled him like a stricken deer. Panting noisily, the survivors looked down on the young King's body, still twitching on the floor.

And I'm sure, thought Isabeau as she chose her words kindly and carefully to give a brief and expurgated version of this scene to Richard's widow, I'm quite sure his last thought was of Anne whom he was re-joining, not of the Little Queen. But she was compassionate enough not to voice that thought.

Aloud she said: 'If there's any truth in that story, it was a valiant way to die – worthy of any Plantagenet. I hope he felt he was going out on a blaze of glory. Poor Richard!'

There was a long pause. Then Isabella's voice came softly: 'Yes – much better than being starved to death.'

'Oh – so you heard that too?' retorted Isabeau. 'We were also told that he'd voluntarily starved himself. Hah! Everyone did protest too much that he'd not been murdered.'

'*That* would have been most unlike Richard,' said Isabella proudly, '*he* was no coward.'

Listening, frozen, immobile, Isabella was shedding no tears except in her heart. At each theory as to Richard's end, she felt as if she'd turned the page of a manuscript to the sad sound of wind sighing in a barren tree – a book of which soon nothing would be left but the blank covers – not even illuminated.

'No, of course he was not. . . . So, in due time, it would be far best for you to re-marry,' said Isabeau decisively. She felt – at last the worst is over, we have talked it out.

But now Isabella turned and looked directly at her mother.

'You haven't even mentioned the possibility I cling to,' she said clearly, 'all *that* may be mere rumour spread by Richard's enemies. I still believe that he escaped and is sheltering in Scotland. Hadn't you heard that too? Creton is so joyful at knowing this – he's writing a poem of welcome to the returning King...Ah, Madame! it is my one hope.'

Incredulously Isabeau stared at her, thinking, what a fantasy world my daughter is living in; she has to retreat from a reality too grim to bear. 'We shall soon discover the truth of that,' she said briskly, 'I promise you not to press you further till we *are* sure. . . . I know – we'll send Creton to Scotland to ascertain the truth. You can trust Creton surely?'

And Isabeau was thinking sardonically to herself that it was typical of the Scots to keep England on the *qui vive* with inventions as to a poor distraught Richard who'd fled there for sanctuary. After all, such legends always circulated around great figures who had died or disappeared – mankind demanded immortality, or least the promise to return, for all its heroes.

Creton? Why, of course, Isabella would trust him utterly.

She had the greatest affection for this French squire of Richard's who had accompanied him on that last disastrous foray into Ireland, had composed elegant rhymed verses to sing of his loyalty to his King and rage at his betrayal, and had tried to guard her through the route at Cirencester.

'We shall arrange that then,' said Isabeau easily. Suddenly another thought struck her. She stood up abruptly, spilling the bright silks in a cascade of glorious colour: 'But, my child – we heard that thousands of people saw his body in its coffin, paraded through the London streets. Wasn't that so? We were told that already there'd been so many revolts that Henry had to *prove* him dead.'

'But don't you see,' retorted the child passionately, 'it could have been Maudeleyn's corpse – once they'd captured him – and sealed his body up in lead – leaving only his face on view. Yes – it could easily have been Richard's double – whom *our* side had used to make Henry give himself away – now, after death, being used as a public denial that the true King has escaped to Scotland.' Her voice was trembling.

'Well, we shall send Creton,' promised Isabeau thoughtfully, knowing that Isabella was still at the stage of life where one awaits a miracle.

But of course the strongest proof that Richard was dead and that Henry was aware of this but anxious to disclaim his planning of it, was the new King's quiet relentless pursuit of a match between Isabella and his own son – whom he certainly would not have allowed to commit bigamy! At an impressionable age, the younger Henry was very much taken with the tragic Little Queen, who had been a bride so long seemed ripe indeed for love, and who yet, in stark reality, remained un-mated.

'Listen, my child,' said Isabeau now, 'let me tell you what was happening here. The news of that funeral procession – faked or not! – and of your capture, sent your Royal father into frenzy of insanity. The Council of Regency we were obliged to set up at once demanded your restoration to your own family here in France. The usurper wouldn't hear of it – answered that, like other Queen-dowagers, you should reside in England in great honour. And that *if* – "if" mind you – your husband had died, you would be supplied with another, more suitable to your age than Richard of Bordeaux. Described as young, handsome, and in every way desirous of your love, this paragon is none other than the Prince of Wales.'

Isabella smiled faintly. 'Yes, he was most persistent. I was –

inflexible – in refusing to entertain him. Once he tried to get at me by bringing Math – but no! but *no*! not even then.'

'Ha! no wonder the commonality is captivated by your constancy! I hear that you're the heroine of many an English ballad. That must enrage the usurper. For after all, the direct line is extinct with the deposition of your Richard. . . . Perhaps I should tell you, child, that Louis d'Orleans is sending a challenge to the so-called Henry IV, defying him as the plunderer of your dower and the murderer of your husband – and offering to fight him at single combat in the lists.'

'He won't accept that challenge. He'll say that kings can only fight with their equals,' said Isabella calmly. 'You'll see.'

Leaving her daughter, Isabeau encountered her nephew, young Charles d'Orleans, who was hurrying swiftly from the King's apartments, 'Charles,' she called, 'I don't believe you've paid your devoirs to your cousin since her return. Were you looking for her now?'

'No, Madame, I had not thought of it,' he said coolly.

'She's here – I've just left her – at least give her your greeting,' replied the Queen, hastening off down the corridor with a frou-frou of silken skirts. Strange, the barrier between the generations today! She was thinking, in defiance of all faint memories to the contrary: Why, I'm sure when we were youngsters we deferred to our elders in every way, there was no gap at all between us. Yet Charles now – I sometimes feel he's judging us. Even Isabella hasn't the imagination to put herself in my shoes – yet I can see myself in hers simply by a feat of memory. Ah me! that's why we make more allowance for them than they'll ever do for us.

Charles d'Orleans hesitated and stood gazing down the long corridor towards his aunt long after the swishing echo of her soft footsteps had died away. He was at that point of adolescence when heart and imagination combine in sensitivity to idealism and beauty. It was only recently that the corruption of the Court had dawned on him; and though some young men swallowed and digested this as a stage on the development into manhood, to him it was as yet quite unpalatable.

Of course he'd never forgotten her, she was an ineradicable part of the warp and woof of his childhood – but she belonged in that never-never-land of unrecoverable past to which we can only return in dreams . . . When he was told she was coming back to France after – how many years? – he'd dreaded terribly the idea of meeting her. Why, he thought, she's had aeons of experiences about which I know nothing and is – to all intents and purposes – the Queen of England. And a year and a half older than I, to boot. No, no, let me keep my dreams. Let me cherish a few illusions. . . . I'm always being told I have a fine mind – usually by those who wouldn't emulate me for the world. I don't know about that, but I do know that I don't like our modern manner of sharing coarse and bawdy jokes with our women-kind. Yes, I'm sure I'm being very old-fashioned for an extremely young man; that we're now in the fifteenth century and everything's very go-ahead; that the women themselves like to talk of the more carnal side of love as if that's all there is to it. But surely we've fallen below the standards set all those years ago at the Court of Eleanor of Aquitaine when an elaborate list of rules – *De Arte Honeste Amandi* – was drawn up for the courtly lover. No, I can see that we can't all live on the level of a distant worship of womanhood with religious overtones – but I think I shall still want love idealised even in the act of marriage itself. . . . I always pictured little Isabella growing up into a fragile flower to whom one could address poetic couplets.

How absurd I'm being when one realises all she has experienced.

Young Charles d'Orleans turned on his heel and retraced his steps to the quiet apartments of his Uncle Charles, the unfortunate but well-beloved . . . There was no reason, really, why he should remain permanently at Court. Three or four years ago his father, Louis d'Orleans, had purchased the Countship of Blois and taken possession of the ancient Château de Blois to make it the family seat of the Orleans family. The castle, commanding magnificent views of the Loire and its tributaries, topped the more westerly of two hills some seventy-five miles south of Paris, on a bend in the Rover Loire. Young Charles always thought of it as the very heart of his sweet country and was proud that the whole wooded park-like area was known as the Garden of France. He could be happy there. One day, when he himself was Duke d'Orleans, he would hold his own Court there.

CHAPTER SIXTEEN

EVENTUALLY HE came upon her quite informally. Charles, with a young squire and an even younger page, was returning through burning August sunshine into the Louvre's great Hall after a game of bandy-ball, the page carrying the large ball while both Charles and the squire bore the wooden clubs. All three were flushed with sun and exercise. As Charles glanced around before stepping across the threshold, his eye was caught by a little cascade of rose-petals beyond a low well-trimmed hedge – and then the flash of a long falling sleeve. He hesitated a moment, then gestured silently for the others to go on. If this were she, perhaps he could get their encounter over more easily alone. It would be graceless not to behave with the polished chivalry on which he prided himself, young as he was. . . . He sauntered towards the enclosed garden with the easy grace that was already a part of his urbanity.

Isabella was sitting on a stone bench near a rose-bush whose petals were scattered on the grass verge. Abruptly she scooped up a handful of them, sniffed them luxuriously, then threw them in the air to fall once more in lovely confusion on the grass. She looked lost in a dream world; but not tragic as he had feared.

Although he had been anticipating this meeting, yet now he was entirely at a loss for anything to say. It was, surprisingly, as if the Isabella of the long ago had materialised before his eyes. They gazed at each other in silence for a long moment, mentally bridging the gap of nearly half-a-dozen years . . . Why – she is a lily, a lily of France – not the least bit a rose of England. She is taller, of course – a little paler, more fragile than ever, the embodiment of spiritual beauty, with the air of an unawakened child. The slow motion of her head as she turned to him, her heart-breakingly reluctant smile for which he waited in breathless anticipation, her gazelle-like eager walk as she crossed the grass to meet him – all are poems in motion, he thought in surprised delight.

Something stirred in her numbed heart at seeing her child-hood playmate and finding him so cultivated, suave, and obviously aloof from the coarser dissipations, the brutal noisy pleasures of the average man – an aloofness that would always give him a slight tinge of melancholy even amid his trifling diversions. But, pleased though she was to see him, she told herself that she had nothing to give him; her whole being was a mere empty husk, impervious to pleasure or pain until – until – she knew for certainty what was happening to Richard.

And then, idiotically, they both spoke at once – and spoke so absurdly that almost immediately they burst into unexpected laughter. For, 'Charles, how you've grown!' she exclaimed, recalling the boy who'd longed to go to England with her. And he, as if at random, yet eagerly, burst out with: 'Madame – Bella – tell me – what did you know of Chaucer?'

Chaucer? 'Ah, how strange!' she said, 'I was thinking of him when I plucked the roses. He so loved the flowers – the birds – all nature. I heard him read his poems to the English Court so many times – I remember some of them by heart. . . . I only learned recently that he had died – but he was old.' Death was of course an ever-present acceptable reality, and yet, as regards herself and Charles, so abstract as to be almost inconceivable. For surely they were young and immortal?

'He was fortunate,' said Charles wistfully, 'It's difficult to make one's verses known, to gain any recognition – to have them in a few vellum copies is as much as one can ask. To be eagerly listened to by a noble company – ah! that must be fame indeed.'

She glanced swiftly at him in his gorgeously particoloured jerkin and hose. Nothing could be further from Chaucer's sober long gown and plain black hood – and yet – and yet – Charles's voice too held a poet's melody. When he was talking she found herself listening to the *sound* in a kind of enchantment. Yes – she must tell him what she could of Chaucer.

'Well – the roses reminded me,' she said breathlessly, 'and yet it was the simpler, homelier, flowers he loved the best. I remember one bit –

> "Of all the flowers in the mede
> Then love I most those blossoms white and red
> Which men call daises in our town " –

I may not have it exactly right – but it went something like that.'

'Thank you, Isabella. Yes, he's made poetry spring again to life – in vivid movement – sprightliness. His description of people – d'you remember: "Her mouth was sweet as honeyed ale or mead?" – but no! I've forgotten the rest. . . . Of course he

134

started with the advantages of studying our old French poetry – poems mostly of courtly love-longing and songs of troubadours. England was fortunate in having him. . . . But I mustn't bore you with what is my essential interest too.'

'I knew it – I felt it,' she answered. Her acknowledgement helped to dispel any doubts he felt as to his own métier. For Charles obviously had the quickly-aroused emotional response to ideas and feelings that is the attribute of the poet. So that even his abrupt question regarding Chaucer had seemed almost an inevitable one. 'Yes,' he said now, 'we younger versifiers stumble after him. He will always be our inspiration.'

At first there was so little Charles wanted from her. It became unalloyed happiness just to see her again, to be near her occasionally, to watch her face and eyes light up with the old childish affection when she saw him approaching, and to sit with her in a peaceful harmony of contentment. That there was the barrier of a possibly-alive Richard between them completed the perfection of the situation. For love and marriage were two vastly different relations of life – usually, in fact, were poles apart. The devotion of a knight to his lady was a sort of mystic adoration – sometimes a chaste worship, but not infrequently a paradoxical idealisation of courtly adultery. As far as Charles was concerned, it was poetically satisfying to worship the unattainable.

Some day, as the eldest of the four children of Louis, Duke of Orleans, and his lovely but neglected wife, Valentina of Milan – as indeed one of the most important men in a kingdom of which the king himself was a cipher – Charles knew that he must make a politically advantageous marriage.

But even the Church recognised that love had nothing whatever to do with such practical arrangements as the marriage bond. If liking ultimately developed between a married couple – that was almost the best that could be expected. . . . This newly found platonic rapture with his cousin would be unaffected by such a relationship. And if, in the meantime, any lusty wench momentarily shared his bed, he would not even sully the thought of Isabella by attempting to transpose her mentally into this ephemeral partner. He could not entertain so desecrating a thought – so contrary to his ideals of chivalry – even though he was becoming aware that that same vaunted chivalry of the period was largely becoming a cloak for profligacy.

Queen Isabeau – and even his father, the Duke d'Orleans, regarded him somewhat sardonically. Would he never grow up and recognise the more brutal facts of existence? After all, they thought realistically, maturity is usually a compromise with the corruptions of life - did neither Charles nor Isabella recognise that?

And then, at long last, Creton returned.

He came back in a rougher mood than Isabella ever remembered him. The rattle of his charger and his men-at-arms brought her to a casement from which she looked down upon the courtyard. Creton! She withdrew from the window in instinctive fear, one hand flung at her breast as if in alarm.

She heard him trample roughly through the Great Hall, his steps on the staircase to the solar and the upper chambers. Still, as if frozen into alabaster, she stood, almost incapable of thought. She listened to her mother's swishing footsteps on the flagged corridor, and the one whispered word: 'Creton.'

Then they retreated and there was silence.

A long while later – or was it long? time had ceased to have any meaning – a flurried page came timidly and spoke to Isabella.

'Madame?'

'Yes – what is it?'

'Madame – Her majesty would speak with you within her chamber.'

'Thank you, Francis.' She managed to smile at him.

Creton was bowing. Her mother stood imperiously behind him. Both were staring at her.

'Tell her, Creton.'

His eyes burned as he looked her in the face.

'Madame of France.' (What did that mean? That he no longer regarded her as Queen of England? That she was the ex-Queen of England and Madame of France?) 'Madame – your servant. I again would like to issue a call to action – but this time – this time – it is a call to avenge the blood of the true King of England.'

She felt as if there were nothing in the whole world but herself and Creton's face. A face down which the tears were silently coursing. An expression of agony from which she could never avert her eyes.

'Ah! poor Creton,' she said.

'Do you understand what he's telling you, Isabella?' came her mother's voice, harshly.

'I understand.' In a way she felt as if she'd known all along. Now there was no pretence or evasion possible. She would like to wipe away Creton's tears, though she herself could shed none, even if it were expected of her. She had been a child asking for the moon, positive, as are we all, that happiness was her due, that

136

misfortune was an injustice of fate. Now, with infinite pity for Richard, she was able to accept the thought that he was dead and that she was truly alone . . . How stupid, how slow I've been at understanding. The sun will rise and set, endlessly, for ever. No day will see Richard return to me. No sunset will see us embracing at long last as we had promised. I should say the words aloud to make them penetrate my consciousness: 'I am alone.'

She knew, too, that soon a marriage would be arranged for her. She would accept now whatever was advantageous and best for her family and her country in whatever business-like contract was suggested for her – most probably with a bridegroom who was a stranger. What did that matter? the choice of marriage partners normally had nothing whatever to do with affection, let alone love. But let it not be Henry Bolingbroke; never that unspeakable alliance with the murderers of her husband.

So she was alarmed at the arrival of the English ambassadors with Henry IV's last determined offer to obtain the 'sweet young queen' as his daughter-in-law. In this final desperate bid, the English king even made the astounding offer to abdicate the throne in favour of his son if Isabella would consent to be the queen. With vast astonishment, Isabella heard that Louis d'Orleans in peremptorily refusing had stated categorically that her hand was already promised to his own son, Charles . . . Dear God, she thought frantically, if this too is merely a commercial transaction I would rather wed a stranger; our relationship is too ideal to become one of barter.

No sooner had Queen Isabeau broken the news than, with one backward glance, she left her daughter alone in the solar. Isabella was suddenly aware that it was Charles who had raised the arras and now stood gazing at her with an uncertain, an imploring, expression. She stood silently in front of him. Suddenly he thought – why, I believe she is shy, and the thought gave him confidence. As he approached, gently and tentatively, she took a few steps backwards as if totally unsure of herself.

'Isabella?' he said questioningly. And then, 'What are you thinking about?'

Her gaze fell before his. He thought that if she replied, 'Richard,' he would not be able to bear it, beat so harshly in his mind that he wondered fleetingly if he'd said the words aloud. Now she looked up at him consideringly. Strange, she'd never felt shy with Richard till just before they'd parted – but with Cousin Charles, yes, she did a little. But then, most of the early time with

137

Richard she'd been just a child with the unselfconsciousness of childhood. Until – until – just before the end.

'Childhood,' she answered softly, knowing, with a woman's subtlety that to say the rest would wound his self-esteem. His face lit up with pleasure.

'Ah! Isabella, we had happy childhoods together, didn't we?' and then he thought – is it really impossible to preserve the bond of courtly love within the state of marriage? If not, in marrying her he would lose what had already become the most precious thing in life, a part of life's dream more real than reality itself. He knew now how much his fastidiousness had been repelled by the extreme sophistication of the Court.

And from then on, formal arragements took over and whirled them into a dream world in which they were puppets manipulated by another hand.

By early June of 1406, Queen Isabeau, with her daughter Isabella, Louis d'Orleans and his son Charles, moved into the palace near the great forest of Compiègne in north-eastern France, forty miles north-north-east of Paris. This favourite hunting-ground of the Kings of France covered thirty-five thousand acres of forest-land, and the tiny town of the same name stood picturesquely on the Oise, a little below the inflow of the Aisne. Here proceedings for the betrothal, and immediately-subsequent marriage, of the bemused young couple, went on apace. For them, everything took on a substance of unreality. But at least they were now able to get to know one another better.

It was a time of year when one could practically live out of doors, and they wandered hand-in-hand through the greenwood which was like an enchanted forest in a fairytale. The trees were weighted down with the heavy drapery of their summer foliage, casting deep purple shadows pierced by brilliant circles of sunlight, while the constant murmuring of the river made an intensely sweet music. The trunks looked so darkly fantastic that one could imagine witches and warlocks behind every tree. When Isabella remarked this, Charles grinned secretively and retorted: 'Why not, indeed?' since witchcraft was an ever-present reality, and then, taking her by the hand set her on a fallen log at the end of a glade. 'If you think this beautiful,' he went on, 'wait till we're at the Château de Blois. Ah! there we shall be near Orleans and in the sweetest heart of France.'

Obliquely, Charles inevitably began talking about weddings. Prognostications hedged the ceremony so tightly that one had to beware of many omens; on the way to the church, if one encountered a monk, a hare, a lizard, a serpent, or even a dog or cat, the happiness of the union was imperilled. But to see a wolf, a spider or a toad on one's wedding day was a forecast of bliss. Well, at least they were being married in June – always considered the most propitious season for weddings since Roman times. And the moon would be full.

Hesitatingly, Isabella began to refer to marriages that had managed to evolve into a deeply affectionate companionship – and to some that even – exceptionally – commenced as love matches. Turning her head away she spoke of Richard's adored mother, Joan of Kent, who had died when she herself was four years old and whom, of course, she'd never met. But Richard had talked of his mother so much and of her ecstatic love match with his father, the Black Prince: 'I've always felt, from that, that Joan is a lovely name,' added Isabella softly, and went on to speak of Richard's happiness with his first wife, Anne. She could afford to grant that now, even though she added wistfully, 'I think I could have made him happy too. . . .' Charles did not argue the point though he thought his, as an example of conjugal contentment, was entirely different, since Richard and Anne had married in the usual state of complete indifference, and had only by great good fortune attained to happiness within the marriage bond. His mind flicked briefly to his own parents; he'd always added mentally to his mother's name, Valentina, the poetical description: 'the gracious rose of Milan's thorny stem', But he could hardly mention her in the present conversation as she was grossly neglected by the elegant unprincipled Duke Louis – as their son was becoming increasingly aware.

'Never mind – our marriage will be entirely – completely – different,' he said consolingly to a startled Isabella to whom the remark seemed a total non-sequitur. She was becoming accustomed to the rapier rapidity of his changing thoughts, so she merely smiled back and moved her hand comfortingly under his warm clasp. His face had assumed a tinge of melancholy at the thought of his mother for she had been banished to Neufchâteau on the River Loire. The physicians and sorcerers who were totally unable to cure King Charles's mental condition had now declared their inability was due to the fact that he was being enchanted by pernicious herbs. The sorcerers affirmed that the devil had appeared to them revealing that their pathetic patient was under the power of sorcery; pressed to be more explicit, some of these conjurers definitely stated that the Duchess d'Orleans was practising the black arts and that as long as she was in Paris near the King, he could not possibly recover – hence her present banishment, though her husband remained at Court. . . . Not that his mother's absence seemed to have wrought any improvement in the King's condition, thought young Charles wryly, and, after all, the King was her brother-in-law. Yet stories of her alleged pact with Satan eddied through the streets of Paris, believed, with a delicious thrill of fear, by peasantry and nobility alike.

As the wedding drew rapidly nearer, Charles surprised himself by wondering how Isabella would stand up to the accepted boisterous buffoonery that followed the marriage ceremony. He had taken part in some of these scenes before, and had considered them excellent sport and part of the heritage of legend. But now – now – not only would it be his turn to submit with a good grace – but also to do so for a partner as sensitive as Isabella. He hoped she was tougher than she appeared – as tough, indeed, as this modern age demanded. Occasionally this tomfoolery got terribly out of hand; he recalled hearing that the festivities at the marriage of his uncle, King Charles VI, when twelve years of age, had been quite incredibly violent . . . One couldn't altogether evade these age-old customs whose significance was rooted in the long-ago, but more than one bridegroom had been obliged to protect his mate from turbulent rough-and-tumble. Well, he would do what he could for Isabella without making them both appear too squeamish. He shrank from excesses of vulgarity for his womenfolk, and since he had already learned to love Isabella with a depth of passion that surprised himself, he was peculiarly vulnerable to the thought of her being affronted. . . . If he could, he would even clothe the prosaic realities of life in a little romantic illusion to satisfy Isabella's quest for beauty – and his own, if the truth were told. Perhaps that came of being a poet.

On the 29th of June, Isabella awoke before the dawn to hear the first twitterings of birds gradually crescendo into a deafening chorus. . . . So this was her second wedding day – though in real actual fact to all intents and purposes t'would be her first. She was technically a widow with no right at all to wear her hair loose and flowing as only unmarried girls, by custom, were supposed to. But she felt that Charles deserved not only the truth, but the appearance of it.

As he awaited her at the altar, he found himself trembling. Behind him, he could hear the whispered conversations, the slithering footsteps, all the suppressed susurrous of the crowded chapel, punctuated by the occasional sharp jingle of a spur and clangour of armour. He had time to hope that the poor King would, with many promptings, manage his small part in the proceedings, when a sharp intake of breath rustled, like a zephyr through standing corn, warning him that Isabella had arrived.

He turned his head. All the simplicity and sweetness for which he worshipped her seemed summed up in her guileless appearance. At first he only took in her vivid face, but a second later he realised that she was approaching the altar wearing her hair loose and flowing around her shoulders to emphasise the fact that she was a virgin bride. On her head, she bore a coronet of the fleurs-de-lis of a French princess: its design was repeated on her blue bodice, trimmed with white miniver. She was the embodiment of delicacy amid all the flaunting ostentation of the Court.

The burst of music confused him. He came to himself abruptly when he had to repeat the age-old words of the marriage ceremony. Yes, indeed, he did take her 'for fairer, for fouler, for better, for worse,' – and next, her softer voice promised 'to be buxom and bonny' to him, her husband. He fumbled a moment, then found the ring, held her small left hand in his and placed the ring on each finger in turn, saying at the first, 'In the Name of the Father,' at the second, 'In the Name of the Son,' at the third, 'In the Name of the Holy Ghost,' and, at the fourth, 'Amen,' – lastly returning the ring to the ring-finger, the third, with a warm clasp of his hand.

It was then that the incredible happened.

Noiselessly at first, Isabella began to weep. Tears flooded her face, and suddenly she tasted the salt of them upon her lips. These were the tears, bitter as brine, she'd been unable to shed for Richard's death – and, at the thought, she began to sob aloud, so that the startled church was filled with the mournful sound, which went on and on as if it would never stop. Ah! Charles, she thought, you should not be jealous – I realise now the love I gave to Richard was the passionate adoration of a child in the first stirrings of unrecognised sensuality. . . . But perhaps she was weeping too for the infinite pathos of lost childhood. She hardly knew.

In all the heat of the crowded chapel, among the brilliant colours and extravagances of costume, above the music of the portable organs, of the shrill rebecks, of the double pipes with their repetitive notes, of the deeper-toned citoles and the sweet voices of the choristers, the heart-breaking sobs went on and on. Charles felt a wild resentment – but this was quickly swallowed by passionate sympathy. Somehow we must manage better than this, he thought quite violently. Our wedding day mustn't always stand out in our memories as such a débâcle . . . And by the time the King had performed the symbolic act of taking the bride's slipper, and handing it over to his new son-in-law for him to use to tap his wife on the head as a sign of transferred authority, Isabella's sobs had muted to an occasional ridiculous sniffle.

And things went marvellously better at the wedding feast in the great Banqueting Hall of that Palace of Compiègne. Isabella and Charles occupied the canopied seats at the long main table, while guests sat along the benches, and the love seats below the windows were filled with amorous couples. (Nothing stirred the senses more quickly than a wedding!) The credence and the dressoirs were groaning with dishes of delectable whale, porpoise, swordfish, hedgehog, squirrel, rooks, magpies, a vastly resplendent peacock, and even humble sparrows. This was an excellent time of year also for fresh meats – in a few months the cattle would have to be killed and salted down, and the monotony of living on salt meat for half the year would recommence, with its resultant toll of scurvy and other skin diseases.

Proudly exhibited by bustling pages at the end of every course was some elaborate pastry device, moulded into a fantastic shape and loudly acclaimed by the guests: 'Look! here's a subtlety – 'tis a bride and groom, no less!' Or, 'Ah! here comes a ship in which we'll invade the coasts of England,' followed by gay laughter since the south of England and the Isle of Wight resounded with rumours as to Isabella's intended invasions against the House of Lancaster.

Charles glanced anxiously now and then at Isabella. Her usually pale face was flushed and she was smiling brilliantly. Good! No doubt the muscadel and malmsey wines, the ale fermented from their own grain, and the delectable mead of ginger, sugar and honey – all of which were circulating now so freely – helped her present a glittering façade. Perhaps they would also fortify her against any excesses in the ritual buffoonery to come!

Fools, jesters, tumblers, buffoons, and a favourite dwarf made merry between the tables, sometimes timing their antics to the instrumental music and the songs which echoed around the hall. It was well known – recognised even by the leeches and physicians– that to be gay while eating these long and heavy courses aided digestion. Mental light relief was as efficacious as herbal medicine!

The heat – the torches – the candles – had intensified the smell of the bayleaves and rosemary which were extensively used so that their powerful scent might dispel infections. Looking round at the light-hearted company, Charles noticed fleetingly that most of them were sporting the *livrées de noces* – the knot of ribbons or favours distributed to the wedding guests as a momento – and that reminded him that when Isabella was disrobed the trimmings of her dress would be torn to shreds and eagerly seized upon by her ladies. Worse yet would be the moment when the young gallants, those bachelors who were bride-men, would fight for her garters, so that they might sport them in their hat. He must remind Isabella to be prepared. Soon it would be time.

Now the bishop made a sign to Charles that he was going in state to bless the nuptial bed. Charles jumped up to whisper to him something about the little bower off the courtyard rather than the grander solar. A surprised look crossed the bishop's ruddy face; but Charles always did have his own ideas. It would make no difference to the benedictions.

Coming back to the table, the young bridegroom leaned down and whispered to Isabella. He noticed that her face was luminous with sweat. Some of the candles were guttering. Everyone was on the *qui vive* looking in their direction. He put one hand upon hers on the table.

'Everything will be all right, I promise you. Try to relax, my sweet. In a moment, all your ladies will be rushing you, carrying you to the bower and there undressing you.'

'Yes – I know,' she said between stiff lips.

'Don't resist anything, as sometimes a crowd gets rough. Take it all as a game . . And one more thing: stoop down in a moment and untie your garters. Let them hang down – however untidily – that doesn't matter. The thing is – the bride-men,' (those laughing bachelors over there who were eyeing her expectantly after their evening's drinking) 'those bride-men will demand their right to pull off your garters. Make it easy for them,' – so easy they won't have any excuse to attempt liberties, he was thinking carefully.

The next moment they were both surrounded by hilarious guests. The bride-men struggled with each other, till the two strongest gallants were left victorious with the loosened garters. Isabella laughed sweetly up in their faces while they proudly attached the garters to their hats as trophies.

Then her bridesmaids lifted her on crossed arms and carried her, laughingly, lovingly, towards her bower. This was a reminder of barbaric times when the reluctant bride was forcibly seized and empounded. She looked back once to see Charles being hustled off to another room and wished she could call to him reassuringly. Sometimes he was too sensitive on her behalf; that was the penalty of being a poet. He forgot all she'd gone through at the rout of Cirencester. But no! this was no time to remember Richard? She thrust the thought resolutely aside before tears could sting her eyelids.

One of the ladies was carrying a silver candlestick. Flickering lights and shadows fell on the cosy wall-hangings of the bower, (an apartment on the ground floor that could be entered from the court through a croisée) as the bride was being rapidly stripped. 'Hurry, hurry,' her ladies were urging 'the others will be here any moment.' The coverlet was pulled back and she was lain naked on the feather-bed. The bolster and pillow were comfortable enough, and she drew the thin cool coverlet up to her chin.

Then suddenly the apartment was crowded with jostling people – and – yes – that was Charles coming hesitantly towards her. How young he looks, she thought in his plain long dressing-gown; a moment and even that was snatched from him and he slid naked under the coverlet beside her. His face was turned away, but she felt his hand seek hers in re-assurance. This moment of being bedded in public that both of them had dreaded, though accepted by custom, would surely soon be over?

Someone had brought in the bride's cake then broke it, and everyone scrambled for the largest crumbs to bring them luck. Then the search began for her stockings: 'Look here they are – on top of this chest,' – and the ceremony of flinging the stockings began.

The bride-men sat on the foot of the bed with their backs to the newly-wedded pair, and beside them crowded several of the bridesmaids, giggling irrepressibly. The latter had snatched the bridegroom's stocking from the men, while the bride-men now held those of the bride. Each in turn, with great guffaws, threw the stockings backwards over their heads – the bridesmaids hoping devoutly that the masculine stockings they threw so blindly would fall on the bridegroom's head – the bride-men wishing to hit the bride with her own hose.

'There – there – didn't I hit you, Madame?' shouted one of the bride-men: 'sure sign I shall be the next to be married.'

'*I* hit the bridegroom,' insisted the girl next to him, 'did I not, Sire? Besides, I'm already affianced.'

'No – no – I shall be the next bride,' giggled another lady-in-waiting.

If only they would go, thought Charles wearily. But he himself had joined in these follies often enough to know that though it was merely an entertaining sport, it somehow mattered that such prognostications should be made. And the crowd had thinned out a little which surely meant that some of them were already preparing the posset of milk, wine, yolks of eggs, sugar, cinnamon and nutmeg for formal presentation to the bridal pair. After all, one couldn't break entirely with tradition; he was probably absurd in thinking some of the jokes a little coarse. Exposed to bantering sibilant advice, Isabella was managing to look uninvolved, a spectator at an absurdity.

Now at last came the sound of loud music and of marching feet along the corridor; once more the room was crowded as a grand procession halted at the bedside, ceremoniously presenting the posset.

'There! that should help you to sleep,' soothed a deep masculine voice, and a shrill soprano broke in: 'I can't imagine that they really want to!'

'Now – *go*,' said Charles, grinning engagingly, and handing back the empty pewter mug. 'Go – go – GO – or I shall throw this at you,' and he fingered the other heavy mug that Isabella, silent beside him, had passed to him.

'We'll leave you,' they laugh back at him, 'and we'll be here with a serenade at dawn.'

'Don't you dare,' scoffs the young bridegroom.

And then at last the noisy scampering footsteps echo down the long corridors, leaving Charles and Isabella to the quiet night. The welcome silence was only broken by the occasional sibilation of the scraping of fiddles far away in the Great Hall, where dancing, carousing, and romping games would, for once, go on until the morning – though usually everyone went to sleep with the birds.

This was the moment Charles had been waiting for. He turned his head on the bolster and, in the luminous darkness of reflected moonlight, ran a finger lightly down the nose, mouth, chin, of the girl who was his bride. She was shivering, and he wondered fleetingly whether this were nervousness – or excitement – or revulsion. So next he took her slim left hand, kissed the palm, then turned it over and ran his lips over the wedding-ring.

'Isabella,' he whispered, 'tell me, d'you share the universal fear of the night air?'

'Mmmm?' Caught in a confusion between romanticism and a faint-hearted distaste, she looked astonished at his question.

He jumped from the bed, slung his abandoned robe lightly around him, and flung the croisée – the casement window known as *fenêtre à deux battants* – open to the night. The air rushed in, cool and sweet in the hot stuffy room, and brought with it the mingled rustling of leaves, the sound of the river, and, astonishingly, a huge full moon swinging above the trees, making it light as day.

'Come, Isabella,' he said, the excitement of adventure in his voice, 'didn't you realise why I chose this bower room? We can escape for a while into the forest.' He laughed like a young boy.

She sat up in bed, covering her bare breasts with spread fingers, and gazed at him questioningly. This was like a game of make-believe from the past.

'Come – put on your warmest cloak,' he urged, holding a surcoat up for her to slip into. How ethereal her naked body looked in this unreal light.

She moved beside him into the edge of the forest as if in a trance. The moon hung like a great lanthorn in the sky, the man-in-the-moon clearly smiling down on them. Great pools of moonlight broke the dark shadows in the foreground, and, beyond, the serried leaves were etched against the darkly glowing sky where faint stars hung in clusters. Rustling in the underbrush, and occasional startled squawks, betrayed night-denizens of the forest alarmed by human presences. . . . It was too beautiful to endure, an almost unbearable rapture.

'Oooh – oooh!' soft as a sigh came a flute-like repetition as a whirr of wings broke from a near-by tree. Isabella shrank against Charles. The sound, eerily repeated, sounded ghost-like from a distance: 'Oooh! oooh!'

'What was that?' she whispered, startled.

'Must have been a long-eared owl – people often mistake their cry for that of pixies – or wandering spirits. . . But are you warm enough, my love?'

They had arrived at a glade, half in darkness half in moonlight, where soft dead beech-leaves from the previous autumn still lay in the deeper clefts. 'Are you warm enough, my love?' Charles repeated, slipping her surcoat from her trembling body and laying his hands gently on her breasts. Speechless, she gazed up at him,

146

outlined against the moon, as he spread her cloak upon the drifted leaves – then knelt and held her naked body to him before urging her gently to this forest bed.

Theoretically of course she had known what to expect. Yet it was all completely different. There was pain – but there was ecstasy – and astonishment that she had never realised before that physical passion was a part of love. And he had clothed it in magic and romance for her. For both of them.

When at last he whispered in a small voice: 'Isabella?' she cradled his head with both hands, murmuring a lullaby. Never had she felt so contented, so at rest and yet so gay.

Suddenly, beyond them, from a deeper thicket, came a startling liquid sound: 'Wheet – wheet – *tack*,' and then, loudly, 'Kerr, kerr, kerr.' There was a short pause before a bubbling, 'Chook – chook – chook,' rose to such a brilliant crescendo of music that it was almost impossible to believe so small a bird as the nightingale could produce such richness and variety.

'Hush,' said Charles softly, 'we are in luck. It's late in June to hear the rossingnol philomèle – that's the rich lovesong of the male – he's as ardent as am I.' He laughed quietly. Then both were silent again, caressing one another as they listened to the slow, 'Piu – piu – piu,' rising once more into a loud musical intensification that broke one's heart with beauty.

The moon sank towards the west. Isabella stirred, and Charles murmured sleepily that they must return before the sunrise. He pulled the edge of the cloak towards her bare shoulders, asking, 'Are you cold?'

Shaking her head wordlessly, she gazed up at the sky where the infinite night was the only ceiling, the dangling stars their witnesses. 'How strange to think we are the centre of the universe,' she said now.

'Mmm?' he murmured sleepily, 'yes, of course – astrology has proved that this earth is the hub of the entire universe: the stars – the sun – the whole vault of heaven revolve around us every day.' Abruptly he pushed his head up once more to gaze smilingly at her. 'Why? Does that make you feel important, Isabella?'

'No,' she said, tracing his mouth tenderly with one finger, 'it's you that make me feel important, Charles – as long as I'm the centre of *your* world.'

'Ah, Bella, Bella, Bella – never leave me.'

'We have our whole long lives together,' she comforted. The future compassed an eternity.

How strange it was, when stealing back hand in hand to the bed in the bower beyond the courtyard, to hear the now-rackety music and the romping sound of games and dances still echoing from the Great Hall. Only on such exceptional occasions as this was night turned into day . . . No one would ever learn of their escapade though it set the tone of their tender, intense, yet tragic life together.

When she awoke at dawn from a half-sleep half-waking trance, she found Charles propped on an elbow watching her. 'What is it?' she asked, alarmed.

'Hah! I'd almost forgotten. What do you choose for your Morgengabe, my love? You have the right to ask for anything at all after such a night.' He was smiling.

She frowned in concentration. Yes of course, the Morning present could, by established custom, be anything she chose to mention. This was the modern civilised mode that had usurped the barbaric rite of symbolic acquisition when on the wedding night, the bridegroom used to press into the bride's hand a wallet with the purchase money for her body. Isabella smiled now at the thought. She could easily demand gold – or an estate – anything at all she wished in this up-to-date fashion of the fifteenth century, even though marriage was ceasing to be a commercial transaction.

She turned her head as the scent of honeysuckle rose to her nostrils. There was the long tendril Charles had brought in when they returned before the dawn.

'Give me the honeysuckle,' she said, 'it's like fairy gold.' This too was part of the shared magic of the night.

CHAPTER SEVENTEEN

AND FROM the first moment that Isabella had sighted the great two hundred-year-old donjon of the Château de Blois rearing its impressive bulk above the Loire, she knew that Charles was right. Nothing could be more beautiful than this valley of Touraine, mantled with trees and flowers like a well-wooded park and watered by the river's tributaries. The view from any part of the château was breath-taking.

At Blois that September the days were the perfect blend of departing summer and approaching fall when all nature seems to stand on tip-toe of anticipation. The very apex of the year is reached. A faint, almost imperceptible, mist softened the landscape into a silvery haze that only dissolved under the midday sun. The autumnal light that struck through the thinning foliage was tender with an almost ethereal gaiety that gave to the shortening days a feeling of urgency, of the transiency of loveliness itself, without which it becomes as boring as a woman whose beauty never varies . . . To Isabella the very fact of existence had become a miraculous gift; and if it were transient too – well, one accepted that as part of the price one has to pay for life itself. Happiness was almost a tangible thing as Charles became not only increasingly perceptive in his love-making but also more and more companionable in the ordinary happenings of every day.

They knew, for a few short months, the winged ecstasy on which one soars to heaven. At first Isabella was too distrustful of the jealousy of fate to dare acknowledge her happiness even to herself. Could it be true, she wondered, closing her eyes against the outer world, that at last heaven was granting her a bliss akin to intoxication?

Not that she was idle. From being a guarded child she had now become the chatelaine of a world on its own – a castle which operated as a hive of industry. From 5 or 6 a.m. when the huge household assembled in the oratory for devotions, the whole building hummed. Scullions rushed to and fro in the kitchens, spits were turned, cooks prepared gargantuan meals, the stables, the mews, the granary, the kennels had to be supervised, herbs and simples stored ready for use, and the ladies kept employed on their spinning, weaving, tapestry, embroidery. Often the light musical voices of Isabella's waiting-women could be heard singing, or gossiping, over their looms. Dinner – the big meal of the day – at 10 a.m., supper at five or six, and in bed again by nine. They were happy with the day-to-day urgency of living; to run the Château de Blois was a life's work in itself in supervising clothing, food, furnishings, medicinal herbs for a multitude of people. Isabella felt that at last she was stepping out of her *château en Espagne* to come to terms with real life.

Sometimes when Charles came into the solar or the Great Hall he read his poems aloud while they worked – or told them of forthcoming jousts and tourneys. The voices of the ladies, gay and excited as parroquets, questioned as to which of the knights would be in the lists, when the events would be taking place, and what brilliant costumes they themselves could plan to wear. And after supper sometimes there was an hour or two of boisterous fun: hoodman-blind played with much buffeting and laughter, hot cockles, and the chanted rhymes of such processional arch-games as London Bridge is Falling Down – which indeed it had started to in the previous century.

When they were tired out and bedtime was near, sometimes they dropped to the floor in a rough circle to play the age-old word games, teasing each other about their beaux.

'You start, Philippa – then go all round the circle.'

'All right. Here goes . . . I love my love with an A – because he is amoureux.'

'Affectionné.'

'Aisé.'

'Un Adonis!'

'Adipeux!' – loud laughter at this and cries of protest from those who admired slim muscular men. And so on to the end of the circle. Then –

'I love my love with a B – because – because – he is bien bâti.'

'Beau – that's an easy one.'

'Bon,' and again to the end of the line.

'Your turn to start, Frances.'

'Yes. Well, I love my love with a C because he is charmant.'

'Calme.'

'Chevaleresque,' – and all around again before it reached –

'I love my love with a D because he is doué.'

'Un *drôle* de garcon!'

'Doucet.'

150

'I love my love with an E because he is *explicite* – mon Dieu, how explicite he can be!'

'And I because he is ennuyeu!' – whereat they all dissolved in laughter. Each time the initial letter reached towards the end of the circle, the descriptive words grew more and more frivolous, and increasingly difficult to think of instantly. Whereupon the hesitating maiden would be pounced upon to pay a forfeit.

Life provided little time for solitude or introspection.

With a look, Charles would sometime silently ask Isabella to come with him. They would retreat to his Study next to the Oratory. Here, with Charles's high chair placed carefully in front of La Scriptonale (the inclined board for writing,) next the revolving desk for his manuscripts, she would sit on cushions at his feet, her face serene yet eager between the swathes of hair confined in a caul of golden thread. He would talk of astrology, of magic, of alchemy – of all the wonders of natural science being spread abroad in the form of folk-lore. Simples and charms – the first forms of medicine – the developing use of the lancet in blood-letting – safe enough surely if you went by the moon's phases in the timing of it? – fomentations, plasters, decoctions of all kinds made from pennyroyal, wormwood, male-fern, sage and many another native herb – everything profoundly intrigued the young poet-duke.

And then one evening she leaned her bright head against his knee as he read to her, and said: 'Charles, listen a moment.'

'Yes?' he asked, still fingering his manuscript.

'Charles – I think we're going to have a baby. The first of many, I hope. Oh, Charles!'

The precious manuscript dropped unnoticed on the rushes. 'My love, my love, how wonderful.' He pulled her up and sat her, head cradled, against his shoulder: 'We must take good care of you.'

'Nonsense. It's the healthiest occupation in the world – bearing a child.'

'What shall we call it?' He was grinning with delight.

'Well – what a question! "*Charles*" of course,' she said. And then, for one terrible second, their eyes met in alarmed self-consciousness which both immediately tried to hide. He had had the thought: 'If she says "Richard", I shall not be able to bear it.' While to her, even before she got out that heart-felt 'Charles', had flashed the terrible doubt as to whether Charles had indeed overheard her talking in her sleep that night weeks ago when her own voice had awakened her. Was that what that fleeting expression across his face this moment meant? Now she would never know.

The simple happening was still as vivid as if it had occurred last night. Charles had made love to her, tenderly caressingly; they'd fallen asleep embraced. Much later, she was startingly awakened by a clear childish voice saying one word: 'Richard!' Stunned with surprise, after a moment she'd realised that voice must have been her own. Had she been dreaming of Richard – Richard dead and gone? If so, she had no remotest recollection of it. Then, terrified at the possibility that Charles might be awake and feeling humiliated at her cry, she held her breath to listen. Somehow she *felt*, by his utter stillness, that he was indeed awake; if so, then was the moment to laugh and say: 'Poor old Richard – how strange for me to say his name.' But Charles gave no sign – and to wake your husband to make such a comment would lend it too much significance. . . . Yet now she would never know. How difficult complete communication was, even between two who loved each other.

And yet – he had no reason to feel jealous of poor Richard who'd deserved so much of life and got so little. If indeed she had dreamed of him it was the fruit of an intolerable pity. She would always lament his fate.

The moment passed. Now Charles said lightly: 'And what if the first one is a girl?'

She hesitated. Then, 'I would like "Joan",' she said. Surely Richard's mother would be an excellent choice? That much of remembering was allowable?

And what fun it was to plan for their burgeoning little family. In the Bed-and-Sitting-Chamber, near the built-in armoires, they would place the gilded cradle on rockers which, when winter came, could have a fur coverlet, and which a nurse-maid could easily rock with one foot when baby cried and while she soothingly sang it to sleep. . . . Isabella remembered with relief the charms and spells, appropriate to this pre-natal period, that would ensure the well-being of her child. Then, a plentiful supply of swaddling bands must be made and packed away in the armoires so that the baby could be tightly swaddled like a mummy directly after birth, to enable its limbs to grow straight. But there! the excellent mid-wife whom they'd employ would know all the important points of child-care – such as seeing that the babe was carried *upstairs* before it had ever been carried *down* – and the best method of massaging little limbs with oil of roses to strengthen them before adjusting the tight swaddling-bands. . . . And although Mother Church was always at hand to guard them against evil – well! – just to be on the safe side – the midwife would also know charms and incantations against witches, hobgoblins, and other monsters that lay in wait outside the homely limits of their own safe world of the château . . . Naturally, the priest would see to it that the babe was baptised at least the day after its birth, for child mortality was necessarily high and the souls of the unbaptised, however innocent, were inevitably destined for limbo – that borderland of Hell specially designed for those who had not been christened. Isabella shivered at the thought.

Nevertheless, that summer of 1409, filled as it was with a sense of expectation, was the height of happiness for Charles and Isabella. The very earth seemed to burst with promises. Beauty was everywhere – not least in his beloved's face, thought Charles, as he watched her grow more and more etherealised even though her body thickened. He was glad he lived in this modern age when romantic sentiment was creating – and recognising – a feminine ideal.

In August she retreated for the last few weeks, as custom dictated, to solitude in a private Chamber. But Charles broke the accepted convention by often being there with her: for he found that when she no longer invaded his Study, loneliness came upon him like a premonition . . . By September when the trees were beginning to shiver off their brilliantly-variegated leaves and shake gnarled limbs against a lowering sky, he thought, this unusually early autumn is like unanticipated death. But such morbidity was senseless and he thrust it from him.

The last few days seemed endless, as if she would contain the child for ever within her body . . . Then suddenly her time was upon her, everything rose to its momentous climax and the whole château seemed alerted. A leech scurried down the long corridors with additional herbs and nostrums, a friar-observant began involuntarily intoning fragments of Latin prayers as he paced the flagstones, and most comforting of all to Charles's relieved gaze, the stout unhurried midwife materialised before his eye like the competent figure of wordly experience in a morality play. Her very appearance was reassuring in her calm acceptance of such recurrent and blessedly-natural events as giving birth – a welcome contrast to the excited chattering of Isabella's ladies.

It was the 13th of September 1409. In a little less than two months the young Duchess d'Orleans would have reached her twentieth birthday. What double celebrations they would have, both for her natal day and the arrival of the child.

'According to the zodiac, this is an auspicious date for the birth of your heir, Sir,' the physician remarked, giving Charles an encouraging look as he measured sedative nostrums; even the patient managed a brilliant smile towards her young husband between the expected – and welcomed – bouts of pain. He had not realised that birth could entail so much suffering, or, indeed, any difficulty. Now he felt as if each of Isabella's pains racked his own body.

At last the protesting wail of the new-born babe echoed thinly through the birth-chamber. Smiling broadly with satisfaction, the midwife received the child from the physician's hands, dipped her finger in honey to rub the tiny mouth and gums, and proceeded with anointing the little limbs preparatory to the expert swaddling. 'A perfect little girl-child,' she murmured, remembering with relief that they'd engaged a wet-nurse in case the Duchess's milk did not come abundantly. Just as well, she thought now for she must admit that the patient didn't seem to be rallying very rapidly. The buxom wet-nurse would at least be a stand-in till the young Duchess had recovered her strength.

Charles had fallen on his knees by the bed. To him, his sweet Isabella looked like a bruised flower, barely raising the level of the coverlet. He was dimly aware, on the borderline of consciousness that was directed exclusively to his wife, that the physician was saying; 'We are giving the Duchess a herbal draught, as you can see, Sir, out of the Church Bell, and if it seems necessary to do a little blood-letting, I shall use my lancet. I can assure you that every omen is exactly right for that by the moon's present phase.' On the far side of the bed, the priest's mumbling voice attempted to augment the cure with the prayer finishing: '*Domine sancte, Pater omnipotens,*' while the assistant leech was applying heat to the patient's feet by inserting hot bricks under the coverlet.

Charles was staring at her pallid face and thinking desperately: Blood-letting? Surely she has lost too much blood already? Supposedly, the physician must know best – after all, medicine was at last making great strides, especially with all its improved knowledge of herbalism.

But he could not contain himself. Still kneeling beside her bed, he laid a soothing hand on her breast, and was startled to feel her heart beating as wildly as a thrush in a fragile cage. Making a supreme effort, she turned her head and looked into his face, so close to her own, her pupils widely dilated. At that moment, their

154

silent communication was absolute. And he realised at last, with horror and dismay, that the thread that held her gentle spirit to him – and to the world – was of gossamer. He loved her so tenderly that he longed to reassure her of its cable-strong consistency.

He found himself falling further down, with his face against the coverlet, silently repeating over and over: 'Mary, Mother of God, if she must go, let her parting be painless.' Yet, despite the leech's now desperate words as he bled her still further, despite the priest's administration of extreme unction, Charles had not really accepted the fact that this was the end.

He did not accept it until – until she lifted her head from the bolster and said, in a startled wondering voice: 'I'm not – not – dying – am I, Charles?' A reply was more than he immediately could manage. So that, after a moment, she continued, bewilderedly, gazing at him in frantic appeal: 'I can't – I can't be dying – I've just learned – with you – to be so very, very happy.' She panted a little, before adding in a tiny voice: 'We have been – happy – haven't we, Charles?' And at last he knew for certain, when it was far too late, that long ago he had taken Richard's place decisively in her heart. Now as he cradled her in his arms and reassured her that in eight week's time they would be celebrating her twentieth birthday, he thought his own heart would break.

A ghost of a smile lit her face the second before all life left it. Desperately he felt that in abandoning him for death she had committed her only act of infidelity; never had he anticipated so tragic a betrayal. For him, the future stretched ahead like a barren desert – an infinity of tomorrows in which he must learn to live – alone. . . . Perhaps happiness, that elusive state, was always either a hope for the future or a memory of what had been enjoyed, so unthinkingly, in the past? Ah, no! he *had* for a time realised his happiness. At least he had that. It was only the hope of growing old together that had become a bitter unrealised dream.

Suddenly Charles put his face in his hands and wept.

Somewhere along the periphery of pain, he reached out a hand for God's pity. And the thought formed in his subconscious that he could not *endure* her death unless – unless – he clothed it, expressed it, as something beautiful, transmuted it into a different form . . . Almost against his conscious wish, words began to form as poetic lyrics in his mind:

'Come, death – my lady is dead.
It kills me – my distress.

155

Oh misted eyes, why fail ye not your sight?
Since Death, alas! hath taken my lady bright.'

Charles d'Orleans had found his own immortality as France's poet-duke, in immortalising his love for Isabella out of his rage of grief and despair.

RICHMOND
AND ELIZABETH

by Brenda Honeyman

Elizabeth of York, wife of Henry Tudor, Earl of Richmond,
was complicating her marriage by an incestuous love for
her uncle, King Richard III.

Richmond, however, was destined to wrest the crown
from his crookback cousin. But his reign, complicated in
turn by his resentment of Elizabeth and her ways, was also
haunted by the ghosts of his two young brothers-in-law,
the 'princes in the Tower'.

RICHMOND AND ELIZABETH is a New English Library
historical novel in the 'Shadow of the Tower' series.

NEW ENGLISH LIBRARY

NEL BESTSELLERS

— — — — — — — — — — — — — —

NEL P.O. BOX 11, FALMOUTH, CORNWALL

Please send cheque or postal order. Allow 6p per book to cover postage and packing.

Name..

Address ....

....

Title ....
(SEPTEMBER)

THE SYLVIA SCARLETT TRILOGY

by Compton Mackenzie

D. H. Lawrence considered the Sylvia Scarlett saga to be Sir Compton Mackenzie's masterpiece. Covering the same colourful period and including many of the same characters as the classic SINISTER STREET, this story breaks brave new ground in its exploration of a heroine acclaimed as 'one of the few really great women in fiction'.

Sylvia is a beautiful girl with a bitingly sharp tongue. She is married at the tender age of nineteen to the dashing Philip Iredale, and their three-month whirlwind of passion drives their relationship to cataclysmic destruction in SYLVIA SCARLETT. Shattered by a brutal divorce, she throws herself into a hedonistic life in Europe, which prepares her for the second great passion in her life – SYLVIA AND ARTHUR. Finally, in SYLVIA AND MICHAEL, she fights down despair only to be confronted by the horror of the First World War, and her last and greatest love.

'In the great tradition of English picaresque novels – in many ways it is a twentieth century *Moll Flanders*.'
—*Antony Sampson*

SYLVIA SCARLETT
SYLVIA AND ARTHUR
SYLVIA AND MICHAEL

NEW ENGLISH LIBRARY